TALES OF
BREKH'CHA

Beware the dragon mist.
—Ian Vroon

THE FLAMES CHRONICLES

PREQUEL TO BOOK TWO

IAN VROON

ISBN: 9798478513764

Visit the author's website at

www.ianvroon.blog

Cover Design

by Piere d'Arterie

CONTENTS

ACKNOWLEDGEMENTS

I'd like to thank my Lord and Savior, Jesus Christ, for giving me the ability to write this book. As Isaiah 26:12 says, "Lord, you establish peace for me; all that I have accomplished you have done for me." I'd also like to thank God because he created an amazing world to inspire me as I write.

Furthermore, I'd like to thank my mom. She did much of the editing, and should go recognized. Margaret Kay Maloy—my high school teacher—was instrumental in expanding my lexicon and educating me.

My sweet, beautiful wife Nicole—you have been the greatest blessing in my life, blowing me away with wonder! My family and friends, particularly Andrew Detwiler—you rock.

And finally, incomplete sentences. Because that's how acknowledgments are done.

I WRATH OF THE FLAME DRAGON

The 5,654th year of the Okúmba Tree (5654 OT) • 12 years old

"Kel!"

Dad was calling. Kel didn't care. He wanted to stay and keep looking. Running his stone fingers over his chair, his desk…taking in the room he'd grown up in.

He gazed into the bronze mirror. A smooth, perfectly round boulder with long arms, short legs and emerald eyes frowned back at him—his glossy rock skin shifting from jade to blue as he turned, gleaming in the firelight. His face was part of his boulder body's surface, but could pop out like a turtle's at any time.

He studied his reflective skin. A labradorite if ever there was one. The torch let off sparks within its portico a few feet away, and Kel flexed his arms.

It wasn't fair. He'd never wanted to move. This wasn't the kind of thing that was supposed to happen. He and his family were supposed to win.

"Kel!"

That sounded slightly more urgent. Most likely serious. He could dillydally a wee bit longer, though. He let his eyes wander the room again.

His bed. A marble bowl stuck to the ceiling. He reached up to touch it—and gravity shifted around him. He fell into the bowl, the surface he'd been standing on becoming the ceiling. That never got old. It likely never would, no matter how long he stayed.

"Kelmor Ketarn! Come out here now!"

The way everyone rolled their r's was always comforting. Even

1

when he was a wee bit late, listening to people speak was great.

"Kel!" A boulder rolled in from the tunnel. As it halted, legs and arms sprouted from its sides. Its eyes opened—just Kolath. Kel's father. A shiny hematite with a perfect sense of time. "What're you doing lying in bed! We have to leave *now*!"

"I know." Kel felt the words escape his stony lips—but he didn't understand them. He didn't want to. "Because of the dragon."

"That's right." Kolath waved a finger. "The Flame Dragon could show at any second. We cannot be here. You understand?"

Kel let his head pop out from his boulder body, stony neck supporting it. He gave a small nod. "I understand."

"So let's go! Now!"

"Dad, I'm only ten. Give me a break."

"Lives are at stake here." Kolath put his hand against the tunnel's archway, narrowing his eyes. "And you're twelve. Come on."

Kel's eyebrows creased, and he sat up. "Twelve?"

"Great boulders, lad! Do you have no perception of time?"

"Maybe." Kel shrugged. "I don't care, dad."

"Why not?" The dragon was forgotten. Dad spread his arms. "Your dad's a timekeeper, and you can't be bothered to keep track of anything?"

Kel swallowed. "I don't see a need to."

"You don't—" Kolath crossed his arms, shaking his head. "Listen, Kel. What'll you do when I'm gone?"

"We live for centuries, dad. Who cares about time."

"*I* care!" Kolath indicated himself with his thumb. "And you can't—" he pressed his palm to his forehead, closing his eyes. "Nevermind that. Let's go."

And that was the final warning. When dad got calm, Kel needed to roll. "Fine. Lead the way."

"That's the right attitude."

Kolath turned around, tucked in his limbs—and rolled off down the tunnel. Kel approached the tunnel's threshold, then glanced back at the room. This was it.

He tucked in his head and limbs, clenched his abdomen—and burst into a roll. He could go forty miles an hour on a good day. Maybe fifty.

Today he was going twenty.

He bumped into the wall and ricocheted to the ceiling. Gravity shifted, and now he was rolling on the ceiling. Twelve years, and he was still figuring out how to roll without bumping into things. That nanosecond of information—when his eyes were facing ahead during the roll—wasn't a great deal. At least on the run, he'd have the opportunity to practice.

☆ ☆ ☆

Boats. Helenberry shells like canoes dotted the lava river, geolites tucked in them like peas in a pod. One pea to every pod. Families beside one another. Some labradorites, rhodochrosites… But all dark against the lava's glow. Most had their hands in the lava, ready to paddle.

Kel's stomach knotted. The whole of Ticora was here—or at least the last evacuation party. Everyone else had up and left.

"Charges in place?" Kolath waved to geolites sitting in clefts far above the river. They waved back. "Great. Aim to blow them when the last boat is twenty meters out! We'll stay on the shore and roll out through side routes."

They were collapsing the exits. No way the Flame Dragon could follow them to their new habitation. Only a few hours from here—but with all the wide tunnels in pieces, an eternity as far as the dragon was concerned.

At least, that was their hope.

"Kel, find your mother and hop in a boat."

"Aye." Kel rolled down the bank, uncurling at the bottom. Mom was somewhere here—

"Kel!" A fiery opalite waved at him, not five meters out—Mom. She grinned. "About time."

Kel cracked a smile. He took a spare helenboat and set it on the lava. Tucking his legs in, he set himself inside—and there. His muscles relaxed. Floating on the lava was great. Not that he wouldn't sink like the stone he was if he tumbled off the boat.

"Come here!" She beckoned with one arm. "Quick, before we leave!"

Somehow she seemed less pushy. Kel had never minded her. "Aye." He paddled out, dipping his hands in the warm lava. It hissed a little, and he leaned forward. His helenboat brushed between others, but everyone was oddly silent. Holding their breath, almost.

"Alright! Let's go!" Kolath motioned—and every geolite began paddling as he watched from a ridge above the shore. Like lily pads drifting along, helenboats floated down the hissing lava river. Bubbles formed and popped around Kel, pillars of lava rising to the ceiling just ahead.

"He's not a villain, you know."

He glanced at his mom. "I know."

"He's just looking out for us. Keeping the hour so we don't have to."

"I know."

Mom turned to him, concern running like cracks through her stony face. "We need timekeepers, Kel. Years turn to decades. Decades turn to centuries. We don't know time—and only a few of us can keep track of it very well."

"I know."

"Stop saying that! Do you really know?" She glanced back. "He's heading the evacuation team for a reason. People depend on him. And that's something to be proud of."

Kel shrugged. "I suppose that's true."

Mom shook her head. "You know it is."

Kel gave a loud, drawn out sigh. Not that she was wrong…

Then he heard it.

A metallic shriek. Like steel scraping steel. Echoing through the cavern, making his back tighten into little bumps.

"Dragon!" A voice far behind Kel. "Approaching the river!"

As if no one could tell. Geolites started shouting. Everyone was paddling, digging at the lava, wide strokes as boats bumped each other. No one could move fast enough.

"Dispatch the fighters!" Kolath was practically screaming his orders. "Stall it best as we can!"

Kel looked behind them. Purple light gleamed on the cavern's walls, growing with the sound of rushing flames. Some fighters rolled toward it, while others picked up rocks.

Then he saw it. A funnel of twisted purple flame, blue ridges lining its back as it twirled through the air. Serpentine, its body a blur of fire. Blue flames like eyes burning in hollow sockets. A forked tongue of flame testing the air.

4

The Flame Dragon had arrived.

"Hurl the stones!"

Rocks sailed through the air, passing right through the dragon's body. No effect. The dragon shrieked again, and Kel flinched.

What could they even do against such a thing? Stones were useless. Fists would be too.

Twin flames launched from the dragon's body—its legs. One snatched a geolite, enveloping it in flame. The geolite melted as Kel watched, her silvery drops hitting the cave's floor. The dragon closed its jaws—and its burning pupils seemed to settle on the boats.

It approached the bank, legs withdrawing into its body. Kolath glanced back at the boats, fear carving his face. The approaching flames gleamed off his hematite skin, purple mingled with blue. He turned to face the dragon—and clenched his fists. "Blow the charges!"

"No!" Mom reached for him, though they had to be twenty meters out by now. "Kolath!"

The geolites up in the clefts nodded—and struck their fists together to make sparks. Earsplitting explosions shook the cavern, sending rocks plummeting into the lava. Kel gripped the edges of his helenboat, gritting his teeth as more explosions shattered the tunnel.

The dragon was floating toward the bank, past Kolath, flame body hovering over the ground as if gravity had no effect. It opened its jaws, shrieking as stones fell through it. Its flames wavered—and it turned back just as the tunnel collapsed. Kel's last glimpse was of his father facing the dragon as purple flames enveloped him.

Then stones blocked his view.

"Kolath!"

Kel stared, still gripping the helenboat. He let his eyes fall to the lava, which was foaming with debris. He blinked, lips pressed together.

Sobbing. His mother's body was shaking. She was trying not to wail—he could tell—but her hands were pressed against her eyes.

What had just happened? Kel glanced at the debris. His dad was gone. That was it.

And it had happened so fast.

"My Kolath." Mom sniffed. "My love, I wish we'd had more time."

Time. Kel tightened his grip on the rim. If he'd cared more about time, maybe...

5

No. The dragon had no concern for time. It came and went as it pleased. That was the reason they'd left. No society survived without structure.

And Dad knew that.

Kel inhaled deeply, turning to face ahead. Paddling a little, he cleared his throat. "Best get going, I suppose."

Mom was still weeping—but she nodded, wiping her face. Her voice was small. "I know."

Kel swallowed hard, hands dipped in the warm lava. He felt numb inside. "I'm sorry, mom," he whispered, voice cracking. "I'm so sorry."

2 CONTRAPTIONS

5655 OT (one year later)

Back and forth...back and forth. Kel ran the sander along the helenboat's exterior, stony muscles tight. Easy there...and perfect.

He set the sander on the obsidian bench—then raised the helenboat, turning it so the green lava pillar's light could gleam off it. He tilted it, narrowing his eyes. Smooth edges...almost perfectly curved...good.

His surfboard was finished.

Well, mostly. He ran his thumb along it. Not his best work, but...he was still learning. For now, it was pretty good. Might even be worth surfing on.

Legs popped out from his body—and he stood with a grunt. Great boulders...his muscles were tense. He was a rock, but somehow he could still get stiff. How long had he even been sitting here? Hours? Days?

That was the problem with requiring no sustenance or sleep. Time went fast.

He scanned the cavern. Silver globules of lava floated in midair, like bubbles suspended in place. Giving an eerie glow. No magma dragonflies here, though—so he was alone.

He swallowed, checking the surfboard again. Testing it out would be fine. Though it wasn't quite high tide. The red lava river a few feet away was flowing smoothly enough...

Giggling. His eyes darted over to see a pair of sapphire-eyed lasses enter the cavern—one a milky halite, the other a silvery kimberlite. They were covering their mouths, whispering like some

7

secret was unfolding. The halite noticed him and stopped.

Great. Now he had an audience.

"Is that a surfboard?"

Kel glanced at the helenberry shell in his hands. His mouth dropped, and he blinked twice. Stupid. He looked really stupid. "Eh...yeah."

"Oh it is! That's so cool!" The halite lass giggled again. Her friend nudged her, and she cleared her throat. "Can you *ride* it?"

Ride it...Kel's mouth felt very dry. That made no sense, because he was a stone. Stones were always dry. But he knew little of his own anatomy—so dry it was. "Aye."

"Oo! Can we watch?" Without waiting, both lasses took their seat on the lava river's shore. "We've never seen anyone ride the waves before."

"Well, it's not high tide..." Why was he so nervous? It's not like they were here to kill him or anything. This was stupid. "You can't really surf when it's not high tide."

"But you can try—right?" The kimberlite lass's sapphire irises glittered in the lava's light. "I'll wager you could pull off *some* surfing."

Kel swallowed—pretty loudly. He was gripping the surfboard much tighter than he needed to. "I, I suppose I could...eh..."

The kimberlite giggled—but the halite batted her eyes at him. "Please? We'd *love* to watch, lad."

Now he knew his cheeks were turning red. He didn't even know if labradorites could blush—but the heat alone had to be making his face melt. "Aye."

"Yay!" They were probably in their teens, by the way they were acting. They dipped their feet in the lava, leaning forward.

Kel approached the river, footsteps awkward on the jagged obsidian. Suddenly it was hard to keep his balance. He set his surfboard on the river, trying to keep his hands steady. What was so hard about surfing now that people were watching?

"How long have you been making surfboards?"

"Since—well...I don't know."

They giggled, covering their mouths. Then they leaned forward again, eyes glittering. Waiting for him.

"Alright then." Kel waited as a strong surge rippled through the river. The "wave" was coming his way—and all he needed to do was hop on at the right time. "Ready?"

They nodded in unison. "Waiting!"

What was it about women's voices that were so singsong? Kel shook his head—then hopped on as the surge hit.

His stomach lurched as the tide lifted him. He was balancing, teetering on his surfboard. It was tilting a little to the right—he'd need to sand that out—but so far not bad. Now for the flip.

Kel grabbed the surfboard—then leapt, twirling in the air. For an instant he spotted the lasses staring, hands cupping their cheeks. The wave of red lava burned beneath him, its reddish-orange glow filling his vision.

Wait. How was he going to land? Why couldn't he remember how—

Kel plunged into the lava, clutching the surfboard. Heat enveloped him, pressing at his body. He dared not open his mouth.

The tide was carrying him—he could feel himself being thrust along. But he didn't know which way was up. Only lava met his eyes.

Then a current ripped the surfboard from his hands. He flailed, streaks of red and orange swirling around him. His stomach lurched—

And he flew onto the bank, tumbling past boulders with a grunt. Lava hissed on his forearms, heat tingling across his skin. He gasped, spitting out searing droplets. Where was he? Where were the lasses?

The world was spinning a little. All that turning must've made him dizzy. He tried getting to his knees—then closed his eyes, inhaling sharply. Any more tilting and he might throw up.

Stupid. Why'd he forgotten how to land? Was it a matter of being in front of others? He was better than this.

"There he is!" Giggling. Both lasses rolled up to the opposite bank. "Nice move, labradorite!"

Now that was uncalled for. Kel got to his feet, brow furrowed. "I was just—"

"Trying to impress us?" The halite giggled again. "We know. It was *almost* great."

"Almost." The kimberlite pinched air between her thumb and forefinger. "This close, lad."

"We loved watching, though!"

Now Kel's cheeks burned with a heat that had nothing to do with the lava. "I—I tried…"

"That you did!" The halite shook her head. "Not quite there,

9

though!"

He opened his mouth—but suddenly had nothing to say. He could just stammer all day, or—no. He turned from them, fists curled. He put a palm to his forehead—then turned back. "You don't—I know how to surf—"

"Sure you do!" Now they were laughing again. "You just need a bit better balance!"

His surfboard hadn't been ready. The tide hadn't been right. So much could have been different. "Don't mock me." Kel's voice trembled a little. "Stop it."

"Oh come on." The halite put her fists on her hips, a grin twisting her lips. "It was entertaining and you know it."

Kel swallowed, lowering his eyes. "Whatever." He turned to leave, their giggles following him. He could find his surfboard another day.

He'd make a better one anyway.

☆ ☆ ☆

Kel came out of his roll inside their new house. Table on the ceiling, fires burning in porticos on either side—not much, but home for now. This new city was still being chiseled out—even a year after settling here, a stone was lucky to have a home at all.

"Good day?"

He turned to Mom, nausea nearly crushing him. Tears welled in his eyes—why did he still feel embarrassed? "I—not really."

"What happened?" The opalite had her back to him. She was pounding away at the wall with a corundum hammer, no doubt chiseling out a storage portico. Fiery streaks danced in her back as she moved—tricks of her opal skin. "You don't sound well."

So she could tell. Moms were like that. Kel rolled his shoulders, cracking his neck. What was there to say? "I fell when I was surfing."

"Oh?" Mom turned to him, setting down the hammer. "You alright?"

Kel opened his mouth—then swallowed. "To be perfectly honest…" Could he tell her about the lasses? The flop of a trick? "I wanted to impress some lasses. And I—I didn't do it quite right—"

10

"Oh m'dear." Mom put her hands to his, then laced her fingers through his. Their version of a hug. "Don't mind that. Mockers mock—that's their way."

Kel closed his eyes, cheeks warm. Really, Mom hadn't been there. But he wouldn't say that. "I could've done better."

"Then do better! But don't worry about them." She raised her eyebrows. "Their opinion doesn't matter."

He'd tried to tell himself that. He really had. But something about laughter was so hard to ignore... "I know."

"Anyway, what were you doing surfing?" Mom stepped back from him, picking the hammer up. "You don't know what's out there. The wilds can be dangerous."

"All the more reason to explore them. And what better way to do that then surf?" For some reason the subject cheered up Kel. "Wouldn't you agree?"

Mom shrugged, a smile tugging at her lips. "I suppose. That what you've been doing when you disappear for days?"

"Aye." Kel grinned. So it had been days. "Any problems with that?"

"No." Mom shook her head. Then she pressed her lips together. "But Kel..."

Uh-oh. She was worried. "What's the matter?"

"I'm simply wondering." She set the hammer down again. "You and your contraptions. Making surfboards and all that."

"What about it?"

"Isn't it...a little trivial?"

So that was it. She thought he was wasting his time. "It's what I like to do."

"What you like to do?" She studied him with her eyes, red irises glittering in the firelight. "Are you sure."

"Always have been."

"And this doesn't—" she lowered her voice, "—this doesn't have anything to do with Dad? And his timekeeping."

Kel curled his fists. Why would she bring that up? "No. I'm fine."

"It's just..." She narrowed her eyes at him. "You're isolating yourself in the wilderness, barely speaking to anyone. You spend days away, busy with your contraptions." She started listing things off on her fingers. "But you're a friendly stone, Kel. I know you like your contraptions—I don't doubt that. But being alone like this..."

11

Kel's eyes wandered over to a portico. He turned slightly, flexing his muscles. "I'm perfectly fine, mom."

"No, you're not." She put a hand on his shoulder. "You're broken, Kel. And no one can smelt new parts for you."

"And what am I supposed to do?" Kel spread his hands, voice raised. "Dwell in it? I have to move on, right?"

Mom shook her head. "No, Kel. Brokenness isn't a burden. It's a badge. You never move on."

What did that mean? "Am I supposed to just sulk all the time then?"

"No. But you don't forget it."

"Really." Kel turned from her, facing the tunnel. "Alright, mom. I won't forget."

"You'd better mean it."

Kel swallowed, loosening his fists. What was it about this that was so hard? "Right."

3 SURFING THE MOLTEN WILDS

5656 OT (one year later)

Massive lava waterfalls poured in the distance—green, silver and red, flowing into the same basin. The colors swirled, churning in a lake between the falls. A dark red—almost brown—lava was the result, running down the ridge between rocks and crevices. Near the bottom, it was an all-out rapids.

Perfect for surfing.

Kel nodded to himself, hefting the surfboard in one hand. Now this was a board. Perfectly fine in every way. He wouldn't be tripping up this time.

A spot in the lava rapids before him erupted. A ball of flame and magma rose from it, shedding sparks as it uncurled. A long, fiery tail, tipped with a stinger dripping with lava—and at the front, the face of an insect. White-hot dragonfly wings sprouted, sparks flying from them as they fluttered. Buzzing filled his ears as the magma dragonfly hovered in place.

"Hello there." Kel held out a palm. This one wasn't too big—only a bit larger than Kel. "You gonna ruin my surfing?"

The dragonfly just stared at him. Dumb thing couldn't understand a word he said. Then it shot off, zipping through the cavern and out of sight. Pretty fast, those creatures.

"Didn't think so." Kel approached the shore, giving a contented sigh. The tide was perfect. *Perfect*. If he hopped—

"Oy! What're you up to?"

He turned to look up at the ridge. Standing at the top was an ebon geolite with yellow freckles on his cheeks, fists and knees. Probably

13

an ilmenite with sulfur impurities, though Kel couldn't be sure.

The ebon geolite called out, cupping his hands to his mouth. "You out here all alone?"

Kel scratched his head. "Not anymore, I suppose. Who're you?"

The geolite grinned—then picked up something beside him. A helenboat! Shaped just like a surfboard. "Name's Grekham." The geolite hopped in and skidded down the ridge, letting his fingers drag along the rocks to slow himself. Pebbles skittered after him, and he spun a little to halt. "I'm an ilmenite, if you can't tell. Who're *you*?"

"Kelmor Ketarn. And I could ask what *you're* doing here." Kel arched an eyebrow, approaching Grekham. "Quite an odd place, this is."

"Not if you're looking to surf the molten wilds, eh?" Grekham punched Kel's shoulder playfully, winking. "That's about what I thought, lad."

"Alright. You got me." Kel shrugged. "But it's not illegal or anything."

"Aye. If anything, you're playing it a wee bit safe." Grekham got off his surfboard, eyes wandering across the cavern. "I see you pick your spots well. But couldn't you be riding wilder waves?"

"Perhaps." Kel glanced at the lavafalls. "Though not without going deeper into the wilds."

"Precisely." Grekham picked up his own board with one hand. "And that's why I'm here, lad. Heard a stone was surfing the Western Wilds—and knew that was my chance."

Kel ran his fingers along his board, brow furrowed. "Why not surf alone?"

"Because I need a backup, lad!" Grekham slapped him on the back. "Going deep into the wilds isn't safe. This way we watch each other's back!"

Finally, this stone was making sense. "Not a bad idea."

"No. Not bad at all." Grekham raised his eyebrows, grinning. His eyes darted over to the lavafalls. "So? Shall we start searching?"

Another stone that really liked surfing…Kel hefted his board. He could get used to this. "Aye."

☆ ☆ ☆

14

Purple quartzite crystals jutted out from the domed walls of the cavern. It was like they were standing inside a globe, a massive pillar of pale silver lava twisting through its middle. Centipedes made of red fire floated lazily through the air, flame pincers clicking as they sniffed the rocks. Their light danced in the purple crystals, mingling with the lava's silver glow. They wouldn't be a problem.

No, it was the center of the globe that had their attention. That pillar...the lava was rushing fast, but not fast enough to be a lavafall. Just to a point where it was clear it was rushing uphill.

Kel took aim, then hurled a stone. The rock sailed through the air, plummeting into the lava with a hiss. It cascaded up the pillar, like trout leaping up a stream.

"That's pretty fast," Grekham whispered, surfboard under his shoulder. "Think we can maneuver it?"

Was he kidding? "It's perfect." Kel put a fist on the part of his body some might call a hip—though to outsiders, it looked just like part of the perfectly round boulder that was him—and nodded. "Let's surf here."

"Aye." Grekham cast him a mischievous grin. "I'd have recommended it if you didn't."

Spoken like another tide experimenter. Kel approached the pillar, stepping carefully between quartzite crystals. "Quite perfect."

Heat swept across his stony skin as they neared the pillar. Its coruscating silver lava sparkled with a metallic glow, flowing toward the ceiling. Kel held out his surfboard with both hands, lining it up with the current. "Ready?"

"Let's do it."

Kel set his surfboard on the pillar—and hopped on. He jerked back as the current launched him upward, hands gripping the board. The pillar twisted around, diving through a tunnel in the ceiling. He tried standing—there. Now he was really surfing.

"Whoo! Now this is a ride!"

He glanced back to see Grekham surfing just behind. The geolite had his hands out, crouching as he gained speed. Kel followed suit, scanning the tunnel. Red rhodochrosite lined the walls, sparkling in the silver light. They burst from the tunnel—

The new cavern was a void. No walls in any direction—only darkness. Pillars of silver lava twisted and turned into the abyss, crisscrossing each other like gnarled roots in a dark jungle.

15

Kel tightened his muscles, keeping his arms out. Might've been a good idea to scout the current. Too late now. "And down we go!"

They both hollered, bringing one hand down to steady their boards as the current took them into the abyss. Nothing too difficult. The flows were whipping them around a little—but that was the way of surfing. They'd adapt.

Then the pillar swerved up—and Kel spotted a bigger current running just above them. "Grekham! Let's try this one!"

"Agreed!" Grekham reached up with two fingers, touching the new lava river. He flipped his board around as gravity shifted, landing perfectly on the current. Now it appeared he was surfing upside down. "Following?"

"Of course!" Kel grinned, tapping the current with his finger. He flipped his board around and landed easily, laughing. "This is great!"

"What a current!" Grekham adjusted his course so they were surfing side-by-side. "We should—"

"Just ahead." Kel's smile disappeared. The current was ending—or so it appeared. More likely it was running over a cliff into a lavafall. Depending on where that went, they could be in trouble. "Brace yourself."

"Aye."

They shot over the lavafall's edge, twirling through space. Green globules of lava hung suspended, and Kel let his hand pass through one. Each globule had its own weaker gravity zone—and by touching them, he was slowing himself with their pull. Better than nothing, anyway.

Grekham smashed into the wall as Kel flew into a tunnel. Kel tumbled off his board, rolling down—down, down into darkness. He tumbled to a stop at the bottom, one arm against a boulder.

Well. He'd have to be repaired after this. Convenient that labradorite parts weren't hard to smelt.

He got to his knees—then braced himself with the boulder and stood. Not the worst that could happen.

Where was Grekham? Kel squinted into the darkness—he could just make out a glimmer of silver ahead. He rolled toward it, bouncing off stones with a growl. Hard enough to roll when you could see where you were going. This was a nightmare.

There. He found the source of silver—more lava, but flowing nowhere near as fast. Not that he could swim in it—and finding his board was a joke of a prospect.

Perfect. He was lost and stranded.

"Grekham?" His voice echoed oddly in the cavern. He cupped his hands to his mouth and tried again. "You hear me?"

A clicking noise. He froze, hands to his mouth. Now his heart was really beating—pounding at his chest, screaming for him to leave. His eyes darted around the cavern—though he dared not breathe. Any sound could be fatal.

More clicking. A scurrying on the rock above him.

Then he saw it. Magma body, obsidian pincers and legs. A gargantuan spidery creature with glowing red eyes, pausing before him. Sparks of flame wavering like hairs on its abdomen. A lavarack if he'd ever seen one. One of the bigger breeds, he'd wager.

It clicked its pincers, coming right up to him. He could feel the heat from its magma body—and he focused on the creature's legs. The legs weren't bad. Pointed wedges of obsidian—capable of stabbing him through, no doubt—but safer than the eyes. Anyone staring into those would be paralyzed. That was their way.

Not that the "eyes" were actually real. He'd heard lavaracks couldn't see. They just had a sprinkling of red dots on their head with the power to stop people from moving. Yet this one looked to be studying him.

If Kel so much as swallowed...

The lavarack clicked its pincers again, cocking its head—then scurried off, crawling over a large boulder and through a crack in the tunnel. It seemed the creature had decided Kel's shouts were just an echo from elsewhere.

But Kel dared not breathe. No sense in taking a deep breath when there might be more lavaracks in the area. He must've been near a hive.

Good thing geolites didn't need to breathe. Air was inhaled, no doubt—for but only for speech.

Kel let his eyes wander over the cavern—the silver lava, the deep rivulets of red lava flowing down the walls—and decided it was time to go. Though how he could leave without making noise was beyond him.

Whispers. Kel's eyes darted over to a tunnel in the ceiling of the cavern. Purple mist poured from it, and some was already creeping along the floor toward him. Tendrils reached out like fingers,

17

enveloping his legs.

Was he still holding his breath? Kel couldn't tell. Having a nose to pinch would be helpful—but his wasn't even big enough for a bump on his face.

More whispers. What was this mist? It seemed familiar...Kel remembered something about the dragon breathing out mist.

The flame dragon. Kel's eyes went wide. Was this his doing?

"Kel."

He nearly jumped. That was Dad's voice! His heartbeat quickened, and he scanned the cave. There. Kolath was standing beside a boulder.

Kel blinked. But—Dad was dead. No way he could be standing here now.

"You stupid wee child. You've gotten yourself lost again, and now you'll get yourself killed." Kolath approached him, shaking his head. "Just like always. You never keep track of anything, do you?"

Kel wanted to ignore him...and this just *couldn't* be Dad, right? But these emotions—everything he'd always hated about his father's lectures, every part of his being that recoiled when he was scolded—no! Kel curled his own fists. "I'm not so irresponsible," he retorted, words clipped, "I'm just a bit lax on keeping track of time."

"Lax?" Dad chuckled. "Oh that's the most accurate thing you've said, lad. Lax is right."

Kel shook his head. "I'm responsible. I just have a different idea of things to be done than you."

"And what's that? Your surfboards?" Dad extended a hand toward the darkness from which Kel had rolled. "Your precious contraptions? Worthless."

Kel blinked. Dad couldn't really think this... "They're not worthless. They're valuable creations."

"And they're all you do—as you fritter away your time." Dad put his fists on his hips. "Isn't that about right?"

Kel took a step back, shaking his head. "No. No, they're worth *something*."

"To you. And no one else." Dad crossed his arms. "Ever occur to you—that might be the case in other ways? That you're a worthless waste of stone?"

Kel's mouth dropped. No. This really couldn't be Dad. Even though...

18

He averted his eyes, swallowing. It was true that Dad might've thought these things from time to time...Kel didn't really know.

"*You* are a waste of time, Kel. Time—that thing you care so little about." Dad moved in close, lowering his voice. "And as days turn into years, years into decades, decades into centuries—little by little time will snatch away everything you love." He snapped his fingers. "Just as it snatched me from you."

"No! No, it—"

"And one day—" Dad raised his finger, "it'll take your mom, lad."

Kel leapt on him, fists swinging. He pounded again and again, growling. He didn't care if anything heard him—he'd just keep pounding all day. "Stop it! Stop saying that!"

"Just how much time will you waste before she—"

"Kel!"

Kel felt himself being jerked back. Someone was clutching his arm! He turned, wild eyed, fist raised, as Grekham pulled him onto a high boulder. For an instant his fist trembled, rage rippling through his arm—then Kel lowered it, blinking. "Grekham."

"Don't inhale the mist, lad. It's the dragon's saliva."

So it *was* the Flame Dragon's doing. "The—the dragon is here?"

Grekham shook his head. "Not a chance. It can't make it through the collapsed tunnels—remember?"

"Then—" Kel swallowed suddenly, "—than what is its saliva doing here?"

"No one knows, lad." Grekham released his arm, eyes on the mist below them. "Maybe the dragon knows it can't reach us, so it sends out its saliva to spite us. The mist has a mind of its own—it creeps as it wills, looking for sentient life to inhale it. Then it spins its illusions."

Kel focused on the mist, still shaking. "That's a lot of saliva."

Grekham nodded. "It must be a very hungry dragon."

"It doesn't eat us, though. We just burn and melt in its body."

"And our life energy sustains it. At least, that's what our scientists supposed."

Kel let out his breath—lowering his shoulders, closing his eyes. Somewhere far out there—he could practically see it in his mind—the dragon waited, mist flowing from its jaws. Eyes burning. "So next time, we scout out the current."

"Aye."

Kel swallowed, eyes opening. He glanced at the silver lava river,

19

clenching his fists. "And what now?"

"We wait for a rescue team to take us home." Grekham turned and hopped to another boulder. "As I made the precaution of informing someone I'd be exploring the wilds. I told the timekeeper to send a team if we didn't return in two days."

Kel nodded, following Grekham. "So we wait then?"

"Aye. And in the meantime, we seek higher ground. For the mist."

Kel's eyes darted over to the mist. It was rising slowly, tendrils reaching out for his feet. "Agreed."

☼ ☼ ☼

"Grekham!"

Kel's eyes opened. How long had he been sleeping? And who had called out Grekham's name? That was a lass's voice.

He glanced down at the mist. Or at least, where the mist should've been. The ground ten meters below them was clear, jagged veins of golden pyrite running along it. Nothing odd.

"Grekham? Are you here?"

"Aye." Grekham's eyes fluttered open, and his legs and arms popped out. "Watch out for the mist."

"What mist?" A rhodochrosite with yellow spikes on her shoulders and legs appeared from behind a boulder. Bright red, with a translucent body. She batted her eyes at them, fists on her hips. "So there you are. And I see you dragged someone else along with you this time."

Grekham gave a sheepish grin. Then he offered her a thumbs-up. "Thanks for coming, Kharema."

"Don't hope for a habit." She began climbing the boulders between them, muttering to herself. "Always getting in trouble, never thinking ahead…"

"And here you are." Grekham flashed her a smile. "Not bad, is it?"

"I had to avoid lavaracks on the way here." Kharema heaved herself over the last boulder and stood beside them. "So yes, quite bad. Thanks for asking."

"My pleasure." Anyone else would be flinching from the glare

20

Kharema was giving Grekham. But the ilmenite was still smiling. "Shall we leave?"

"One moment." Kharema turned to Kel. "Your name?"

"I—eh—" Kel swallowed, blinking. Why was he so nervous?

Well, she was a lass. He hadn't talked to one of those in almost a year. Mom didn't count.

"Come on now—it's not a difficult question." She put her fists on her hips. "Name. Please."

"Kel." Kel swallowed. "Kelmor Ketarn."

Kharema studied him, eyes narrowed—then stuck out her hand. "Nice to meet you, Kel."

Kel took her hand uncertainly—then gave it a shake. "Eh—good to meet you as well."

That was the most awkward handshake in the history of Brekh'cha. Now she'd be giggling at him.

Except she wasn't. In fact, she didn't seem like the type to be giggling at all. She released his hand, then inhaled deeply. "Alright then. No time to lose—let's be going."

Kel blinked—then his shoulders lowered. "Right." Glancing at Grekham, he cleared his throat. "Now's as good a time as any."

"You both should really have some oversight, you know."

A smile tugged at Kel's lips. "I know."

☼ ☼ ☼

Home.

Kel rolled in, hoping Mom was anywhere else. Fires burned in porticos to either side—and for a second, he supposed he might be alone.

"Kel!"

He turned as Mom put her hands on his forehead. She ran her opal fingers down his cheek, concern lining her face. "You've got cracks. What happened?"

Oh no. Kel raised a hand to his cheek. Definitely some damage. "Mom, I—I'll have it repaired."

"Why, though?" She tilted her head at him. "What happened, Kel?"

21

Kel pressed his lips together, averting his eyes. Mom never liked it when he did dangerous things. Really, he couldn't blame her. "I'm afraid I went off a bit deeper into the wilds this time."

"Without anyone to watch your back?"

Kel shook his head. "I had backup."

"Then what's the problem?"

She was taking this far better than he'd expected. "I—I thought you'd be worried."

"Of course I'm worried! But you're a growing labradorite, Kel. You've got to branch out." She nudged him, the fiery streaks in her opal face glittering in the firelight. "And besides, now you have a new friend. I can't stop you from going out—but maybe I don't need to."

That was quite an admission. "You're fine if I go out then?"

"Well not fine exactly..." She let her voice trail off, eyes wandering over to the entrance. "Kel, we dug out this home by hand."

Kel scanned their abode. Sparkling emerald table on the wall, marble bowl of a bed on the ceiling, plenty of storage alcoves...quite cozy—but quaint, in its own way. "Aye."

"But we didn't build it so you could stay trapped here." She focused on him, lips pressed together. "I want you to be free—explore your options." She put her hands on his shoulders. "Even if you have to take risks."

Risks! If only she knew. "I can take risks."

"I know you can. And I'm not telling you to leap into danger," she wagged her finger, "but I'm not forbidding the possibility either. You need a healthy freedom."

That meant quite a bit. Kel smiled. "Great."

"And I know Kolath would've agreed."

Dad...Kel averted his eyes, curling his fists. "Mom."

"What?"

"I—I saw Dad."

She furrowed her brow, stepping back. "Kel—that's impossible."

"I know." Kel inhaled deeply—though he wasn't planning on saying much. But air seemed in short supply when you wanted to say something hard. "He came to me in the dragon's mist."

"What!" Mom's eyes went wide. "No! You inhaled the mist?"

"Only a wee bit." He pinched air between his thumb and forefinger. "Enough to see dad."

"Dad? Bah! That wasn't your dad!" Mom shook her head, hands

on her hips. "The mist spins the dragon's illusions."

"Aye." Kel cleared his throat, focusing on the emerald table. "And he had things to say."

Mom stared at him, concern lining her face again. His cheeks burned a little with her gaze. She could always read him...

She placed a hand on his shoulder. "What did he tell you?"

"I—I don't want to repeat it."

"Of course not. The dragon told you lies—not your dad."

He swallowed, glancing at her. "The dragon wouldn't know those things."

"But its saliva does." She placed her other hand on his shoulder so he would meet her eyes. "You understand, Kel? The mist knows your thoughts. And it brings out your most bitter imaginings."

His bitter imaginings? "Why?"

"Because those distract you. You can't think about anything else when you're bitter. It consumes you." She gritted her teeth. "Just like the mist, Kel. You can't inhale any more. You hear me?"

Now that was firm. Kel gave a sharp nod. "Understood."

"Good." Her face softened. Glittering lines of opal flashed across her skin—and she closed her eyes. "Don't let the dragon win, Kel."

And one day it'll take your mom, lad.

Kel's eyes watered—and he bit down on his lip. Why was this so hard? Now he wanted to cry suddenly. "Mom..."

"What?"

Kel laced his fingers through hers, inhaling deeply. "I love you." He pressed his head to hers and closed his eyes. "Don't leave me, okay?"

Seconds passed. Kel dared not open his eyes.

Then he heard Mom's voice. "I'll try not to, Kel."

4 THE CENTIPEDE ABYSS

5656 OT (two months later)

"Alright. I think it checks out." Kel followed the green lava river's course with his eyes. "You scouted the end?"

"Aye." Grekham came up beside him, hefting his surfboard. "It's a good one."

Kel grinned. "Ready on your mark then."

"Just one moment!"

They both turned as Kharema and a jadeite rolled up. Kharema uncurled from her roll, her rhodochrosite body filtering the lava's green glow. Yellow spikes popped out from her shoulders and legs, and she pressed her lips together. "Don't you go wandering off again."

"Aw, come on!" Grekham spread his free hand. "I told you we'd be off and where we'd be! That's proper safety protocol, no?"

"We scouted the river," Kel added, raising an eyebrow. "C'mon already. What do you want from us?"

"Oversight." The jadeite beside Kharema spoke. Her jagged body was just as translucent as Kharema's, and she wore a pair of loosefitting spectacles that barely managed to rest on a slight bump between her eyes—the nose? Some geolites had bigger noses than others. The jadeite adjusted her spectacles, lips parting. "You'll be operating under my terms now."

"And who are you?"

Kharema opened her mouth, but the jadeite cut her off. "You can call me the Jadess."

"The Jadess?" Grekham chuckled. "That an official title?"

"It's one I gave myself." The Jadess put her fists on her hips,

24

raising her chin. "I don't intend to be suffering your disparagement, Grekham. This is my turf now."

"And who put you in charge?"

"Brekh'cha—a couple hundred or so years from now." The Jadess inhaled deeply. "I have ambitions for this land. I'm going to be the Supreme Declarer of the Ticora Council."

"Oh-ho! And what are you now?"

"It doesn't matter." The Jadess adjusted her spectacles again. "Now I've heard of your little surfing expeditions—and while they are dangerous..." She let her voice trail off, like this was some admonition. "They do intrigue me."

"Intrigue you?" Kel's brow furrowed, and he shifted his grip on the board. "Why?"

"What other reason?" The Jadess pursed her lips. "Each expedition's an exploration of the Western Wilds."

Well, that was something. She actually cared. "Really? That's important, eh?"

"It's valuable to our understanding—especially when those wilds rest between us and Old Ticora."

She couldn't even say the dragon. But that's where the creature was, right? Kel cleared his throat. "Aye. Though we don't intend to go that far."

"I don't doubt it. You'd be foolish to the core."

Kharema elbowed her friend. "For Knoth's sake, Khera, don't be condescending—"

"I told you not to call me that!" The Jadess elbowed her back. "Excuse my sister. I am 'The Jadess' to you."

"Khera, eh?" Grekham snickered. "I'll bet you're no older than twenty."

"That doesn't matter. I—"

"And you're commanding us. I'm thirty!" Grekham indicated himself with his thumb. "And you boss me around?"

"I—"

"Look." Kharema crossed her arms, glaring at Grekham. "Khera—excuse me, the Jadess—and I feel some oversight would benefit the group. Which is why we're creating a formal team."

"A team?" Kel approached them, brow furrowed. "You mean to say you'll be looking to make these outings official?"

The Jadess nodded. "Under our oversight, an official expedition team—you, Grekham and Kharema—will scout out the pathways between New Ticora and Old. Without getting too close to the old city, of course," she added hastily, averting her eyes. "Agreed?"

Not a bad deal. Kel shrugged. "Could be worse, I suppose."

"Only if we get to surf." Grekham crossed his arms. "You don't expect to suck the fun out of everything, do you?"

"It'll be fine." Kharema gave the Jadess a look. "They can surf."

The Jadess rolled her eyes, lips pursed. "Agreed."

"Great! Let's go!" Grekham adjusted the surfboard under his shoulder—then turned to the river. "Now we've scouted this river already—"

"One moment."

Kel noticed Kharema looking away. What was she nervous about? Kel put a hand on Grekham's shoulder. "Wait up, lad."

"What's the problem?"

Kharema looked like she'd rather not say. But after glancing at the Jadess—no doubt to muster her courage—she focused on them. "I'm to be the expedition team's leader."

"Leader?" Grekham burst out laughing, slapping his knees. "You're kidding me, lass!"

"I think she's serious." Kel crossed his arms. He'd be laughing at no one—it was rude, plain and simple. "She's going to be our leader, Grekham. And that's fine by me."

"What? Her?" Grekham indicated the rhodochrosite with his palm. "She's good at finding us, sure—but surfing like we do?"

Kel clenched his jaw. "She can learn."

"Really. What's gotten into you, Kel?"

Kel's voice was low. "We don't laugh at people."

Grekham frowned, confusion running like cracks through his forehead. "No kidding?"

"No kidding."

Grekham hesitated—then nodded. "Alright then."

Kharema looked between them, uncertain. "So it's decided? No problems?"

"None." Kel hefted his surfboard, clearing his throat. He'd worked on this board for quite some time. There was no way anyone would ruin its maiden run. "Shall we go?"

"Let's." Kharema crossed her arms, eyes darting over to the Jadess. "Anything else?"

"Nothing. Update me when you return." The Jadess plucked the spectacles off her nose, folded them and tucked in her limbs—then rolled off, bumping over boulders as she disappeared into a tunnel.

Now it was just the three of them. Kel rolled his shoulders. "Can we surf now?"

"Aye." Kharema made her way to the green lava river, Kel and Grekham in tow. "Any spare boards?"

Kel shrugged. "I've got a stash."

"Really?" She glanced back at him. "How many?"

More than he cared to admit, truth be told. "Plenty."

☆ ☆ ☆

"Now I'd prefer you go a little slower for me—" Kharema hesitated, "—at least, until I pick up a wee bit more skill."

"No problem, love." Kel set his board in the river—then hopped on. He pulled his legs in, and dipped his hands in the warm lava with a hiss. "Just follow our lead."

"Right."

Grekham hopped on after them, smile in place. "Ready, lass?"

Kharema kept her eyes ahead. "Don't call me 'lass.'"

"As you wish, love."

A surge rippled through the river—and in seconds their boards lifted. Now they were riding the wave. Kel stood, holding his arms out for balance. "Easy there. If it's too strong, let me know."

"I'm fine, thank you."

"You sure, love?"

"I can—whoa!" Kel heard nothing for a couple seconds. Then, "I'm fine."

Right. They'd never be able to surf their scouted route at this rate. Kel gripped his surfboard's edges as the wave set them down. "Alright then."

Drops of green lava sprayed past him. Grekham had landed hard. The gold-speckled ilmenite floated just ahead of them, hands hanging in the lava to slow himself.

When was the next wave? This river wasn't as fast as Kel had supposed.

But now they were out of the main cavern, floating through a tunnel of silvery crystals that stuck out like needles. Almost like white sea urchins were perched along the walls and ceiling. The green river was taking them up a wall, and gravity shifted around them. More white urchin crystals grew along the banks. They had a sort of sparkle, like snow under a full moon.

"This isn't so bad."

He glanced back at Kharema. "That's because the river isn't as fierce as we'd thought."

"Aye." Grekham frowned, looking ahead. "Not nearly what we'd hoped for."

"I can accept that." Kharema paddled a little, coming up beside Kel. "How deep is this lava?"

"No one knows. Probably only a few feet."

She turned to him, sapphire irises sparkling in the green light. "And if it's more?"

Then they'd be sinking quite a ways if they fell off. Kel focused on her arms. They seemed more ruby than rhodochrosite—was she a combination? "I doubt it, love."

"Hm." She turned to look ahead, lips pursed. "It shouldn't be a problem. Long as—" her brow furrowed. "What's that?"

What? Kel gazed down the tunnel. Silver globules of lava hung in the distance, glowing brighter every second.

But wait…they were getting too bright, too fast. Like the globules were falling their way. But why would lava be dripping toward them? That was wrong for this gravity zone.

Then he heard it. Buzzing.

"Dragonflies," Grekham whispered, eyes wide. "A swarm."

"Aye." Kharema's muscles tightened. "We need to turn."

Kel shook his head. "Can't turn against the current, love."

"Then we—" Kharema's eyes darted from bank to bank. "The crystals are everywhere."

"Aye." Kel focused on the swarm, now much larger than silver globules. He could just make out the shape of silver dragonflies, buzzing toward them. Some far bigger than the harmless breeds. "Soldier dragonflies."

"And silver." Kharema closed her ruby fists. "The most vicious species."

"No choice but to press through." Grekham leaned forward,

28

gritting his teeth. "Hope they pass overhead."

"Agreed." Kharema glanced at Kel. "Did you not scout for swarms on this route?"

"Truth be told, no."

"And why not?"

"It didn't occur to us." Kel checked behind them. "We might be able to surf through the swarm on this next wave, though."

"Might?"

Kel could already feel his board lifting. He gripped the edges—then grimaced as the wave raised them before the swarm. No choice but to surf.

Silver dragonflies buzzed around him as he stood, heat washing across him. He twisted and turned his body, steering the board between angry dragonflies, dodging silver stingers and fiery white wings.

"Kel!"

Lava exploded beside him. Silver bursts of magma erupted from the soldier dragonflies, zipping past his head. He tucked it into his body, gritting his teeth.

"Kel, I can't surf!"

He dared not look back. He steered his board where he hoped Kharema was—then reached out his hand. His fingers curled around her wrist. "Gotcha!"

"Imbecile! Now we'll *both* flip over!"

She was stressed. Kel wasn't sure how he had the peace of mind to know this—but something about her voice told him she wasn't thinking clearly. "Just hold on. It'll be alright."

"We're about to get buried in lava! And it's both of your—"

"Agh!" A jet of silver lava sliced through Grekham's arm. A dragonfly swooped in, obsidian legs ready to snatch him—and Grekham pulled his board up with his good arm, ramming the dragonfly. He ricocheted off the creature and plunged into the green river with a hiss.

"Grekham!" No way they'd go after him. Kel gritted his teeth, clutching Kharema's wrist as he swerved between dragonflies. As long as she held her balance, they'd be fine.

A silver laser glanced his shoulder. He gasped, searing pain running down his arm—hissing filling his ears. His shoulder was smoking.

"Why are they still coming!" Kharema growled in frustration.

29

"How many *are* there!"

What were silver dragonflies doing zooming over a green lava river in the first place? Were they lost? "I don't know, love."

"How are you so calm! Really!"

"I—" Kel wasn't calm. His heart was pounding at his chest, his muscles tight. Any second and a dragonfly could hit them. Just because he wasn't losing his head… "Could you be quiet?"

"Quiet?"

A fork in the river! Kel twisted his board—and they veered to the right, dragonflies zooming past. Silver lasers exploded in the lava beside them, green droplets spraying his knees with a hiss. Steady—

And there. Just like that, they were through. The dragonflies were well behind them.

Perfect.

Kel smiled, setting himself down in the board. He released Kharema's wrist. "No problem."

"Except Grekham's at the bottom of the river."

"Eh, he'll find his way out. Happened to me once when I was six. Took me a few days, but I pressed through and got home." He put a palm on his head. "Might have lost an inch or two, though. That pressure is something."

"Did you?" Kharema paddled so she was floating beside him. "Were you in the wilds though?"

Fair enough. Kel averted his eyes. "I suppose we could send a search party to comb the river bottom."

"Aye." Kharema pulled her arms out of the lava, expelling a sharp sigh. "Assuming we don't run into another swarm ourselves."

Kel swallowed, staring ahead. Nothing to say, really.

"I'm—I'm sorry if I overreacted."

His eyes wandered over to Kharema. "Are you?"

"It did nothing to help our situation."

Kel shrugged. That was true. "Eh, you needed to vent your fears. No biggie."

"No biggie?" Kharema arched an eyebrow, turning to him. "You're a brave lad, Kel."

Not really. Warmth crept into Kel's cheeks. "Aye."

"I mean it. That was really brave."

What could say? "Thanks, love."

They floated along for a few seconds, bobbing up and down in the lava. Kharema inhaled deeply. Though there wasn't much to say, he supposed.

Then, "Thanks for helping me steer, Kel."

A smile pulled at Kel's lips. "Couldn't have you capsizing yourself, could we?"

She gave a small laugh—more of a breath, really. "That's right."

Now Kel cleared his throat. He was still a little awkward around her—but that was clearing up quite a bit. He tapped the edge of his board.

"You still should've scouted for dragonflies, you know."

And there was the admonition. Kel pressed his lips together, eyes on the current. "Mm."

"Not that—not that I'm not grateful. But..." She hesitated, looking ahead. "You could avoid a lot of trouble, Kel. Just pay attention."

Kel let out a small sigh. Did she have to lecture him? "I know."

"Not that I'm mad. I'd just prefer a little more scouting in the future."

No dragonflies had shown up when they were scouting. And at any rate, this is why they preferred green and red streams to silver. "I'll make a note of it."

"Good." She paddled so her board was closer—they'd been drifting apart. "You alright, lad?"

Kel shrugged. "Been better, truth be told."

"Mm." She refocused on the tunnel ahead—then gasped. "The river's ending!"

Kel's brow furrowed. That made no sense. If they were coming to a lavafall, the current would be picking up. Unless—

Perfect. The river was flowing into a fissure—one too small for their boards. They'd wash up on the opposite shore, landing amidst red rocks. "Looks like we've found our stop."

"Oh." Kharema studied the shore—then nodded. "Good. You can stay put here."

"Pardon?"

They bumped up on the shore, and Kharema handed him her board. "I need to fetch help. For Grekham. If you stay put, that will make it easier to know his general area."

A good plan. "Alright then."

"And I—I'll turn around now, if you don't mind." She let her sapphire irises settle on his feet. "Stay put—if that's alright."

"No problem."

She met his eyes, arms flat by her sides. Then she cleared her throat—and rolled off. Kel watched her disappear down a side tunnel.

Well. Nothing really to do.

He should find some kind of shelter in case the dragonflies returned. He rolled down the main tunnel past the shore, trying not to bump into rocks. Rolling was still a chore. He could spend more time practicing.

Whoa! He'd rolled into a void. He uncurled, feet skidding as he stopped.

He was standing on quartz. Perfectly transparent, so light could shine through it. Except there was no light. Everything around him was totally dark.

Well, not everything. He spotted fiery centipedes of all colors floating lazily in the distance on every side. Twirling as they mined unseen rocks.

The quartzite pillar itself struck through the middle of the abyss like a spear. He could see no end to it—or to the darkness past the centipedes.

He checked the quartzite. Despite some fractures, it felt quite sturdy. But...it seemed almost empty inside. Without light to shine through it, it was like he was standing on a void.

And the centipedes...there were so far away. He could reach out and pretend they were close enough, but that was it.

His eyes scanned the darkness. No walls, nothing of substance. He was alone.

Kel pressed his lips together. For someone without a sense of time, waiting was an eternity.

5 BULLIED BY HERODONS

5754 OT (ninety-eight years later)

"Whoo! What a ride!" Kel flipped the board up with his foot, catching it in one hand. He tucked it under his shoulder—then made his way down the ridge, Grekham and Kharema in tow. "That current was great."

"Aye. Not as wild as last week—" Grekham chuckled, "—but still a ride."

"I'll take ordered over wild," Kharema snapped, glaring at him. "Count your lucky stones we didn't end up at the bottom of some lake."

"Luck had little to do with it." Kel turned to them, grinning. "You've improved your surfing, Kharema."

"I should hope so. Almost a century of practice with you crazy lads."

"We're not that crazy." Kel reconsidered. "Okay, just a wee bit."

"More than a wee bit." Kharema shook her head. "You seek danger."

"*He* seeks danger." Kel indicated Grekham with his thumb. "I'm just here for the ride."

"Whatever." Kharema was smiling, picking up her pace. "Let's get a report to the Jadess."

"Going somewhere?"

They turned to see three creatures approaching them. Armadillo snouts, humanoid forms, rubber lining their backs and the fronts of their arms and legs—clawed toes and hands...definitely herodons. And no doubt here to pester them. Kel narrowed his eyes. "As a matter

33

of fact, we are."

"The Nicota Outpost, we assume?"

"Where else?" Kharema snapped. "Though it's none of your business."

"Isn't it?" The herodon took a step toward her, a smile tilting his lips. His voice was soft as a whisper—like all herodons. "Since you are so close to our own abodes."

"The dragon forced us away from our old habitation," Kharema countered, raising her chin. "As you well know."

"And yet, you keep coming closer to our dwellings in Eastern Brekh'cha." The herodon tilted his head, studying her. "Now you're building an outpost at Nicota. Not very subtle."

"We mean no war against your kind." Grekham curled his free fist, leaning in. "So you can leave us alone."

"Should we?" The herodon barked a laugh. "You multiply over the decades, you claim. Expand for more land." He lowered his voice so it blended with the hiss of the lava. "I think you're just rocks looking to pick a fight."

"And what do you know?" Kharema set her fists on her hips. "Leave us alone."

The herodon motioned to his comrade. The second herodon curled into a rubber ball and rolled down the cavern. When he was about twenty meters out, he uncurled and put a clawed hand against the azure crystals by the wall.

Keeping his eyes on the geolites, the first herodon gave another signal. "Watch."

The second herodon curled into a ball again—then sped up, tumbling down a second ridge farther off. In seconds he was a blur, racing between boulders.

Then he collided with a larger boulder—one about the size of Kel—and it shattered. He burst out of his roll, landing in a crouch. Around him the boulder's fragments were littered. He raised his snout—then stood tall, brushing himself off.

"You see, our rubber hides absorb impact quite well." The first herodon arched an eyebrow. "While your stony bodies, like these boulders, typically do not."

"You don't scare me." Though the herodon was a foot taller, Kharema advanced on him. "You couldn't shatter me anyway. My arms are ruby corundum—a hardness rating of nine—my body

34

rhodochrosite."

"Ah, but it is not your hardness which determines whether you will shatter." The herodon put his hands on his knees, bending down so they were eye to eye. "It's your structure. Some rocks—including diamonds—shatter quite easily upon impact."

Kharema didn't flinch. Though Kel knew as well as anyone it was true. He'd spent at least two decades studying his own anatomy. She shook her head. "Irrelevant. We geolites have stronger structures than rocks in the wilds."

"Only somewhat stronger." The herodon beckoned with his free hand. The other herodon rolled toward them, slowing only a little as he bounced up the ridge. "What if my friend shatters you right now? Are you willing to bet your structural stability on it?"

Kharema didn't answer. She just kept standing there, fists on her hips. The herodon was going to hit her!

Kel dropped his surfboard, leaping at Kharema. He shoved her aside—but the herodon uncurled feet from them, claws digging in as he skidded to a stop. The creature gave a soft snort, eyes twinkling in the lava's light.

"My oh my." The first herodon chuckled, smiling. "We have your boyfriend to the rescue."

"I'm not her boyfriend." Kel kept his eyes on the herodon, though his face was surely turning a deeper shade of blue. Blushing betrayed him. "And I'll not have you threatening her."

"Will you?" The herodon cocked his head, straightening himself. "And what are *you* made of, geolite?"

"Labradorite," Kel announced, indicating himself with his thumb, "one hundred percent pure feldspar."

"Ah. And with such perfect labradorescence." The herodon indicated Kel's skin with his claws. "Shining a slight shade of white or blue in the light when you turn—perhaps even other colors. But dark green otherwise. A phenomenon unique to labradorite."

Kel felt uneasy suddenly. "So? What do you know of my structure?"

"Quite a great deal, as a matter of fact." The herodon stepped back, cupping his elbow in one hand. He rested his chin on his other fist. "I know that labradorite, despite being softer than most gemstones, is actually quite durable. I suspect you would not easily shatter."

35

"That's right." Kel hoped it was true himself. He'd studied hardness only briefly. "You can't scratch me."

"On the contrary." The herodon raised a clawed finger. "Softer materials, such as my claw, can scratch harder materials when applied with enough force. Moreover, labradorite is quite soft compared to other gemstones…" He placed his claw on Kel's skin. "Only slightly harder than glass, in fact."

"Stop it!" Kharema pushed the herodon's claw away. "Enough of this!"

"Oh! And now the girlfriend returns." The herodon stepped back, giving a snort of laughter. "Here to stand up for your clueless boyfriend?"

"He's not my boyfriend." Kharema set her fists on her hips again. She might've been blushing, though it was hard to tell with rhodochrosites—especially in red lava light. "And you can leave us alone now. As I'll be giving you more than a scratch otherwise."

"Oh will you?" The herodon chuckled. He motioned to his comrade. "Grab the surfboard lying on the ground."

The herodon rolled over before Kel could stop him. He uncurled, snatched up the surfboard and raised it higher than Kel could reach.

"I assume you don't care about this surfboard," the herodon began, walking over to his friend, "as you dropped it so hastily."

"Give that back!" Kel tried leaping, but the other herodon held it just out of reach.

"Certainly." The other herodon took the board—then jabbed it with his claws. Chunks of helenberry came out. "I simply need to modify it first."

"Stop it! Let go of my board!"

"Your board?" The herodon chuckled again. "Looks like an abandoned helenberry shell to me."

"It's—my—board!"

The herodon struck again—more helenberry pieces fell out. And again, and again—

The creature stumbled sideways as Kharema pushed him. "Let it go. Now."

"Oo." The herodon grinned, tossing the board away. It clattered across the dirt, coming to rest by an azure crystal. "Going to fight me now, are we?"

Kharema didn't answer. Instead, she started spinning. Holding her

36

fists out, she twirled like a ballerina. Then she stepped in close—and tilted her angle upward so her fists pounded at the herodon. Like a ball and chain. But the balls were her fists, the chains her arms. Each blow drew a grunt from the herodon as he stumbled back.

Kharema slowed to a stop, facing him with curled fists. "I said leave us alone."

"So you're trained in geolite combat." The herodon rubbed his jaw, arching an eyebrow. "Not bad, actually. But you've miscalculated. There are three of us, and apparently only one of you trained enough to fight."

"Three, last we checked." Grekham had kept silent, but now he stepped forward—fists curled. "You want to challenge all three of us, it's your bones that'll be breaking."

"Oh, I doubt it." The herodon flexed his hands, claws gleaming in the lava's light. "You have terrible luck, geolites. You're invulnerable to disease as rocks—and swords just bounce off most of you."

"Aye." Kharema crossed her arms, standing tall. "What are you going to do about it?"

"Not only that…" He let his voice trail off, eyes darting between them. "I have heard you're immune to magic."

"Correct." Kharema raised her chin. "So where's our terrible luck?"

The herodon indicated the shattered bolder only forty or so meters from them. "You're not immune to physics. And you've encountered the one race in this world that may be able to shatter you quite easily." He leaned in close, gums pulling back so his fangs showed. Blood trickled along one side—where Kharema had struck him. "And we will not spare you if it comes to war."

"Will you, now?" Kharema held his stare. "You won't need to. We'll crush you."

The herodon pulled back, gums lowering. "On the contrary. We'll shatter you."

"Try it, you fiends!" Grekham shook a fist at them. "Just see what happens!"

"Should I?" The herodon narrowed his eyes, turning to his friends. Kel saw no response—but when the herodon turned back to Grekham, he shook his head. "Not at this time. You can keep your small victory."

"That's right." Kel was feeling bolder. "And you can stay out of our business."

"Can we?" The herodon flexed his claws again. "That depends on you, geolites. And whether you encroach on our space."

"We have no intention of encroaching on anyone's boundaries," Kharema objected, ruby muscles tight, "So don't come near us."

"Hm." He inhaled deeply, chest rising—then turned from them. "See you on the battlefield—eventually."

"Oh really?" Kel raised his fists. "You'd be wise to avoid it, herodon!"

"And you'd be wise to avoid us." The herodon beckoned—and his two comrades followed him. They strolled down the ridge, heads held high. "Goodbye, geolites."

"You—" Kel stopped himself, teeth gritted. "Herodons. No respect for people's property."

"They're a nasty sort," Kharema breathed, arms still crossed. She turned to him. "But we'd best be going. This area clearly has problems."

"Aye." Kel swallowed, glancing at the half-ruined surfboard. No point to salvaging it. "Back to Nicota."

"Not that herodons have any business being here in the first place." Kharema waved dismissively. "Their nearest habitation is miles away."

Kel never thought he'd regret moving to a more isolated location. Ticora had simply grown too crowded. But now he was wondering if Nicota might be more trouble than it was worth.

A hand on his shoulder. Kel glanced back to see Kharema studying him. "Kel? You alright?"

Kel blinked—then shook his head, fists loosening. "Aye."

"Shake it off, lad." She shook her head, sapphire irises glittering. "It's no sweat off our back."

Not like geolites could sweat in the first place. Kel gave a half-smile. "That's the truth."

☆ ☆ ☆

"And they ruined your surfboard?"

Kel nodded. "They—I spent days on that board."

"Weeks, more like. You were excited about it." Mom placed her

38

hands on his shoulders. "But Kel, you can rebuild a board. Lives—
that's a different matter."

That was true. Kel swallowed, eyes on the ground. "I realize that."

"And what about Kharema? Is she okay?"

Another lump in his throat. Kel tried not to swallow. "Aye."

"You should really ask her out, you know. She won't wait for too
many centuries."

"I know." Kel wanted to be discussing anything else right now. "I
just...I don't know, mom. She might not like me that way."

"Of course she likes you that way, Kel. Do you see any other
eligible bachelors in Nicota?"

Truth be told, he did. Kel shrugged. "I suppose so."

"And how about Grekham? She's not dating him."

"Grekham has no interest in her. He's set his eyes on a nice
halite."

"Right. But that's recent." Mom gave him a look like it was
obvious. "She's got plenty of options—but instead, she hangs out
around you. She even moved to Nicota when we did—despite her
sister staying in Ticora." She put a finger in his chest. "You're the one,
Kel. And you get along quite well with her, from what I've heard."

Kel opened and closed his fists. This was no lecture he wanted to
endure after those herodons. "I know."

"Stop saying that!" Mom stepped back, concern lining her face.
"I'm just worried, Kel. It's been a century since moving from Old
Ticora—and you've no one to call your own."

"It's not been—" had it? Kel scratched his head. "It's been a
century?"

"Aye. And here you are, tooling around and surfing." She shook
her head slowly. "Not accomplishing anything."

"What's there to accomplish?" Kel spread his hands, throat tight.
"I just—I want to surf, mom! That's okay, right?"

"It's okay for a decade—maybe two. But this constant tooling
around..." Mom crossed her arms, eyes on Kel's feet. "Kel, you've
got to make something of yourself."

Right. And that's what it was about. "And if I don't want to?"

"I'm just saying—you've got a gift. You can make contraptions
like hardly anyone else. You've got the skill—and most geolites
would beg and cry for those fingers of yours."

Kel looked down at his hands. His fingers gleamed blue as he

39

turned them in the light, then shifted back to dark green. Perfectly smooth, long and narrow. Not bad at all, really. "So what?"

"So put your boards on show! Go to an exhibition!" She pleaded with one hand. "Do anything, Kel! Just stop holing yourself up!"

"I hang out with Grekham and Kharema."

"Aye. And maybe one day you'll end up with her." She leaned in. "If you've got the courage."

Oh—now that was a blow. Kel stumbled back, like she'd hit him. "Do—do you mean that?"

"I—" she turned from him, giving a sharp sigh. "I want to see you succeed, Kel. And I think she's great for you."

That was no doubt true. But—no. Kel couldn't risk it. And besides, he wouldn't know how to start anyway. Could he just go up and ask her out? Not a chance. "I—I don't want to lose her as a friend. You understand that, don't you?"

She studied him, her lower lip trembling. Why was she about to cry? "I know you think you have all the time in the world, Kel," she whispered, blinking. "But one day you'll be out of it. And you'll wish you'd spent it better."

Kel's mouth dropped. "But—" but she was right. He swallowed, averting his eyes. "I suppose so. But give—just give me more time, okay?"

She sniffed, drilling him with teary eyes. "Alright, Kel. You can take your time."

6 THE GREAT DEBATE

5912 OT (one hundred fifty-eight years later) • 12 years old

Behind the podium the herodon stood. Short snout, rubber hide covering the top of his nose and head, the front of his arms and knees—and his back, of course. Claws gleaming in the chandelier's light. Bronzed chest, shoulders back as he stood straight. Watching the humanite finish his speech behind the opposing podium.

Hrossar enjoyed watching his father debate.

Silence. The humanite was finished. Father adjusted his spectacles, letting them rest a little lower on his snout than one would expect. That was more optimal for reading notes. As many in the crowd might see note-reading as a weakness, subtlety was essential.

Father cleared his throat. "Thank you for your presentation, Mr. Sorensen."

The crowd leaned forward. Now came the rebuttal.

"I see you've made the mistake of equating correlation with causation." The herodon tapped his podium with a claw. "But that is a non sequitur. In this case, the theft of crops and the arrival of newcomers are not necessarily related. A thief could easily seize the opportunity to frame said newcomers."

Murmurs. Some nods in the crowd.

"Now as you have no direct proof the newcomers are involved in any way, shape or form with the theft of your client's crops, I fail to see where your argument rests."

A smile pulled at Hrossar's lips. His father could take people apart quite easily—even when they appeared to have the edge. His voice, soft as silk, never rose an inch to dismantle his opponent's arguments.

41

"Perhaps you would care to offer some real arguments—but as this is near the end of the debate, I doubt you have any." Father's eyebrows went up. "I, however, have many points to restate, none of which you have bothered to address. Observe."

The crowd waited as Father strolled over to an easel with drawings on it. He flipped back the page, then ran his clawed forefinger along it. "As you can see, Diagram A exhibits the arrangement of shrubbery beside the plantation in question. Based on this, it is likely an intruder would come from the east—not the west, as there is no cover there." He allowed his point to sink in, addressing the audience. "The new neighbors reside in the west."

The people knew this already. That Father was restating facts was simply a rhetorical tactic. *Many times it is said before many people understand,* as Father put it. *As people ask the same questions, the same answers must be given.*

"Now as my opponent has not addressed this, I assume he has no counterargument. In which case he should concede the debate." A corner of Father's lips lifted. "But as I suspect he does not wish to forfeit his payroll, that would be impossible."

His opponent stood there, fingers laced on his podium. The humanite didn't even flinch.

"Moreover, since the debate is coming to a close, it is irrelevant. The point is, as I am certain the judges and audience will see, my opponent has no case—and I do." Father flipped another page, indicating the next diagram. "I could continue, but there is little point to refreshing your memory. The newcomers are innocent."

Perfect. A conclusion delivered with all the dryness of a census taker. The killing thrust, soft in tone but not power.

Hrossar loved it when Father won.

☆ ☆ ☆

"Not as challenging an opponent as I'd hoped," Father admitted, putting a hand on Hrossar's shoulder, "but still enough to refresh my skills."

Hrossar watched the crowd pile out of the debate house, snout raised. His claws dug into the cold grass, and he gave a soft snort. "He

42

was foolish. But an easy victory is still a victory."

"Correct. Though it is no friend to the lax."

"Agreed." The softness of Hrossar's own voice still surprised him at times. Puberty truly removed the hoarseness from one's vocal cords. Now it was soft as a whisper. "Perhaps your next opponent will be more challenging."

"Perhaps." Father sniffed at the air, eyes narrowed. "It seems we ended late, however. It is almost six-thirty."

"Is it?" Hrossar sniffed at the air. He was still distinguishing the elements of scent that told him the time...the subtleties were *exceedingly* complex. But he would learn it eventually. "I could tell it is afternoon—but that observation could be discerned just as easily from the sun."

"You will improve with time." Father patted his shoulder. "Now your mother will be expecting us. So—"

"You! You herodons!"

Hrossar turned to see a humanite boy with red hair and freckles running toward him. "Are you referring to us?"

"You bet I am—you rogues! You miscreants!"

Strong words from someone who knew nothing of them. Hrossar arched an eyebrow. "Are you certain of this?"

"Of course I am! You and your kind are always getting in the way!" He skidded to a stop before Hrossar, pointing back at a woman. "See her? She's my mother."

"I see."

"She was robbed out of her life savings by a thief a few years ago." The way he spat the word "thief" made it clear he believed Hrossar inhabited that category. "And what did the thief do? Take one guess."

Hrossar glanced at Father, who indicated him with an open palm. Part of being an adult was defending oneself. Hrossar would be on his own—and he'd prefer nothing else. "A thief steals."

"'A thief steals.' Oh, how precise and pristine!" The kid repeated Hrossar's words in a mocking tone. "'A thief steals.' Just the perfect answer, isn't it?"

Hrossar's brow furrowed. "I fail to see the source of your animosity."

"Of course you do! You know why?" The kid stepped closer, looking up at Hrossar. "Because the thief hired a herodon to defend

43

himself. He got the fanciest herodon he could—using our money—and guess what happened next."

Hrossar could see where this was going. But he would humor the child. "What."

"The herodon beat us in a debate. We couldn't afford anyone to debate for us, you see—not exactly made of money." He pulled out the inner linings of his pockets, as if that would demonstrate his financial deficiency. "So no sophists on our side. Just yours. And guess what the judges did."

Hrossar's claws dug tighter into the grass. "I assume by your attitude that the judge allowed the thief to keep his money."

"That's right!" The kid pointed at Hrossar. "Because of you! Because of people just like you and your stupid father!"

Hrossar arched an eyebrow. "We had no part in such a travesty."

"No part? You're debaters for hire!" The kid thrust his fists on his hips. "You just work for the highest bidder, don't you? It could've been *you* debating my mother out of her life savings!"

"I am not old enough to debate—"

"But you will be—won't you!" The kid thrust his finger in Hrossar's chest. "And then you'll scam other people out of whatever they own. Whether you defend a villain or a hero, you don't care—" he rubbed his fingers against his thumb. "As long as there's money involved for you, it's fine—isn't it."

"If I may."

Hrossar glanced at his father. The herodon cleared his throat. "It is true that some of us will take on any case, provided the price is acceptable."

The kid blinked at him. It was clear he hadn't expected such a frank admission.

"However, not all sophists operate according to the same values. For instance, I only debate when I believe the viewpoint I am presenting is plausible."

"Plausible?" The kid's lips curled. "Say whatever you want, farce. You're only—you're only making excuses."

"It is clear you have been wronged. Perhaps if I took up an appeal—"

"Oh yeah! If I pay enough, right?"

Father blinked. "I occasionally offer my services for free—"

"Too late! That was years ago!" The kid shook his fists, a vein

44

bulging with rage. "Years later, and we're barely scraping to survive! All because of you!"

"We—"

"I'll tell you what I'll do. Because I can't do anything else." The kid spat on Father's chest. "There. Hope you appreciate it."

Hrossar flexed his clawed fingers. No point in attacking a child. But this disrespect was intolerable. "Careful."

"Or what? You're all the same, you stupid herodons." The kid spat on Hrossar's chest. "Some of you debate, some of you fight. Mercenary or sophist, fighting verbally or physically, always slaves of the highest bidder. Beasts of burden that can talk and steal people's money. You're no different than the animals that scrounge for scraps outside our door."

Hrossar raised an eyebrow but said nothing. No point in responding.

"But you'll just be fine, won't you. Until the day everyone gets tired of you."

Hrossar kept his gaze even, refusing to blink. Blinking might indicate weakness.

"And when that happens, good riddance." The kid spun around and walked off, head held high. He joined his mother, who'd been involved in another conversation. As loudly as the boy's voice carried, it had not been loud enough to dominate the crowd's noise.

"Well." Father took a deep breath, turning to Hrossar. "That's unfortunate."

"Truly." Hrossar turned to the plains, ears flattening with a breeze. How much of that diatribe had been true? "Father?"

"Yes?"

"Is this the general sentiment toward herodons in Newílderashe?"

"Only in Dovrenol." Father smiled. "For now, at least. But discrimination never hides for long."

That was a curious way to phrase it. "Discrimination?"

"Correct."

Hrossar narrowed his eyes, studying the grass. "But if the boy's words were true, he would have good reason for anger."

"Not quite." Father faced him squarely, putting his hands on Hrossar's shoulders. "Listen, son. When you look at me, what do you see?"

What an obvious question. "My father."

"Precisely. But when others look at me, what might they see?"

Hrossar considered. "A debater. Perhaps even an opponent, if they are a debater themselves."

"Or—a herodon." Father tilted his head. "You see? And if they've been wronged by a herodon—that is *all* they see."

Curious. Hrossar's brow furrowed. "That makes no sense. You were not the one who wronged them."

"Correct. However, most people think collectively."

"Collectively?"

Father's eyes searched the crowd—then he turned back to the plains, beckoning. They strolled away from the crowd, flies buzzing along the tall grass. Now just twenty meters from the debate house, each blade of grass was coming to Hrossar's knees.

"Collective thinking." Father inhaled deeply, chest rising. "Defined as placing people and races into collectives."

"Which means?"

"When an individual places people into collectives, they will view each person according to the way they view the collective." Father indicated the flies buzzing around them. "For instance, if I see flies as a collective, and one bites me…" He gestured at Hrossar, as if his son should finish the sentence.

"You shall see all flies as violent."

"Correct. Which might be somewhat accurate," Father chuckled, "but would be a hasty generalization nonetheless."

Hasty generalization. "A common fallacy of logic in which the one is used to characterize the whole."

Father nodded. "If people view herodons as a collective, they will *judge* herodons as a collective. When *some* herodons create problems for them, *all* herodons become evil to them."

"But what if most herodons are in fact this way?"

Father shrugged. "Most humanites are evil as well—at least, by their own standards. They steal, they kill, and they pursue wars for no other end than to expand their territory. But they don't see each other as uniformly evil."

"Because they don't think of each other as a collective."

"Correct. They make distinctions when it comes to each other— but not when it comes to other races."

Hrossar shook his head. "That is incredible."

"Hypocrisy is common to all species. I won't pretend we are

46

immune to it." Father waved aside a fly. "And besides, we do resemble their beasts of burden. I have heard us likened to armadillos with rubber hides before. It is not entirely unthinkable to see us as such."

Father refused to even raise his voice. Hrossar narrowed his eyes. "Does it not disturb you?"

"Of course. But not overly." Father stopped, looking out over the endless plains. "What's important is that I don't fulfill whatever prejudices are set against me."

Hrossar nodded. "I understand."

"But it does disturb you."

Hrossar let his claws dig into the grass. One fist opened and closed. No point in denying the truth. "Naturally."

"I understand. Discrimination is difficult to deal with."

Hrossar gave a sharp nod. "It is."

"But you must not become what they fear." Father put his hands on Hrossar's shoulders again. "Do you understand? No matter how much they hurt you, you must not hurt back."

Hrossar nodded, swallowing a lump in his throat. "I understand."

"Excellent." Father stepped back, glancing at the crowd. "Now your mother was expecting us half an hour ago. We—"

"But what if you took a job, then realized it was the wrong side of the debate? That you were facilitating evil?"

Father blinked at him. The words had left Hrossar's lips before he could check them. That had been careless. Hrossar dipped his head. "I apologize, father. My words should be more measured."

"It is irrelevant this time. You have done well to ask this question." Father glanced back at the crowd—then took a seat in the grass, facing away from them. "Sit beside me."

Hrossar obeyed. This always happened before Father taught him something important.

"Do you see the sun?"

As it was roughly six-thirty, the sun would soon be in their eyes. "I do."

"What about tonight? Will we see the sun then?"

Hrossar shook his head. "No."

"Precisely. So if I ask you at night where the sun will rise, can you point it out?"

Hrossar considered. This was a test...he'd studied this only recently. "I would discern the presence of various markers—and use them to identify compass directions. After that, I would simply point west."

"Correct. But what if you were in a new land—with no markers?"

This was difficult. Hrossar had never considered that. It was foolish to overlook such an obvious flaw in his solution. "I apologize, Father. What could I do?"

"You could do several things. First," he raised a clawed finger, "you could wait until the sun rises. But this solution is inefficient—and if you are on a long journey, will cause you to become delayed as you linger."

"An ineffective solution."

"Correct. You may also attempt to use the stars—although this is less reliable on a cloudy night."

Hrossar nodded. "Naturally."

"If it were early or late enough in the night, you could check which direction the sky is darkening or lightening."

All good solutions. "Understood."

"But ultimately there will be some difficulty—and with that difficultly, those who oppose you. You may have to debate them to prove your point."

What did this have to do with taking the wrong side of a debate? "And?"

"And eventually the sun will rise," Father raised his hand as if demonstrating, "and one of you, if not both, will be proved wrong."

Ah…a smile tugged at Hrossar's lips. He understood where this was going. "Indeed."

"In real debates, the truth is not always so clear. Some things are obvious, while others are not. But at the end of days—when the sun of truth rises, so to speak, and the night of our ignorance is over—we will all know every detail of our ineptitude."

The way Father spoke…it was so majestic. Hrossar constantly sought to emulate it. "I see."

"So when I accept a job and end up on the wrong side, I am partaking in this nocturnal discussion. A discussion which some herodon philosophers have called, 'The Great Debate.' A continual search for truth."

"And can it be found?"

Father nodded. "Absolutely. When we engage in debate, the purpose is to discover the truth. If we cannot find truth, debate would

48

be pointless."

"What if some people debate simply to win?"

Father's body stiffened. He gave a soft snort, gums curling back as he spoke his next words. "They have no honor."

So this had happened before. Hrossar scratched his snout with his knuckles. "What if you knew for a fact your side of the debate was wrong—but you only discovered it after taking the job?"

"Then I would continue."

Hrossar's eyebrows rose. That was certainly an admission. "Why?"

"Because it is my duty." Father closed his eyes. "I should have been more careful when I accepted the hire. But a herodon's first job is to his duty."

"Even if the duty is wrong?"

"Wrong?" Father's eyes flew open. "Understand this, Hrossar. Not fulfilling your duty is wrong. All other matters are secondary. If the duty makes you uncomfortable—choose a different duty beforehand."

Fulfilling one's word. It was important to Father. Hrossar lowered his gaze. "Understood, Father."

"Herodons as a race spent centuries debating each other, tossing around different systems of morality—this is the only one we could agree upon." Father's eyes burned. "You stand by your word."

"Why couldn't they agree on anything else?"

"Because murder might be justified in certain situations—war or justice, for instance. Stealing might be appropriate when there is no other way to feed your family. Lying could protect those close to you. But breaking your oath of duty—" he shook his head. "All you *have* is your word. No moral you hold means anything if you do not stand by it."

Hrossar swallowed, dipping his head. "I see."

"Hrossar."

Father's voice was softer than ever now. Hrossar could barely hear it over the rustling grass. "Yes?"

"Stand by your word."

Hrossar studied Father for a few seconds. This truly meant a great deal to him.

"Understood?"

Hrossar nodded, never breaking eye contact. "Understood."

7 PROVOKING THE DRAGONFLIES

5914 OT (two years later)

Hiss. The pebble sank into the magma dragonfly's molten body, smoke rising. Hrossar hefted a larger rock in one hand—then lobbed it.

Hiss.

Perfect accuracy. A corner of his lips lifted.

"Incredible tosses. You're up by two."

Hrossar glanced at Foran. The herodon was gathering stones, eyeing the magma dragonflies buzzing overhead. So far the swarm had paid them little attention. Not surprising, considering magma dragonflies typically ate rocks. Only geolites needed to be concerned.

At least, that was his assumption. But assumptions could be wrong.

Another stone sailed through the air. This one narrowly missed a green dragonfly, plopping into the lava pillar behind it with a hiss. Smoke rose from the pillar as the stone floated up it. In seconds the pebble was gone.

Hrossar studied the pillar. It was bright—almost too bright to stare at, and red like a live coal. Rushing strands of lava wound around each other to create the pillar, like the wind in a tornado. But the structure was stationary—and come a century from now, it would still be here.

Fascinating. Brekh'cha's formations never ceased to interest Hrossar. He lifted his snout, eyes wandering the cavern. What else was here?

"Agh! Missed again. Your turn."

Of course. Hrossar smiled, picking up a pebble. "Watch." He

lobbed the pebble again, keeping his eyes trained on the largest dragonfly. The pebble flew into its molten hide, disappearing with a hiss. The dragonfly turned his way, multifaceted eyes throbbing red.

"Whoa! That's one of the big ones."

Hrossar arched an eyebrow. "I see that."

The dragonfly eyed them, wings buzzing as it hovered only meters away. Its fiery tail dipped, stinger dripping lava on the rocks below it. The dragonfly tilted its head—Hrossar stood perfectly still—then buzzed up to the ceiling.

"Well then." Foran stepped back, hefting a stone. "We could stand to go somewhere else, I suppose."

"Perhaps we should cease, Foran," Hrossar whispered, turning to his friend. "As we may be pressing our luck."

Foran shrugged. "Perhaps."

Not that either of them had any such intention. Tossing stones was far too diverting. "We might also investigate the lifeforms further down these tunnels."

"Which ones?"

Hrossar picked up a stone. "Lavaracks."

"Oh. Now that's fearless." Foran rubbed his jaw. "Though I'm not entirely sure how wise it is."

"Oy! Herodons!"

They both turned as geolites rolled down the ridge behind them. A milky halite and a pearly pink dolomite uncurled at the bottom, glaring at them. "What're you doing here, herodons? Come to make trouble?"

Hrossar refocused on the dragonflies. "We have no intention of troubling you."

"Oh, but you're content to come near Nicota!" The dolomite crossed his arms. "We know what you're up to. No more heckling, you rogues."

"We have no intention of heckling, accosting or castigating any geolites."

"And yet you're here." The halite tilted her head. "I thought your kind was leaving Brekh'cha."

Foran opened his mouth—but Hrossar raised a hand. "Some herodons, including my family, have resettled in Newílderashe in the last six years—which in our case, was the result of my father's profession. Commuting for two or three days to a job is inconvenient."

51

"Then what're you still doing here?"

"I grew up here." Hrossar arched an eyebrow. "And as we still have settlements in Eastern Brekh'cha, it is appropriate to occasionally visit."

"So what are you doing so close to Nicota? We've seen you around before—bullying our kind at every turn."

"I apologize." Hrossar dipped his head. "I did not intend to roam this near the Nicota Outpost. I will depart momentarily."

"That you will!" The dolomite made a shooing motion. "And good riddance!"

"You have no prerogative to kick us out!" Foran finally spoke. He stepped forward, fists raised. "And you still call Nicota an 'outpost'— even though it's a full-blown settlement! Maybe it was an outpost a century ago—but now you're practically forcing us out!"

"Oh-ho! That old argument again!" The dolomite's eyes widened, and he stepped toward Foran. "You really think we're invading you, do you?"

"Through sheer population. It's a simple calculation—you live for many centuries, while we live for only two or so. You'll multiply and replace us."

"Except we only *reproduce* once every few centuries." The dolomite put his fists on his hips. "And as we've made clear to your leaders, we've no interest in your territory."

"You're only attempting to flee the alleged 'Flame Dragon.'" Foran's gums curled back, baring his fangs. "A clever invention to excuse your populous invasion."

"The dragon is real! Just because no one's seen it in centuries—"

"We have no doubt there is a creature roaming the bowels of Brekh'cha," Hrossar stated, stepping between them. "And we are certain you have excellent intentions. Please excuse my friend."

"Oh, you're certain? Could've fooled me." The geolite curled his fists, jaw clenched. He stepped back from Hrossar, eyeing them. "Seems like you're biding your time."

Foran opened his mouth—but Hrossar raised an arm again. "We will now depart. Please allow us to leave in peace."

"Oh you'll leave—back to Eastern Brekh'cha. And we've no interest in it."

Hrossar should seize the opportunity to exit...but his curiosity burned. "And what would occur if the herodons vacated Eastern

Brekh'cha?"

"Don't know." The geolite crossed his arms with a shrug. "We'd only move in if you totally abandoned it."

Hrossar gave a soft snort, narrowing his eyes. "I see."

"Now off with you! Both of you!" The dolomite made another shooing motion. "Now, before we call a patrol!"

"As you wish." Hrossar put a hand on Foran's shoulder, letting his claws dig into the rubber hide. His eyes met Foran's—and Foran's shoulders relaxed. The herodon nodded.

"Go!"

Hrossar curled into a ball—then burst into a roll, weaving between rocks, his ears picking up vibrations to steer him on his path. He was still discerning how to navigate through hearing alone. Similar to a bat's sonar, but operating off lower sonic frequencies. He'd been told few other species could even hear on that level.

He ricocheted off a boulder—but maintained his roll, aiming for a tunnel he could hear ahead. This was not a safe area to experiment with the dragonflies.

☼ ☼ ☼

"So they didn't harm you in any way, shape or form?"

Hrossar shook his head. "No, Father."

Father leaned back in his chair, running his knuckles along his lower snout. "Hmm. You were wise to avoid their ire."

Hrossar arched an eyebrow. "Indeed?"

"There's been several incidents this week alone. This and the general attitude between our peoples is leading many herodons to consider alternative habitations."

Alternative? "Such as Newílderashe?"

Father nodded. "Of course, herodons have been immigrating to Newílderashe for over a century now. First it was one or two families..." He let his voice trail off, waving with one hand. "Eventually it was most of the population. Only a shadow of our people remains in Eastern Brekh'cha—and scattered at that."

A shadow. Hrossar straightened, hands behind his back. He shifted his footing, giving a small snort. "So they have driven us out."

"Not truly." Father hesitated. "Perhaps there have been...*tensions* that motivated our exit. But it's a mutual, if unspoken, agreement. Things are simply better this way."

"With us exiting Brekh'cha."

"And the geolites replacing us. I know," Father raised a hand, clawed fingers glistening in the firelight burning from porticos, "it looks suspicious. But it is better this way. With tensions as they are, we are avoiding war."

Hrossar let his clawed toes tap at the ground. "War is sometimes necessary."

"Not when we have a community in Newílderashe. And the humanites there have been more welcoming than the geolites here."

"Though there have been some who resist our presence."

Father shrugged. "There always will be. But we've established ourselves there. It's not a bad arrangement."

Hrossar raised his snout, studying the ceiling of the cavern. Purple quartz ran along in mineral deposits, mingling with rivulets of lava that glistened deep red. "Will we still visit Brekh'cha?"

"Of course." Father averted his eyes, tapping the armrests. "As we have no real quarrel with the geolites, they'll allow us to visit."

Hrossar studied his father. "And our kind will leave."

"Every last one of them. One analyst projects that by 5925, every settlement will be abandoned." Father shook his head, giving a small snort. "Brekh'cha will belong to the geolites."

"And they will have their wish."

"What else can we do?" Father met Hrossar's eyes, voice soft as silk. "Should we stay, war may occur. And we have better alternatives. Would you have us shed our blood?"

Hrossar's shoulders lowered. He turned his head, considering. "Can we not simply remain here?"

"Not with the geolites unable to expand westward. The dragon patrols that area."

"Allegedly."

"She exists and you know it."

"Are you certain?"

Father nodded. He leaned back, tapping his fingers against each other. "In fact, the Flame Dragon is extraordinarily hazardous. We have our own tales, and one speaks of herodon pioneers a few millennia ago—before the geolites migrated down here—who came

54

across a terrifying creature made of purple flame."

That did sound similar to the geolites' myth. "But that is foolishness. Ancient tales."

"Is it?" Father cocked his head. "You should know, Hrossar, that many ancient tales exist for a reason. This one should not be regarded lightly. The creature was referred to as 'beautiful like a serpent, glittering with rushing flame—but hotter than the lava, and swifter in her fury.'"

That father could simply recite this from memory was impressive in itself. Hrossar nodded. "And if such a creature were now dead?"

"Truly? If you were the geolites, would you accept that risk?" Father spread his hands. "Expose everything you've worked so hard for? Lead the creature to your new home?"

"No." Hrossar raised his snout, inhaling deeply. Much as he regretted it, this argument made sense. "But might we still live in harmony with them?"

"Not in our current state. Herodons continually provoke geolites—and geolites continually provoke herodons." Father leaned over, plucking a stone by his feet. The light gleamed on his rubber hide as he cleared his throat. "Listen, son. Remember this well."

Hrossar straightened, arms flat by his sides. Father only spoke this way when he was about to reveal an important truth. "Yes, Father."

"If I toss this stone at a magma dragonfly once, it will not mind." Father tossed the stone, then caught it in his other hand. "Twice or thrice, it may glance at me."

Hrossar tried not to shift his footing. Was Father also rebuking Hrossar's diversions? "I understand, father."

"Do you?" Father raised an eyebrow. "That is precisely the problem, Hrossar. When we are young, we are foolish. We believe we can provoke forever—and nothing will come of it." He plucked another stone from the ground. "Now which of these stones do you believe is harder?"

Hrossar studied the stones. "The one on the right is chalcopyrite—a hard mineral."

"And the left?"

"Olivine. Roughly identical in hardness."

"Correct." Father brought them together. "Now what should happen if I smashed them hard against each other?"

Hrossar adjusted his footing. "They should shatter each other."

"Precisely." Father released the rocks, and they clattered by his feet. "Now what would happen if the herodons and geolites provoked each other enough times?"

Hrossar flexed his claws, trying to keep his arms still. The answer was clear. "They might approach each other in war."

"Might?"

Hrossar met Father's eyes—unblinking, burning in the light of the porticos. He gave a small nod. "We would shatter each other."

Father leaned back, keeping his eyes on Hrossar. His next words barely rose above the crackling of the flames. "That is correct, son."

8 STUBBORNNESS

5917 OT (three years later)

Now came the opponent's turn. Hrossar leaned back in his seat, arms crossed. The humanites and herodons beside him dared not make a sound.

"Thank you for your argument. However, I noticed certain flaws in it." The herodon facing Hrossar's father cleared his throat. "You used fallacies of reasoning throughout your speech."

Father adjusted his spectacles. The light of a hundred candles from the chandelier above made it look like his glasses were burning. He raised his snout, appraising the other herodon.

"Your assessment," the foe enunciated his words, "flouted the implausibility of being struck by lightning at the Foreth Region. There are no lightning storms there, and never have been."

Father raised a finger. "Actually, historical records from two hundred years ago show lightning storms there. They've been inactive in the last two centuries."

"Ah, but those are ancient witnesses, are they not?" The other herodon grinned at him, baring his fangs. It was more of a challenge. "Quite unreliable. And reporting something we've never witnessed."

"Lightning storms?"

"In the Foreth Region." The opponent tapped his podium with a claw. "Never seen by my eyes, certainly."

"And what does that matter?" Father leaned forward, pressing his palms against his own podium. "There is no reason to doubt the witnesses."

"Uniformitarianism, opponent." The herodon turned to their

audience, spreading his clawed hands. "If it does not abide by our experience, the account must be false."

"Experience—" Father cut himself off. He leaned against the podium with one elbow, an impatient snort escaping him. "These accounts are the *experience* of others. Is only your experience valid?"

"Not quite." The herodon raised a finger. "But my experience is the rubric by which I grade other experiences."

"And so you discount any experiences which do not line up with yours?" Father mumbled something that sounded like "pathetic," though with such softness that Hrossar doubted any humanite could hear him. "Your perception of reality is determined by how sheltered you are. Not a very accurate filter for evaluating empirical evidence."

The herodon blinked—then shook his head. "I am merely following the logical principle of uniformitarianism."

"Uniformitarianism does not determine history—it is the other way around, fool. Otherwise you are employing the hasty generalization fallacy by assuming your experience constitutes the whole of reality."

"That's not quite—"

"It's exactly true. That's where your idiotic system fails. It requires you to limit other people's experience by your own."

The other herodon leaned forward, arching his eyebrows. "And what other experience should we assess testimony by?"

"The collective experiences of peoplekind determines what we view as uniform—not your hopelessly provincial experience of reality." Truly Father was infuriated by this herodon. Such harsh phraseology rarely passed his lips. "Otherwise reality would be indistinguishable from individual to individual. Testimonies must be scrutinized on their own terms rather than our limited experience."

"But then you might believe everything." The herodon spread his hands again. "What if I claim I flew to the moon yesterday?"

"Judging by the fact that you appear to be inventing this fable, and knowing through context that we have no way of getting to the moon, and also by identifying you as a lying mongrel beforehand, I can easily determine that you are equivocating."

"But what if—" the opponent gave a snort, "—what if you had no means of verifying me as a liar?"

"There are *always* means." Father jabbed a finger at him. "And that is what you refuse to acknowledge. Do you think the study of history is a coin toss? A guessing game?"

"Well, I suppose there is archaeology…" The herodon let his voice trail off. "But yes, basically."

"You idiot. Tell historians that. Tell them their accreditation is worthless." Father gripped his podium, clawed fingers digging into the wood. "Talk to them and they'll educate you on the many methods they use to determine whether an ancient source of information is lying or reliable! History is a science, you fool!"

"Well I suppose some things are reliable." The opponent seemed much less confident now. Father was getting to him. "Certainly the records of no lightning in the Foreth Region are fine."

"So that's it? You only regard history when it's convenient to you?" Father huffed and snorted, throwing up his snout. "Just by coming here, you acknowledge an individual's claim that this building existed. You evaluated their words, scrutinized them by context and discerned that they were honest!"

"Yes, but that's different—"

"No! It's not." Father raised a finger. "It was *outside* of your experience, and you trusted them. You show by your actions that you *do* trust alternate sources. When it's convenient to you."

The other herodon smirked. "And yet *you* don't trust the sources that say there is no lightning in the Foreth Region."

"No such sources exist. They simply reported no lightning in their time. Which I believe completely." Father barked as the other herodon opened his mouth—everyone in the audience stiffened. Herodons rarely barked. "And how dishonest do you have to be to distort that? Reporting the *absence* of lightning is not the same as reporting the *impossibility* of lightning. You know this."

"I—well, I—" the other herodon shook his head, clutching the podium. His muscles were trembling—he was right where Father wanted him. He'd gambled with a few logical fallacies, and Father was ensuring he paid for it.

"In their day, no lightning. In an earlier day, lightning." Father slammed the podium with his fist. "I believe *both* sources. You believe only the sources convenient to you."

"Now—but that's—" the other herodon licked his snout, gesturing wildly with one hand. "I have—I—"

"Did you think you would undermine history as a source of knowledge? That you would so lightly dismiss it?" Father shook his

59

head, straightening. "You have only played the fool. And shown your own intellectual hypocrisy."

The other herodon wiped his snout—then stared at his podium, blinking rapidly. There was, of course, nothing he could say.

That was the nature of debating Father.

☆ ☆ ☆

"Stubbornness," Father spat, pacing outside the building. "Sheer stubbornness. I expect such deceptive tactics from humanites—but herodons?"

Hrossar swallowed, standing straight as the night's breeze swept him. Father rarely displayed such anger. "He was simply trying to defeat you."

"I am *aware* of what he was attempting!" Father rounded on him, clutching the air with trembling claws. "He was twisting logic!"

"He may not have intended to."

"That much is obvious." Father shook his head, glancing at the debate building. "It seems people are losing competence with each passing day. They pervert logic in such a way that even a child could apprehend them."

"Then this only serves to make your task easier."

"And if that were all, I would not mind." Father scratched his jaw with a claw, focusing on the crowd. "But it seems as though they are doing it on purpose. I never doubt my intuition—and it informs me they know better. They know better!"

Hrossar placed his hands behind his back, raising his snout. "And?"

"And what do you do when you know a position is wrong? Do you take it up? Do you make yourself a scoundrel by arguing for that which is wrong?"

Hrossar shook his head. "Obviously not."

"Correct. But these rogues know no shame. They defend sides they know are wrong, then confuse the facts with—with—argh!" spittle flew from his mouth, "—with clever, logical-sounding equivocations! It takes intellect to come up with arguments like that. Abused intellect."

60

"So you are proposing they should know better because they are intelligent. But they choose not to know better—in order to accept a position they should know is wrong."

"Precisely!" Father expelled a breath, shaking his head again. "They have no shame."

Hrossar arched an eyebrow. "But they are doing their duty."

"They should never have chosen that duty!" Father pointed at Hrossar. "Listen, son. Simply because your highest calling is your duty does not mean all duties are good to choose. Some are preferable to others."

Hrossar nodded. "You have told me this."

"And have I also told you that we have a kind of duty which compels us to choose only those duties that are morally acceptable?"

Hrossar shook his head. "Not in so many words."

"But my example has been sufficient." Father held up a finger. "Correct?"

"Correct."

Father inhaled deeply, closing his eyes. The crowd's chatter was dying down—humanites were dispersing, herodons rolling off. Rubber hides gleamed in the moonlight, grass rustling as they sped off. The opponent was nowhere to be seen. "It is...difficult to explain."

That was unsurprising. "Especially considering herodons cannot agree on what is good, other than holding to a duty."

"Just because they cannot agree does not mean they do not know." Father put his hands behind his back—then began pacing to and fro, giving an impatient snort. "Honor has been written on their hearts. They know which duties to shun and which to accept."

That was a bold claim. "And do we?"

Father stopped pacing. He met Hrossar's eyes, muscles tense. "I believe so."

Truly? Hrossar averted his eyes. Was his father's certainty warranted? Precisely what constituted an honorable duty? "Much would hinge on that knowledge."

"Indeed."

Wind rippled through the plains. Grass rustled, leaves shaking on a nearby tree. "Follow my example, son." Father dropped his voice to a whisper. "I will show you."

"By example?"

Father nodded, eyes on the plains. "By my duty."

☼ ☼ ☼

ONE YEAR LATER (5918 OT)

"You speak so often of logic—of ascertaining the evidence." The opposing herodon sneered, claws drumming the podium. "But that's so unenlightened."

Father adjusted his spectacles, arching an eyebrow. Sunlight streamed in through the skylight, gleaming off his mahogany podium. "Exactly how is that?"

"You can't really know anything." The herodon gestured at their podiums. "These podiums, for instance, could be an illusion."

That seemed ridiculous. Hrossar snorted, crossing his arms.

"In fact, this whole conversation could be a dream I'm having—a very vivid one, to be sure, but still a dream." The herodon grinned. "So you see, you can't really make firm conclusions based on the evidence."

This was nonsense. But the people next to Hrossar were leaning forward, transfixed. Couldn't they identify foolishness?

"While I admit that our senses do not produce absolute knowledge," Father began, speaking slowly, "we are able to produce reasonable and reliable results by assessing what is most likely. Based upon our surroundings, we can reach reasonable conclusions."

"Not necessarily." The opponent leaned forward, claws clutching the podium. "And without absolute knowledge, you have no real argument to go off."

"Then how did you get here?" Father gestured at his opponent. "Obviously you used directions and your eyesight. You are willing to submit to your five senses—when it's convenient to you."

"And?" The herodon almost seemed to be baiting Father. Surely he knew where this would lead.

"And that is inconsistent. You cannot rely on your senses in one situation and doubt them in the next—when they are inconvenient to your case. That is illogical."

The opponent raised a finger. "Ah, ah. That's where you're

wrong. You see, logic is relative as well."

Father adjusted his spectacles. Though his face was expressionless, Hrossar could tell when he was irritated. "Truly?"

"Truly. You see—"

"How, then, are we having this conversation—if logic is relative? Such a statement is insanity—we cannot reason with one another if our idea of logic is simply relative."

The opponent shrugged. If he was perturbed by the interruption, he was disguising it quite well. "Well, that much is true. We really can't convince each other of anything."

"Then what," Father bared his fangs, "is the purpose of debate?"

"To prove who's stronger at rhetoric. It's a sport." The herodon smirked. "And here we are, two champions in our field. Ready to engage in a battle of wits."

"I don't engage with the witless." Father pointed at him. "And your statement is idiotic."

"How is that?"

"First, if we could not know anything—logically or empirically— you could not know that statement. Every word coming out of your mouth might as well be gibberish, because you couldn't know anything."

"Well, as you've said, we can still have an approximate knowledge—"

"Close your eyes."

The opponent's brow furrowed. "Excuse me?"

"Close your eyes." Father's voice was even softer than usual. He bared his teeth again. "Now, if you will please."

"Very well." The herodon closed his eyes, placing his hands behind his back. "Now what?"

"Now tell me how many fingers I'm holding up."

"What kind of game is this? You know very well that I cannot."

"That is correct." Father wasn't holding up any fingers. His hands were resting on the podium, claws gleaming in the filtered sunlight. "And why is that?"

"Because my eyes are closed." The herodon gave an impatient snort. "Now what are you trying to prove?"

"Some people think of approximate knowledge as an old man trying to see without glasses. Your eyesight may be blurry—" Father spread his hands, "—but ultimately you can roughly make out the

63

shape of a tree."

"More or less."

"But that requires a frame of reference. You must know what a tree is first. You must have an ultimate basis off of which to approximate knowledge." Father pointed at his opponent. "If all logic itself is relative, you have no frame of reference. Nothing to help you determine reality even in an approximate sense."

The foe's eyes flew open. "Good observation. I agree."

Hrossar blinked. The opponent was agreeing? What tactic was this?

Father seemed taken aback as well—though only Hrossar could tell. One finger was tapping the podium, and Father cleared his throat. "Do you."

"Which is why we can't know anything. Because logic is relative."

"Including that statement, I suppose?" Father's eyebrows rose. "Again, you speak gibberish."

"Not at all." The opponent raised a finger, turning to their audience. "You see, terms of logic can be redefined at will—even that two and two make four. Under different terms, they can make five."

"So I'm the unenlightened one?" Father snorted. "Redefine terms all you wish, fool. Logic and reality will remain the same, regardless of how you describe them. Add this amount of sticks to that amount of sticks, and you will get the same amount of sticks—regardless of which words you choose to describe the amounts. Reality does not change based on your descriptions of it."

"It certainly does. We define our own reality."

Father coughed—or maybe it was suppressed laughter. He shook his head. "Truly?"

"Truly. With no ultimate knowledge to go off, we can define our own perceptions and live in the world we desire." The opponent spread his hands. "And how would you dare to disprove me? I can repudiate the validity of any approach you take."

Quite a bold dare. Hrossar arched an eyebrow, arms still crossed. What would Father do?

"Any approach?"

The herodon nodded, grinning. "Give it your best shot."

Father inhaled deeply, straightening. He gripped the podium, one thumb scratching at its wood. "Very well."

The audience waited with baited breath, leaning forward. Someone in the back row coughed—but otherwise, silence.

"Design for me," Father began, voice softer than a whisper, "a reality in which you are perfectly at ease."

The opponent chuckled. "That would be particularly easy."

"I can see that." Father's lips curled—though more from revulsion than any attempt to intimidate. "Now design a reality in which you are perfectly secure and safe from harm."

"Done."

"Close your eyes again."

The opponent did so. He raised his snout, fingers drumming the podium idly.

Father strolled over to him, clawed feet clacking lightly on the wooden floor. He stood before the fool, fists balled. "Are you still at ease?"

"Yes?"

"I am standing before you. Do you feel no threat to your well-being?"

The herodon shook his head. "None at all."

Father seized the fool's snout—and jerked it down. The herodon bounced off the podium, eyes fluttering open as Father pulled back his fist. "Now design for me a reality in which I am not punching you."

No one in the audience gasped. Hrossar assumed they were simply in shock.

"Design for me that reality!"

"Well—I—"

The first blow landed. The herodon stumbled back, blinking.

"Design it!"

Another blow. The herodon staggered, opening and closing his jaws. No words would come.

"Come on, you fool! Tell me about your designed world—where you're perfectly safe and at ease! Tell me!" Father's voice was a hoarse roar, like roaring flames. "Or can you?"

"I—I—"

"You see—" Father grabbed his foe by the shoulder, "—you can design all you want, but reality does not change. It comes for you all the same. Pretend that this fist is not here, it still strikes you. Pretend death does not arrive—it still comes for you. Then what will you design?"

"This is all—your conduct is inappropriate—"

"What else am I to do! Such insanity cannot be reasoned with! You know better!"

The foe wiped his lip, where blood was trickling. Then he grinned. "Cannot be reasoned with?"

Father stepped back, eyes widening with realization. "I see. You mean to debate me to the point where only reality itself can disprove you—not any words which I say."

The foe chuckled. "In my mind, we are simply having a friendly conversation." He wiped the blood on his leg, then raised his snout. "No fight occurred."

Father shook his head, jaw hanging open. "You're insane."

"Insanity is relative to sanity. Both are relative. Prove otherwise."

"I—that's illogical."

"Logic, shmogic—all relative. Or would you try to prove otherwise? But that would be impossible—since you cannot use something to prove itself." The herodon gave a light shrug. "You cannot use logic to prove that logic is logical. You can't prove anything."

Father took a step backward, baring his teeth. "But would you live in a world of such madness? No one would."

"To me, it is not madness. And you have no grounds to say otherwise."

"On the contrary." Father raised finger. "To you, it *is* madness."

"Oh?"

"You stumbled back when I punched you. And insisted that my conduct was inappropriate." Father kept his finger raised, barking as the herodon opened his mouth. "You eat when you're hungry, follow directions to buildings, make arguments and counter-arguments. These are not the actions of someone designing their own reality—rather, it is the conduct of someone adhering to an external perceived reality." Father barked again to cut him off. "You show by your actions that even you don't believe your own nonsense."

"And how does that disprove what I'm saying?" The herodon spread his hands. "What does any of that have to do with anything?"

"What you are saying cannot be proven—by your own standards. Obviously you can't use logic to prove it, correct?"

"That is correct."

"Then you have no way to prove it. And without any way to prove or disprove it, the only relevant factor is whether you actually believe it or not." Father pointed at him. "Which, as I have just proved, is not the case."

The herodon raised his snout. "That assumes you can prove something."

"In order to assume I cannot, you must use a logical argument. I believe it went, 'You cannot use something to prove itself.' But if logic is relative, I deny your argument. What will you do about it?"

Of course, the herodon could do nothing about it. He had dug his own grave, and the fool was about to lie in it. He cleared his throat. "The onus is on you to prove it, not on me to disprove it."

"Really? By what principle of logic."

The herodon stiffened. There was no response—and he knew it.

"You set yourself up for defeat, idiot. You're trying to use logic to make your point—but your point is that logic is relative. Your argument is futile by nature—and therefore must be dismissed."

"I—well—" the herodon closed his mouth. He had no options. He had closed every door available to himself—including the path to making his own argument. Father had forced him into a corner, then impaled him with his own argument.

Father bared his teeth, leaning forward so his face was inches from his opponent's. "So tell me I'm wrong."

Hrossar nodded, a smile tugging at his lips. Typical form—other than the violence.

"I can't." The opponent shook his head. "You must first prove that you're right."

"If that's true, don't you first have to prove your own argument?"

This was going in circles. The other herodon had nothing new to offer to the conversation. He scratched the back of his neck. "I suppose in the interests of consistency, if I believe you have to prove your own argument, then I believe I have to prove mine. But that leaves us in a state where neither of us proves our argument. Which I'm sure you would agree favors me."

"No, I don't agree." Father arched an eyebrow. "It merely leaves us at an impasse. The problem is, neither of us believes your position. Otherwise, you would live very differently."

"So?"

"So look around you. Everyone appears to operate under logical principles—including you. Based off our best ability to conjecture, I'd say *you're* the one who needs to prove *your* case. You have a lot of behavioral explanation to do. How do we all operate under the same logical principles if logic is relative?" Father threw up his hands. "The *natural* position is that logic is objective—as if it's programmed into our psyche. The counter-position—that logic is relative—must therefore be proven."

"Well—"

"Especially since you don't even believe your own nonsense— just by *making* an argument, you show that you believe in objective logic. Otherwise, you wouldn't expect it to be compelling."

Hrossar scratched his jaw. He assumed much of the audience was no longer following the conversation at this point. It dealt with difficult topics.

The opponent's smile had long vanished. He raised his snout, inhaling deeply. "That's your opinion."

"Is it? Then you share it."

"No I don't."

"Then design for me a world in which I do not visit my fist upon you."

The opponent closed his eyes. "Designed."

Father's next punch connected with a crack. The herodon fell to the ground with a grunt, tumbling across the wood stage.

Father strolled over to the herodon. He cleared his throat, glancing at the audience. No one moved—it seemed that no one even breathed.

Then father spoke—his voice soft as silk. "You are disproved, fool."

☆ ☆ ☆

"The judges did award you the victory." Hrossar kept his eyes on the debate building, now thirty meters out. Privacy was optimal for this conversation. "Your points were granted."

"Yet I gave into violence. I proved myself the fool in my actions."

"Perhaps not. Your opponent was insane."

"That is what disturbs me." Father was pacing, making gestures as he spoke. "Deprive a foe of reason and sanity as options—and what can they do? Only the undeniable force of reality—manifested so often

68

as violence—remains available."

"But it would not be available if reality was relative and indiscernible."

"Which is why I won the debate. Yet it disturbs me." Father shook his head, grass crunching beneath his feet. He swung around and paced the other direction. "If I can engage in such violence, why not be a mercenary? It is clear reason accomplishes nothing with the stubborn."

Hrossar blinked, straightening. "You don't mean that."

"I certainly do. What can I accomplish with *reason* against such stubbornness?" Father stopped pacing. He balled his fists, looking past Hrossar. "I took up debate to speak the truth—to convince others of what is real. But now I see I was mistaken."

"You were victorious." Hrossar's brow furrowed. Why this doubt? "Is it not clear you are accomplishing something?"

"No, it is not." Father hesitated—then his voice grew low. "Not clear at all."

How could this be? Hrossar had never seen his father experiencing such doubt. He flexed his claws, averting his eyes. What encouragement could he possibly hope to offer? His father was an intellectual monolith—a giant of Newílderashe. "Perhaps stubbornness will lose in the end."

"When the sun rises on our nocturnal ignorance?" Father glanced up at the sky, where the sun sat square in the center. "And until then, I'm done debating for hire."

Hrossar's eyes widened. He took a step back, jaw dropping slightly. Then he recovered, straightening. "Pardon?"

"I'm done with debate. If my opponents cannot be reasoned with, there is no point to debating them. Perhaps I can still debate with the reasonable—but not for money." Father bared his fangs, growling. "They're increasingly stubborn. This is how they operate. Debate has simply become a sport—the one with money hires the best debater, and truth is rarely triumphant."

Hrossar arched an eyebrow. These not unfamiliar objections. "And yet you fight for truth. Is that not worthwhile?"

"Not if it accomplishes nothing." Father began pacing again—then stopped. "No…nothing at all."

Hrossar swallowed, keeping his eyes on Father. This was a mistake. "You enjoy debating."

"Not anymore." Father hung his head, licking his snout. He raised a trembling hand to his spectacles, adjusting them ever so slightly. "Not professionally."

"So the stubbornness of opponents will drive you to retirement?"

Father nodded. "It is clear I am accomplishing nothing with them. They will have to wait until the sun of truth rises—then their stubbornness will be dashed." He enunciated his next words. "They. Know. Better."

Hrossar tapped the grass with one clawed toe. "And what will being a mercenary accomplish?"

"We will fight for what is right. For what is true." Father raised his fist. "We will only take the jobs which struggle for virtue and truth."

Hrossar dipped his head. "I see."

"And we will not engage in the futilous 'game' that debating has become." Father spat on the ground. He glared at the debate house— then rubbed his spit into the grass with one foot. "I am finished with this line of work."

Hrossar kept his hands behind his back, arching an eyebrow. "As you wish, Father."

9 IN TRAINING

5918 OT (one month later)

Hrossar raised his arm. The stick bounced off his rubber hide, and he threw a jab.

But his trainer blocked. The response came before Hrossar could blink—and he stumbled back, gasping as droplets of blood pooled on his chest.

"Very good." The trainer nodded. "You prioritized blocking the sword—in this case a stick—and paid for it by having your chest ripped out."

Hrossar clenched his jaw. "I was distracted by the stick."

The trainer raised his bloodied claws. "No matter. It was not a fatal strike—and what does not kill a herodon will hardly matter in the end."

"Truly?"

"Truly." The herodon narrowed his eyes at Hrossar, twirling his stick in one hand. "It is time I showed you something."

Hrossar wiped his chest. Though it was still stinging, most of the pain had subsided. "Very well."

"With your permission," the instructor began, plucking a sword from the weapons rack, "I'd like to stab you through with this sword."

Hrossar blinked. "Pardon?"

"Not in any important organs, of course." The trainer hefted the sword, studying it. He twirled it once, the rising sun's light glinting off its blade. "Well?"

This seemed foolish. "Of what use is this exercise?"

"Trust me and see."

71

Hrossar arched an eyebrow. "And do I trust my enemies?"

"As your trainer, I am your friend. If you cannot trust your friends, you will never be able to lead a mercenary army or participate in one." The trainer set his stick on a bench. "Understood?"

That was acceptable. Trust was integral to a team. "Understood."

"Now may I stab you?"

Hrossar inhaled deeply, closing and opening his fists. "As long as it will teach me something of value."

The trainer stepped up to Hrossar—and thrust his sword through Hrossar's side. Hrossar gasped, clutching the sword's hilt. It was nearly buried in the thick hide of his abdomen. He spat blood out, coughing—then dropped to his knees.

"Do you feel that pain?"

Hrossar could not nod. Searing fire flowed through his body, igniting his limbs. Every breath was a gasp—and with the white-hot pain came more fire. He spat more blood, eyelids fluttering.

"I am sure you also feel the fire."

Hrossar gave a quick nod. His fingers closed around the hilt, muscles tight. Should he pull the sword? Could he?

"Let it course through you…feel it."

Hrossar felt he was on fire. Every ounce of him was screaming to roll—to dive into water, to do *something*. His limbs were burning down to the marrow.

"And…now. Pull the sword out."

Hrossar tightened his grip—then yanked the sword from his abdomen. He gave a hoarse cry, nearly falling over. He spat more blood, wincing.

"Now keep concentrating. Hold the fire in your mind."

Hrossar squeezed his eyes shut. The fire filled his thoughts…almost as though his brain was burning. He touched his fingers to the wound in his abdomen—and a hissing noise escaped. Like touching the stones lining a furnace. That heat was coming from him?

"Keep concentrating…"

He coughed again. Less blood came out. He clutched the wound with both hands, breathing heavily. The fire had become a tingle. Searing needles were still shooting through him—but the pain was subsiding.

"Good." The instructor knelt so they were eye to eye. "Now look at your abdomen."

Hrossar forced himself to look down—and gasped.

The wound was closed up.

"You see that? That is the herodons' ability to heal." The instructor picked up the sword, then stood. "Simply by heating your body to incredible temperatures, you are able to instantly heal almost any wound or disease."

Fascinating. "All herodons have this gift?"

"All herodons. Though you would need more time to heal if I had pierced a crucial organ."

A crucial organ… "could I have recovered if you had pierced my heart?"

"No. That and your brain are the two organs you cannot instantly regenerate." The instructor wiped his sword off on a towel. He replaced it on the rack. "Your heart is what creates the 'fire,' of course. And your brain regulates it so you don't burn up entirely."

Hrossar nodded. "Understood."

"Now since you have come early, I believe it is appropriate to let you rest—that is optimal for full recovery." The instructor took a seat on the bench, leaning over so his elbows were on his knees. "Feel free to ask me any questions in the meantime."

Hrossar got to his feet—sharp needles jabbed at his abdomen, and he flinched. Swallowing, he closed his eyes. "Very well."

The instructor watched as Hrossar limped to an adjoining bench. "Anything at all."

Hrossar took a seat, trying not to flinch again. The pain truly was subsiding…but it was still there. A small tingling sensation. "How is my father doing?"

"Teros Feodon is advancing quickly." The instructor gave him a smile. "As are you, Hrossar. You are standing on your own, as I knew you would when I separated you from him."

That was reassuring. Hrossar nodded to himself. "Excellent."

"Do you require a towel? Healing can really make you sweat."

"It would be appreciated." Hrossar accepted a damp towel from his instructor. "I do have a number of questions."

"Fire away."

Hrossar wiped his forehead. He dabbed his chest—the bleeding had stopped—then pressed the towel to his abdomen. "How do I block multiple strikes?"

"Look at my eyes."

Hrossar turned to the instructor. The herodon was pointing at his own eyes with two claws. "You see what they're doing?"

"They are studying me."

"Yes!" He waved. "But what are my hands doing?"

"Waving."

"How can you tell?"

Hrossar shrugged. "Peripheral vision."

"Precisely. Now look at my hands."

Hrossar studied the trainer's hands. What was the point of this?

The trainer jabbed at him. Hrossar tried to block—but the fist was a blur, and it bounced off his chest just before he could catch it. He gave a soft snort, shaking his snout.

"Killed you."

Hrossar narrowed his eyes. "If you are intending to prove that I cannot block even a single strike, you have succeeded."

"Now look at my eyes again."

Hrossar gave another snort—then stared at the instructor's eyes. A few seconds passed. Then—

The instructor's fist was a blur—but Hrossar caught it. His claws closed around the fist.

"Good! What was the difference?"

Hrossar's brow furrowed. "I was focusing on your eyes?"

"Precisely. You see, peripheral vision detects movement *before* your central vision. If your gaze is fixed upon my arms, you will not be able to stop them." He pointed at his own eyes again. "Focus on your opponent's *eyes*—the one thing that cannot strike you."

That was quite the revelation. "And you did not tell me this earlier because…?"

"I was teaching you other things." The instructor leaned back, smiling. "One cannot assimilate too much information at a time."

Hrossar shook his head, pulling the towel back from his abdomen. Very little blood. "Perhaps."

"Now that your system has cooled, it will accept water." The instructor handed him a bowl of clear liquid. "Do not drink water immediately after healing, as it may boil inside you."

"Very well." Hrossar lapped the bowl with his tongue, letting the cool water run down his throat. He was apparently still quite hot, as steam escaped his mouth. But most of the water made it to his stomach.

"Thank you."

"Why thank me? You're paying me to instruct you." The trainer grinned. "But I understand the sentiment."

Hrossar lapped more water, closing his eyes. Not a bad start to the day. "I thank you anyway."

☼ ☼ ☼

"So? How did you fare?"

Hrossar strolled beside his father, parting blades of grass that rose to his waist. The buds were flowering, and cricket chirps filled the air. "I did well. I was stabbed."

"Stabbed?" Father arched an eyebrow. "How is that doing well?"

"It was on purpose. The instructor wished for me to learn how to heal through heat."

"Ah." Father nodded, keeping his eyes ahead. "That *is* an important lesson."

"You know of heat healing?"

"I do. In my younger days, I was more careless. I once impaled myself by accident." A corner of his lips lifted. "Needless to say, I learned what the term 'fire through your veins' meant that day."

Hrossar glanced at him. "It does seem like a useful trait."

"Oh, it's very useful. It works even in combat—though if you fight while healing, the healing will be less efficient."

"I see." Hrossar ran his knuckles along his jaw. "That would explain why the trainer instructed me to concentrate."

"Correct. The harder you focus, the faster you heal."

Fascinating. "So it is at least partly a conscious process."

"Like anything else." Father shrugged. "There is always a mental component."

The sun was setting. Hrossar had to squint just to look at his father. He sniffed at the air, trying to isolate the odors. "It is…six thirty. Correct?"

Father smiled. "Six thirty-five. You have almost mastered that particular skill."

"Thank you." Hrossar focused on the plains ahead of them. Grass crunched beneath their feet as they walked—and for a moment, all he

75

could hear were the crickets. Chirping constantly, each vying for a mate. "I appreciate this trek."

"Good." Father placed his hands behind his back. "Most herodons would simply roll home. But I believe it is important to relate while we have the opportunity."

"Agreed."

"In mercenary work particularly, you do not know if you will have the next day together."

That thought hadn't occurred to him. Hrossar scratched his jaw, raising an eyebrow. "Understood."

"Time must be taken together as a conscious decision. Otherwise, we may never see each other again."

Hrossar licked his snout. This was making him uncomfortable. "Father?"

"Yes?"

"We shall serve together. Correct?"

"I don't see why not." Father gave a light shrug. "You are my son, after all."

Hrossar nodded to himself. "Excellent."

"Is that all?"

Hrossar hesitated. How much should he say? "Why do you ask?"

"You seem uncomfortable."

Hrossar swallowed. He placed his hands behind his back, eyes wandering across the fields. "Are you quite certain this is the correct course of work?"

"What? Mercenary work?"

"Yes."

No response. Seconds ticked on, crickets filling the silence. The tall grass nearby rustled as unseen creatures chased each other.

"It is for now." Father cleared his throat. "The world is what it is, Hrossar. I've retired my reading spectacles, as it is time to move on. We must be a different kind of warrior now."

"One that extinguishes life?"

"One that fights for what is true." He raised his fists. "And sometimes, the stubborn—who will not yield to reason—try to shut down the truth. But the truth must fight back."

"With violence." Hrossar let out a soft sigh, eyes on the field ahead. "Is that justifiable?"

"Violence comes, whether you would have it or not. If only the evil are violent, all that is good will die."

That was a cogent argument. Not that Hrossar would be interested in debating Father—he doubted he would stand a chance—but his doubts required a voice. "Yet what if, by perpetuating violence, we become like them?"

"It is not whether the means are violent," Father began, voice soft as silk, "but whether the ends are just. It is our duty to defend the oppressed."

Hrossar raised his snout, considering. Then he gave a small nod. What else could be said? "Very well."

Father put a hand on his shoulder. "Son."

Hrossar turned to him. Father was half-shadowed in the setting sun's light, rubber hide gleaming. Hrossar swallowed. "Yes, Father?"

"I know this is difficult for you. But I will not return to debating again."

"But—" Hrossar cut himself off, averting his eyes. He lowered his voice. "It suits you."

"It does not accomplish anything." Father raised a finger. "Words have failed. Only physical force can defend against those who would crush the helpless. They have no shame."

"And is logic only for those who have shame?" Hrossar could not remain silent. He stood tall, staring his father in the eyes. "Is it only a tool if it is respected?"

"No." Father glanced back at the training house, inhaling deeply. "But it is useless when those who know better refuse to acknowledge it."

Hrossar narrowed his eyes. He opened and closed his fists, studying his father. "As you insist."

☼ ☼ ☼

TWO YEARS LATER (5920 OT)

Sticks clacked as Hrossar battled his trainer. He blocked, struck and leapt back. He circled his trainer—then came in for another strike. Weaving, dodging, striking. The tall grass buds seemed to glow in the setting sun's light, shifting in the fighters' shadows. A breeze rustled

77

the grass, mingling with the cricket chirps.

Click, clack. Click, clack.

Hrossar deflected the trainer's stick—then put his own stick to the herodon's throat, advancing on him. "Point," he whispered, chest heaving. "I win."

"Perfect." The trainer smiled, lowering his stick. "You truly have made progress."

"Thank you." Hrossar dipped his head—then stepped back and tucked his stick beneath one arm. He gave a slight bow. "Next match?"

"Not yet. I have something special." The trainer raised a finger. "Wait here."

Hrossar watched as the trainer rolled off, still trying to catch his breath. Sparring was truly an exhausting sport. And he'd been doing it for three hours already.

But that was irrelevant. Hrossar shook his head, giving a snort. On the battlefield, he might be battling for longer.

The instructor stepped out of the training house. He held two small scythes, which caught the sunlight as he beckoned with them. "Come, Hrossar!"

Hrossar obeyed. He curled into a ball—then burst across the field, grass parting before him. In seconds he was beside his trainer. He uncurled, eyeing the scythes.

"These are known as *kama*." The trainer raised one, turning it so Hrossar could study it. A wooden handle approximately the length of his forearm...an ultra-thin scythe that was even shorter...fascinating.

"I feel you are ready to master their art." The trainer handed him one. "Since you have mastered basic weaponry."

Hrossar balanced it on two fingers. He raised it up, letting the sunlight glint off its blade. Such a light weapon. Curious. "How does it function?"

"An excellent question. It can pierce with the sharp end while slicing with the edges. Originally this device was used to harvest wheat, in fact."

Hrossar arched an eyebrow. "We are using harvesting tools now?"

The trainer chuckled. "Only when they prove useful."

"I see." Hrossar turned the kama, scrutinizing its blade. "It would seem too thin to pierce armor."

"In fact, it is too weak—depending on the armor." The trainer nodded. "Good observation."

Hrossar's brow furrowed. "Then?"

"Armor piercing is not its primary role."

Hrossar nodded. He gave the kama a swing—it made a whistling noise, grass buds flying through the air. They settled like golden snowflakes on the field. "What then is its role?"

"It serves to direct the army."

"Direct it?"

"Listen." The trainer indicated his own ears. "You're rolling in a herd, blue skies above, grass crunching beneath your rubber hide. You steer through hearing. But how do you hear the leader? How do you know when you turn?"

That question had not occurred to Hrossar. "I am not certain."

"These." The instructor tapped his kama with a claw. "As long as you hold them while rolling—you'll need to adjust the position of your arms, of course—they can slice at the ground while you roll." He swept the grass with his kama, sending blades flying. "Your army will follow the sound of the slicing. When you turn, they will turn with you."

Efficient. "That would be highly useful."

"In addition, they double as mildly effective weapons." The trainer shrugged. "Though you, like many herodons, may prefer to utilize your claws."

That was accurate. "Perhaps."

"Now, hold them like this," he demonstrated with his arms, "and roll across the field."

Hrossar accepted the other kama—then positioned both so that when he curled into a ball, their blades would dig into the grass as he rolled. "Is this acceptable?"

"Perfect."

Hrossar turned from his instructor. He set his gaze down the field, waiting as a breeze ruffled the grass. Then he curled up and burst into a roll.

He could hear the difference. The blades whistled around him, slicing grass as he veered and accelerated. He uncurled to a stop, claws digging into the grass as he held out the kama.

"Excellent! Now turn around."

Hrossar turned, letting the kama hang by his sides.

The path he'd traveled was devastated. Fragments of grass and shredded buds littered it, and the sun glinted off the pieces still floating. A gust carried them across the field.

"The effects are incredible, are they not?" The instructor was cupping his hands to his mouth, shouting. "Lead an army with those and your herodons will never go astray."

Hrossar arched an eyebrow. "That is assuming I lead an army."

"It's an excellent assumption." The trainer rolled across the field, grass parting before him. He uncurled beside Hrossar, grinning. "You're one of my best students, Hrossar. You and your father will no doubt lead a battalion."

Hrossar's grip tightened on the kama. "Truly?"

"Truly. And don't forget to mention me." The trainer nudged Hrossar. "If anyone needs quality training, they know who to hire."

"Understood." Hrossar glanced down at the kama. They were light, barely more than sticks. Yet at the moment, they felt quite heavy.

10 OUTCASTS OF NEWÍLDERASHE

5959 OT (thirty-nine years later)

"Let the bride enter."

There she was. Hrossar needed no keen eyesight, no predator's hearing, no instinctive sense of presence. His heart was beating rapidly, and that was enough.

The female herodon stood cloaked in vines and embroidered porcelain armor, braids hanging from her head. She lifted her snout, eyes ahead. It was improper for the bride to make eye contact with the groom until the question had been offered.

"Let the groom stand at attention."

Hrossar straightened, raising his snout. His own porcelain armor fit more tightly than he would have preferred—it was his father's, passed down in accordance with family tradition, but Hrossar had built more muscle through mercenary work. He cleared his throat.

"Let the bride approach."

Holshe dipped her head—then proceeded down the aisle, taking each step gracefully. Her clawed feet fell silent on the red carpet, and herodons bowed as she passed their pews. Within seconds she'd reached the archway where Hrossar stood. Her eyes settled on the officiator, hands laced before her.

"Holshe Rothsen." The officiator adjusted his spectacles. "Do you accept Hrossar as your husband?"

"Yes."

No hesitation. Not that Hrossar was surprised, but it was comforting.

"And you, Hrossar Feodon." The officiator turned to Hrossar. "Do you accept Holshe as your bride?"

"That is correct."

Murmurs of approval from the crowd. The officiator grinned. "Excellent. I now pronounce you herodon and wife. Hrossar and Holshe Feodon, you may now embrace."

It was happening so quickly. Hrossar had spent months preparing for this, yet it was ending in seconds. Admittedly, the speeches from their parents and friends were yet to come. He glanced at Father, who sat in the front row. That would be significant.

Holshe turned to him. Her eyes finally met his—and a warmth spread through his body. Not like the fire of being stabbed…but close. Quite close.

"Shall we embrace?"

Hrossar raised his eyebrows. He'd been caught speechless! He cleared his throat. "Naturally." Though softer than ever, his voice felt hoarse. "Holshe."

She put her hands on his shoulders, lowering her snout. Her eyes rose up to meet his—and in the light streaming in from the stained-glass windows, her irises seemed to twinkle. She drew near him, putting the tip of her snout against his cheek.

Bumps rose along Hrossar's flesh. He could feel the heat of her breath, the wetness of her tongue as she gave him a lick. She stepped back, eyes still on him. Hrossar opened his mouth—

The stained-glass windows shattered. Flaming brands bounced in, rolling over the red carpet.

Gasps. Herodons jumped out of their seats as more firebrands sailed in.

"Animals!"

Hrossar needed no special hearing to detect the shouts outside. The church doors burst open as humanites piled in, waving torches and screaming.

"Look at them! They're going to breed and make more of themselves!"

"Stupid herodons! We don't want more of you!"

"Get out of Newílderashe!"

They were overturning tables. Swinging firebrands at guests—breaking pews with clubs, shouting. Four of them ran down the aisle. "Look at them in their wedding garb! Animals!"

One of them aimed a strike at Hrossar—and he caught the fist, jerked the man's arm down and thrust him headfirst into a pew. Another one brought a flaming brand down on Hrossar's shoulder pad. Hrossar twisted the man's arm and kicked him into another pew.

"Woah-ho! This one looks like a mercenary!"

"Doesn't really matter, does it?" A red-haired man sneered. "They all fight—whether with fists or tongues! Robbing us one way or another."

"Please exit." Hrossar held out his hand. "I do not wish to harm you."

His ears detected a swishing sound—and he spun, raising his forearm to deflect another strike. He spun to the first two humanites, blocking their strikes—then kicked one into a pew.

"Hrossar!"

He spotted Holshe being attacked. Humanites were throwing rocks at her, and she was backing into a corner. Barking, hands up to protect herself. "Hrossar, help me!"

Hrossar curled his fists, growling at the humanites. "Leave. Now!"

His voice was still too soft. Even when herodons shouted, most humanites could only hear it as a hoarse croak. If only their voices weren't so low on the humanites' hearing spectrum! "I insist you leave!"

"Or what?" One of the humanites advancing on Holshe swung around to face him. "We have a hundred or so waiting outside. We'll let *you* leave—but don't think you can fight us all off if you elect to stay."

Hrossar's brow furrowed. "This is dishonorable. If you were to engage us in honest combat—"

"But we can't, can we?" The humanite raised a hand, and the others halted their advance. Holshe was backed into the corner, arms covering her face.

"You can easily engage in us in combat."

"And win?" The humanite sneered. "No one can beat the herodons in hand-to-hand. You've mastered combat too well."

Hrossar arched an eyebrow, a harsh snort escaping him. "And?"

The other herodons were leaving. Some rolled out the door as looters waved brands and pitchforks. The rest were listening, seemingly frozen in place.

"And what do you expect, herodon? You control our political

sphere. Any king wants to win a war, he need only hire herodons—and because of your stupid code, you refuse to fight each other." He waved his brand. "So the opposing king simply loses."

That was a fair assessment. "Then the other king should have hired the herodons first."

"Precisely!" The man clutched at the air with his fingers, rage contorting his face. "And it's the same way with court cases! Hiring a herodon or you lose!"

"We are willing to fight each other in debate, however."

"But the poor still suffer—don't you see? Money brings absolute power now. No one can deal with creatures that heal themselves just by heating up. No one can possibly hope to stand against you!" Spittle flew from the humanite's mouth as he spoke. "You are a blight on Newílderashe."

Hrossar scanned the remaining looters. Two of them were circling him, shaking clubs. He inhaled deeply.

"But this is our land! Our *home*!" The man shook his fist. "Our world, you filthy animal! And where're you from?"

Hrossar's shoulders relaxed. He'd heard this complaint many times. "Our abandoned dwellings in Brekh'cha have long been inhabited by geolites."

"Then you should never have abandoned them!" The man spat on the ground. "So out with you!"

"If I may."

They turned to the entrance, where Father stood. The herodon cleared his throat. "My apologies, Hrossar. The moment the raid began, I exited to find the police. A lawful solution must be found."

"And of course," the man's voice was shaking with rage, "you found them in record time because you can curl up and roll."

"Correct." Father gestured at the humanite. "The police are not far behind, however. I suggest you exit."

The humanite raised his firebrand, knuckles white. His lips curled as he faced Hrossar. "You think you're safe because the police chief owes your father a favor?"

Hrossar arched an eyebrow. "I do not believe I am safe at all."

"That's right. You're not." The humanite spat on the ground again—then rubbed it into the carpet with his foot. "Think about that tonight."

Then he turned and left. The other humanites followed him—

84

leaving broken pews, overturned tables and scattered bits of fruit and meat. Father left with them, closing the door behind them.

Sobbing.

Hrossar turned to Holshe. She was on her knees, braids hanging loose, claws cupping her snout as she wept. Cracks ran along her porcelain armor, mingling with the design of flowers and birds. A tear slid from one eye, tracing her jawline.

"Holshe." Hrossar made his way to her, dodging fallen gift baskets and splinters of wood. "Were you injured, my love?"

She shook her head—but kept weeping. He knelt beside her, putting a hand on her shoulder.

"Why—Hrossar, why are they so mean?" She choked out a sob, rubbing her eyes with her palms. "Why should they hate us so much?"

"We unbalance their way of life," Hrossar answered, squeezing her shoulder. "It is understandable."

"But is it justifiable?"

Hrossar kept his eyes on her. The answer was obvious. "I am merely explaining their position."

Holshe wiped a tear—then pulled him into her embrace. "I know, Hrossar. That's who you are—always trying to understand."

Hrossar felt her body shake with sobs. He clenched his jaw, swallowing. "But they will pay for this."

"By whose hand, son?"

Hrossar pulled back from Holshe to see Father standing over them. His eyes were half-lidded—and he seemed wearier than ever. "Revenge is a futile endeavor."

"But there must be justice."

Father nodded. "Justice, yes—revenge, no." He sat down beside them, crossing his legs. "Listen, Hrossar—Holshe. You must not let the sun set on your anger."

Holshe sniffed, rubbing her snout with white knuckles. She shook her head. "Why not? They deserve it, Teros."

"Love is not about what we deserve. It is about duty." Father indicated them with his claws. "Throughout your marriage, you will hurt each other many times—more so than this event. If you cannot forgive the humanites who did this to you, how can you forgive each other?"

More so than this? Hrossar arched an eyebrow. "This is a very special day for us, Father."

"Yet I still must instruct you during it. We cannot give into vengeance. It is our duty to love our neighbor and family." Father leaned in, narrowing his eyes. "And you know this, Hrossar. I have taught it to you many times."

"And I usually am merciful." Hrossar got to his feet, surveying the wreckage. "You have certainly taught me well, Father."

"Excuse me?"

Hrossar hesitated—then softened his tone. "Forgive me. But I have shown nothing but graciousness to those who spat in our faces. My life has been that of a threadbare carpet—knowing only the feet of those who disregard my tapestry. Why should I not seek revenge?"

"Because it is your duty to love."

Hrossar stiffened. It would always come down to duty. Not a bad mentality—but frustrating at times. "Yet why do we have the duty to love them?"

"If we have no duty to love them, they have no duty to love us. In that case, they are not to blame for their behavior. We cannot be angry at them." Father spread his hands, glancing at Holshe. "Do you not agree, Holshe?"

Holshe stared past him, a tear flowing down her cheek. But she nodded, closing her eyes. "I do agree. For the most part."

"Good." Father stood—then held out his hand and helped Holshe up. He turned to Hrossar, voice softer than ever. "This is my last piece of advice as your father, Hrossar. Now you are married—you are released from my charge, your own individual."

Hrossar dipped his head. "Yes, Father."

"If you serve under my authority, it is only as a captain in our battalion. Understood?"

Hrossar prepared to dip his head—then stopped himself. "Understood."

"Good. Remember my words."

"But what about the way people treat us!" Holshe indicated the cracked porcelain of her wedding garb. "This came from my father's grandfather. Are there to be no repercussions?"

"Armor can be replaced. Lives cannot." Father turned from them. His fists opened and closed. "Nonetheless, there are consequences. This sort of trouble is occurring all over Newílderashe."

Hrossar crossed his arms. "I have heard this as well."

Father inhaled deeply—chest rising, jaw clenched. "Then do you

86

know that, in a week, herodons from all over Newílderashe will be meeting only a mile away?" Father turned his head so they could see half his face. "We will discuss the situation—and what we may do to defend our wellbeing."

Hrossar swallowed. "I assume appropriate action will be taken."

"You will be responsible for that." Father began walking down the aisle, stepping over splinters of wood. "Seeing as both of us, being mercenary leaders, have been invited."

☼ ☼ ☼

Voices mingled as herodons offered opinions. To a humanite's ears it might have seemed as though wind were rushing through the meeting hall—such were the whispers of herodons in fierce debate.

Hrossar leaned back, crossing his arms. He was still uncertain as to the preferred course of action.

"Herodons. Please." An elderly herodon rose, lifting a hand to silence the hall. "You have been eloquent in presenting arguments. However, the discussion has gotten out of hand."

A few herodons let out impatient snorts. Most took their seats, eyeing the elderly herodon. His point had been taken.

"I am Derofon. Most of you have not seen me in person but know my name."

Murmurs of assent. Hrossar himself knew of this legend—a mercenary with a list of exploits stretching longer than the Newíldere River.

"We have experienced problems in the past—with geolites, when they encroached on our territory."

"And now they live in our cities!"

"*Abandoned* cities." Derofon raised a finger. "We allowed them to take residence when we left."

The interrupting herodon crossed his arms, letting out a snort. "For the most part."

"We opted to relocate to Newílderashe as a result of tensions between our peoples. Now we face the same dilemma."

"I will not relocate again!"

Other herodons nodded. Some shouted their agreement. "This is ridiculous!"

"Silence." Derofon raised his hand. "I have no intention of finding a *new* land to live. The world is full, and unless we divided and scattered ourselves, it is unlikely we would find a home that we would not overcrowd."

"Indeed." A herodon beside Hrossar raised his snout. "We have no obligation to relocate."

"Nonetheless, this is their land." Derofon swept his hand toward the doorway, which opened onto moonlit steps. "And they greatly outnumber us. If we were to fight them for it, we would have many casualties."

"And what are they going to do? Surround us?"

"Yeah! I doubt they'd beat us ten to one!"

"Don't exaggerate." Derofon glared at them, jaw clenched. "They do possess some skill. It is more likely four to one. Five to one at best."

"So?" Another herodon stood up. He gestured at the herodons sitting beside him. "Most of us are military leaders. We know tactics— we can simply retreat when outnumbered. Even on horses, the humanites don't even try to keep up with us."

Murmurs of assent. Many herodons were nodding.

"If I may."

Hrossar turned to see Father standing. Father pulled a pair of spectacles from his pouch—then donned them carefully, eyes wandering over the crowd. "The question is less one of retreat and more of collateral damage."

The herodon who had just stood blinked. "Pardon?"

"We have our houses here. They contain many belongings. If an army which outnumbered us twenty to one advanced on it with horses, how would we pack up and leave?"

More murmurs. Some herodons nodded.

"Of course, we could not. No one can roll while clutching their life's belongings. We would lose all that we had built—more so than if we had relocated."

The other herodon balled his fists, swallowing. "We could do the same to them. We roll faster than they can relocate their armies."

"And what then?" Father cleared his throat, his spectacles glinting in the chandelier's light. "We would all lose. Both sides shall face extreme collateral damage. Not a preferred outcome."

The other herodon clenched his jaw. "I suppose that's true."

"There is also the matter of mandate." Derofon placed his hands behind his back, snout raised. "Are we to enslave them? Force *their* relocation? Even if we were victorious, do we really have a right to their land?"

Murmurs in the crowd. The herodons seemed torn.

"What atrocities—" Derofon enunciated his next words, claws clutching at the air, "—should we commit to prove we are worthy of this land?"

Father nodded. "Precisely. It would be too costly for us—and we would become the monsters they believe us to be if we were successful."

"Which is why," Derofon began, raising a finger, "we must return to a land that *does* belong to us."

Father closed his eyes. Herodons whispered their agreement around him, many nodding. He took his seat beside Hrossar, letting out a nearly indiscernible sigh.

"Brekh'cha is our home—and a home is worth fighting for." Derofon pointed in the distance, as if they could spot Brekh'cha from here. "If war is coming regardless, it may as well be with those who first antagonized us."

"What of the lava?"

Every head in the room turned to Father. Hrossar could sense their disapproval—their tight jawlines, furrowed brows.

Father cleared his throat, crossing his arms. "You said we could beat the humanites five to one. But geolites are much more difficult. And they exist in an environment capable of killing us with one false step."

"Nonetheless," Derofon countered, raising a finger, "We would be justified to try. And we would be no doubt successful."

"Are you certain?"

"Yes."

Murmurs of assent. Herodons were nodding.

"I disagree." Hrossar stood, placing his hands behind his back. "Battling the geolites is utterly foolish. We are setting ourselves against one of the few enemies which could actually defeat us."

"But it is our home!" Derofon gestured at the other herodons. "Don't tell me you haven't longed for those rolling ridges—twisting pillars of lava, magma dragonflies buzzing to and fro…all the beauties of Brekh'cha."

Shouts in the crowd. "Yes! That's quite true!"

"Derofon is correct. It's time we went home."

"Brekh'cha is perfect." The herodons were finally agreeing on something. "We should have returned sooner."

"Then it's settled." Derofon laced his fingers. "We negotiate with the geolites for our lands. And if they don't relent, we go to war."

The herodons spoke as one. "Agreed."

"Now then." Derofon dipped his head and took a seat. "We have preparations to do. Any ideas on how to discuss this with the kings of Newílderashe? Or the geolites?"

Herodons rose in reply. The chaotic flow of speech resumed—though this time, a war was being planned. Hrossar took a seat, his eyes meeting Father's.

Father studied him—then took off his spectacles, folding them carefully. He tucked them in his pouch—and closed his eyes, expelling a soft sigh.

☼ ☼ ☼

The meeting hall was all but empty. Only Hrossar and his father remained—sitting at their table, staring at the wall. Father was drumming the wood with his claws. Crickets chirped outside—but otherwise, silence.

"So? Will we attempt to reclaim Eastern Brekh'cha?"

Father kept his eyes on the wall. He gave a slight nod. "Of course."

Hrossar's brow furrowed. "But is peace with the geolites not preferable?"

"It is."

"Then?"

Father met his eyes. "We have a responsibility to our fellow herodons, Hrossar. And I doubt they would appreciate our abstinence."

"I see." Hrossar let his eyes settle on the table. He leaned forward, placing his elbows on the wood. "So if the negotiations should fail?"

Father continued drumming the table, inhaling deeply.

"Father?"

90

Father nodded, closing his eyes. "Then we are off to war."

11 TO WAR

The helenbriars stretched before Kel. Vines thicker than his arms curled around boulders and wound their way to the ceiling far above, massive spikes jutting out from them. The thorny shells of helenberries hung scattered throughout the briarpatch. Like pineapples combined with strawberries, but with rhombus hides.

A perfect place for harvesting. Kel grinned—then began climbing the nearest vine.

He reached the lowest helenberry—and punched it off its vine. It tumbled to the ground, and he followed in one hop. He hit the ground in a crouch, helenberry rolling to a stop beside him. "Tohen! Found a good one!"

"Did ya now?" An obsidianite came waddling over, carrying a large glass jar. He set it down as Kel positioned the helenberry between them. "Aye. That's a wee bit smaller than the last, but good enough."

"Not the size! The shape!" Kel ran his fingers along the thorny hide, grinning. "Perfect for surfing."

"Right, then—surfing." Tohen was clearly trying not to roll his eyes. "Certainly."

"You should come with me." Kel punched the helenberry at the side—and it split cleanly in half. He set his half on its shell and dipped his hand into the warm, pinkish-red meat. "I'll be surfing with this tonight."

"I don't have time." Tohen frowned at him. "I'm a traffic director. Remember?"

"As if helenberry harvesting isn't enough. Aren't you a wee bit busy?"

Tohen shrugged, scooping the meat out of his half. "Not really. And don't you have other friends you surf with?"

"Aye. Arnley." Kel dumped his meat into the jar, then took another scoop. "He's busy tonight."

"Alright. What about those other two..." Tohen narrowed his eyes, staring at the cavern ceiling. "Eh—Kharema and Grekham, right?"

Kel hesitated, muscles tightening. "I told you, Tohen—they moved a decade ago. Back to Ticora."

"Ah. I think I remember that now." Tohen's brow furrowed. He stopped scooping helenberry meat and studied Kel. "Seems like you and Kharema were pretty close, though. Anything romantic ever happen between you?"

That was a pointed question. "Why ask that?"

"The few times I surfed with the lot of you, it looked as though there was a—well, a connection."

"Mm." Kel started scooping again, pressing his stony lips together. What was he to say?

"She seemed into you, you know."

Kel swallowed. He wanted no part of this discussion. "Did she?"

"Aye. I'd wager you could've asked her out."

"Eh, I don't know—you don't have the lay of her. She could've been into anyone."

"Could she have? She certainly wasn't into Grekham."

Tohen was sounding like Mom. Kel shook his head. "It's really none of your business."

Tohen blinked. "Well that's a mite unfriendly, lad."

Kel hesitated—then dumped the helenberry meat into their jar. He sighed, staring at his half-scooped shell. "It's not like that. I don't mind you saying anything. I just..."

Tohen studied Kel, one eyebrow raised. "Just what, Kel? Need more time before you ask her out?"

Kel pressed his lips together again. No point to answering.

"Maybe that's why she left. Ever think of that?" Tohen made a wide scoop, glistening red helenberry meat piled on his palm. "Most lasses won't wait more than a century, you know. And I'd assume she's been waiting at least that long."

Kel shook his head. "If she was interested, she'd have asked me out."

"You sure about that?"

"She's an assertive stone."

"Mm." Tohen nodded to himself, stepping back from his shell. "Then she wants you to ask her out to prove you can be assertive too."

"*Or* she's not interested."

"Oh—blistering stones, Kel! I've seen the two of you!" Tohen spread his hands. "It's obvious, lad! What're you afraid of? Are you hoping more time'll make you braver?"

Kel stopped. He stared at Tohen, brow furrowed. "Really got you riled, didn't I?"

"Well—I…" Tohen threw up his hands as if surrendering. "Fine. I see you every day, but I can't give you any advice. You won't listen."

"No need to be impatient." Kel put a palm on his own chest. "I'll listen. You got something to say, I'm all ears."

"I know you are. You're as loyal a stone as ever." Tohen put a hand on his hip, averting his eyes. "But you need boldness, Kel. You can't wait forever, doing nothing."

That seemed altogether too familiar. "You talked with my mom?"

Tohen grimaced. "Yesterday. She wanted to know how you were doing. Said she didn't want to pester you."

"Right." Kel nodded, muscles loosening. He couldn't blame Tohen for that. "I'm fine."

"I'm sure you are." Tohen started scooping again. Their jar was already half-full—but Tohen had more jars nearby. The obsidianite dumped a glop of red meat in and sighed. "Time won't help, you know."

"That so?"

"It is. You hear people say, 'Give them time,' and, 'Time changes people!' Bah!" He waved dismissively. "Don't believe it, Kel. Time changes no one. It only fossilizes your habits."

Kel nodded, swallowing. He scraped his fingers along the bottom of the shell, dislodging clumps of red meat. He let the meat sit in his palm, feeling its warmth. "I suppose so."

"You know I'm right."

"Eh—maybe." Kel inhaled deeply, mouth dry. "Perhaps after a few decades, the hills I wanted to climb have become mountains. Like tectonic plates raised them higher when I wasn't paying them mind."

"Aye." Tohen jabbed a finger at him. "But you know what does change a stone, Kel? Pressure. Heat—events."

Kel kept his eyes on his shell, lips pressed together. He knew this. Everyone knew the science here.

Tohen picked up a stone. "See this piece of graphite? Let it sit there for a thousand years—nothing changes." He cracked the stone against his shell. "Now in a split second, it changes. Events happen in time—so you see your friend after a few centuries and think, 'Oh, time changed them.' But time doesn't do a thing. You just weren't there to see the events happen."

"So I suppose time is like magic to our eyes."

"Eh, more or less. It runs its course, but nothing changes. Only what *occurs* in that time matters." Tohen leaned in, clutching at the air with his ebon fingers. "You hear me, lad?"

"I hear you." Tohen hesitated. "But I can't ask her. I—"

Their shells vibrated on the ground. Kel felt his whole body trembling—no, the ground! The ground itself was shaking!

Tohen's brow furrowed. "We don't get earthquakes down here."

"No." Kel looked past Tohen, where rocks were sliding down the ridge. "We don't."

Then he saw them. Rubber balls about the size of him—rolling at breakneck speed. Herodons.

Over forty, tumbling down the ridge behind the briarpatch.

"Climb the briars!" Kel ran to the nearest vine. "And take the jar with you!"

Tohen needed only one glance behind them. "What in burning stones are herodons doing here?"

"Don't know! Come on, lad! Seek higher ground!"

Tohen snatched up the jar. He plucked its lid from the ground and screwed it on.

"Now, Tohen!"

Tohen scrambled up the vine, jar under his arm. He wrapped his fingers around a spike, resting on his knees. "What's going through their brains?"

"Don't know." Kel was clutching two spikes, trying to keep his feet from sliding down the vine. He stared as the herodons rolled beneath them, dust rising in a choking fog. His teeth rattled inside his head, and he gritted them.

More herodons poured down the ridge behind them. Row upon

95

row, tumbling, bumping off rocks. Advancing in haphazard formation like dark pebbles in a landslide.

Kel coughed. The dust was rising—no point in breathing. Rocks tumbled from the ceiling, and even the lava pillars seemed disturbed. Droplets flew from them, splattering the walls with angry hisses.

Then the herodons were gone. Rolling past them, funneling into a tunnel. The ground still vibrated—but Kel's teeth weren't rattling. He blinked, trying to speak. No air! He took in a breath, shoulders loosening. "Mighty odd."

"Herodons have never ventured past Nicota." Tohen hopped off the vine, landing in a crouch. "What're they doing?"

"No idea." Kel slid down, landing by their shells. Smashed beyond recognition. "Doubt they're up to any good, though."

"D'you think they're looking for war?"

"Wouldn't surprise me." Kel studied the tunnel the herodons had entered. That way led to Ticora. "Seeing all the fights they've already picked."

☼ ☼ ☼

"Hrossar Feodon."

Hrossar rose from his seat, glancing at the administrator. A sapphire geolite reading a clipboard. He cleared his throat. "Present."

"You may enter the council room now."

Curious. The last herodon had exited the council room approximately one hour ago. It was taking that long to discuss the situation between herodons? "Very well."

She beckoned with one hand—and Hrossar approached the massive stone door. It rolled aside before him, grinding as it retreated into the wall. Before him lay a polished marble floor, reflective like a mirror. He crossed the threshold, claws clacking on the marble.

The door slid behind him. Now he was alone in the tunnel.

He took each step carefully, claws echoing in the silence. He was aware of his own breathing—the tension in his muscles, the alertness of his ears. Would the council hear their request?

So far no herodon had commented on the proceedings. No doubt sworn to secrecy.

He exited the tunnel—and found himself in a massive council room with a sloped bowl of a floor. High chairs lined the room's edges, geolites staring down at him. At the opposite wall a large podium rose. A hematite stood behind it, his grainy ebon skin gleaming in the green flames crackling above.

"Greetings, Hrossar Feodon." The hematite studied Hrossar for a few seconds, adjusting his spectacles. "Please stand in the center of the room so the flames may record your testimony."

Hrossar obeyed. He made his way to the center of the bowl, keeping his snout raised. His eyes darted up to the ceiling, where the green flames seemed to be orbiting each other. No doubt a trick of gravity—but these were recording flames. What magic allowed them to record words and events, he did not know.

"Your attention, if you please."

Hrossar's eyes darted back to the geolite. "My apologies."

"Now you and this—" the hematite dragged his hands through the air, as if searching for words, "—*entourage* have come to declare war on us. Correct?"

"Not precisely." Hrossar loosened his fists. He had to maintain composure. "We are here to seek the return of our land—peacefully or otherwise."

"And you chose 'peacefully' first."

"That is correct. We believe we may bargain."

"So you sent an entire army?"

Hrossar gave a soft snort. "This is an inconsequential force. Comprising a few generals, but mostly sophists. For the purpose of negotiation."

"Ah, yes." The geolite gave a sardonic smile. He shuffled through a stack of notes, spectacles flashing in the flames' light. "You are renowned debaters. So of course you would send them. First you try verbal combat—then physical. Debate, then real war. That about right?"

Hrossar dipped his head. "Those are the trades we have mastered."

"Of course." The geolite gave a sigh, straightening his stack of notes by bumping them on the podium. He narrowed his eyes at Hrossar. "Mr. Feodon, do you know why we've summoned you and not other herodons?"

Hrossar shook his head. "I do not."

"We've been told by the previous herodon witnesses that you and your father oppose the idea of war with us. You objected when it was proposed."

"Both of us did." Hrossar arched an eyebrow. "However, my father is a general. Why did you not summon him first?"

"We will in time. We're going alphabetically." The hematite adjusted his spectacles. "Would you say other herodons feel this way?"

Hrossar tried not to shift his footing. He placed his hands behind his back, raising his snout. Composure was paramount. "It is irrelevant. We will go to war nonetheless."

"Despite your objections?"

"Despite our objections." Hrossar closed his eyes, his stomach knotting. What else could be said? "Our duty is to our kinsmen."

"I see."

Hrossar opened his eyes. The geolite was leaning back in his chair, spectacles removed. He was rubbing his forehead, stony black fingers glistening. "This is difficult—but I don't think you understand."

"It is a simple matter of land." Hrossar's brow furrowed. "Or do you wish to precipitate war?"

"I'd avoid it if I could." The hematite gave another sigh. "There's simply not enough land, Mr. Feodon. We went through a reproductive cycle just a decade ago—one occurs every century or so—and there are many more of us than existed before. Far too many to even *begin* fitting in our other cities."

Hrossar raised a finger. "But it is our land."

"*Was* your land." The geolite leaned forward again. "And may I remind you, you surrendered it voluntarily. Your sophists know this— the right is ours, and they must retake it by force or diplomacy."

"Of course. However—" Hrossar gave a soft snort. This was pointless. Every herodon knew their situation—otherwise war would not be threatened. They would simply ask for what was theirs. "We are giving you the opportunity to avoid bloodshed."

"And it is appreciated. But we cannot yield."

"You do not understand. We could have ambushed you—engaged in war without warning." Hrossar softened his tone. "We sacrificed a major tactical advantage for the possibility of avoiding physical conflict."

"And what of rolling through Nicota?" The geolite's eyebrows went up. "Was that for show? Or don't you know that Brekh'cha sits below the Great Plains? You could just as easily roll over Brekh'cha by the plains, then enter Ticora through crevices."

Hrossar dipped his head. "We are aware of this."

"But you needed to intimidate us. To make a point." The hematite jabbed a finger at him. "You're bullies, Mr. Feodon. You were bullies a century ago, and you're just bullying us now."

"That is not—" Hrossar swallowed, shifting his footing. "Our rolling through Nicota was merely a display of capability. To show we still know the lay of Brekh'cha and are able to maneuver it."

"Most call that intimidation." The hematite crossed his arms, standing straight. "We. Will. Not. Yield."

The council members had been silent up to this point. But now a few were murmuring. Hrossar looked around the room, trying not to curl his fists. "This is not what you want. None of us want this."

"Except you do. Otherwise you wouldn't have come here, would you?" The geolite shook his head. "You knew where this was going, Mr. Feodon. Now the herodons can back off—or war will follow."

Hrossar did not respond. He inhaled deeply, closing his eyes.

"So unless you have anything to add—you're dismissed."

Hrossar lowered his snout. Placing his hands behind his back, he let his eyes open. "Understood."

☼ ☼ ☼

The herodons rolled off as Kel watched, dust rising in their wake. He gritted his teeth, fists clenched. "Good riddance."

"They'll be back." Mom came up beside him. "And from what I've heard," she lowered her voice, "they've declared war."

"Aye." Kel turned to her. "And they'll have a thing or two coming if they try it."

"Will they?" Concern lined his mom's face like cracks in barren rock. "Kel, I'm worried. You're a labradorite. Your structural stability makes you an optimal warrior."

"So?"

"So they'll draft you for the war. You'll have to fight."

99

"That's fine. I'm not afraid." Kel crossed his arms. "Let me at them."

"Kel..."

Why was she so concerned? "I'll be fine, Mom. We're rocks. We don't chip easily."

"But the herodons can shatter you. Granted, you're more stable than most..." She averted her eyes. Something glittered on her cheek—was that a tear? "I just don't want to see you die, Kel. There's so much you haven't done."

Kel opened his mouth—then closed it. Odd how even with air in his stony lungs, it could be difficult to speak. "Mom..."

"What about your contraptions? Showing them off at a convention?" Mom faced him squarely, putting her hands on his arms. "What about Kharema? You have so much to do, Kel. What if your time runs out?"

This again. Kel swallowed. "I'm fine, Mom."

"No, you're not. You're empty." Mom released him and turned away, another tear sliding down her cheek. She sniffed, wiping her eye. Fiery streaks danced through her opal skin, flashing in the firelight as she turned back to him. "This is my fault. I raised you wrong."

"Mom!" Kel felt tears welling in his eyes. His lower lip started trembling. "Mom, don't say that!"

"It's true!" Mom spread her hands. "You'll never do anything! You'll just keep puttering on with life—never going anywhere!"

"Mom—"

"And what'll you do at the end? Weep for all your lost time?"

Kel's muscles tightened—and he flexed his fingers. "No, Mom."

"Promise me." Mom took his hand in hers. "Promise me you'll try something after the war is over. It doesn't have to be Kharema—it can just be showing your contraptions off at Newílderashe."

Kel hesitated. He averted his eyes, feeling her hands around his. "I—"

"Promise me, Kel."

He met her eyes. They were still welling with tears, glittering in the firelight. His mouth was hanging open—curse his insensitivity! But what else was there to say? "I...I promise, Mom."

Mom pulled him into a hug. She squeezed him with her long arms—and he hugged her back. She patted his shoulder. "That's my

100

boy. Now make it through the war."

Kel kept the hug going. Geolites could never wrap their arms all the way in a hug—their bodies were too round and big. He stepped back and squeezed her shoulders. "I will, Mom."

✧ ✧ ✧

FIVE DAYS LATER

"Ladies and gentlemen!"

Hrossar stiffened. King Delóren stood on a stage in the street, holding a large scroll. Just as scheduled.

"I have important news this day—important enough to deliver myself!"

Many in the market were turning to listen. Vendors stopped shouting, mothers hushed their children.

Delóren hefted the scroll in one hand, flashing a grin. "They're leaving us. The herodons."

Gasps. The crowd exchanged glances, eyes wide.

"They're going to war with the geolites in Brekh'cha. Seeking to reclaim their land, naturally." Delóren spread his hands, smirk in place. "But they need our help first."

"What can we do?" A man stepped forward, hand raised. "I'll help in any way I can!"

"That's where this scroll comes in." Delóren unrolled the scroll a little. About a page's worth of lines filled the top, followed by blank space. "Each of you just need to sign this agreement—and pay me a small processing fee, of course—and the herodons will be out of your hair."

Processing fee. Hrossar gave a soft snort, shaking his head. Delóren was a businessman, plainly. No such processing fee had been proposed—but leave it to Delóren to turn a profit from anything.

"The herodons, you see, have agreed to leave their families unprotected in Newílderashe—provided we agree not to attack them." Delóren frowned, eyebrows creasing as if he was genuinely concerned. "I'm sure we can all agree that leaving your women and children unprotected while you go off to fight a war is unwise."

101

"I'll treat them like a second family!" a woman shouted from the crowd. "They won't lack or fear a thing!"

"They won't have to fear me!" another man claimed. "I'll guard them myself if I have to!"

As predicted, the peasants were favorable. Hrossar closed his eyes, expelling a breath. Excellent.

"Now I don't doubt the authenticity of anyone here," Delóren continued, raising a hand as if in apology, "but you should know that once you sign this, you agree to enforce the penalty for anyone who doesn't abide by these rules."

Murmurs in the crowd. The people exchanged confused glances.

"Now I've been a fan of the herodons. I enjoyed their company—utilizing them for various endeavors. But I understand some of you have...been less than enthusiastic." Delóren unrolled the scroll further. "After you sign this, you agree to put to death anyone who breaks these terms."

Gasps in the crowd. More murmurs.

Death?

Is he serious?

For simply attacking them?

Sure, murder should get death. But pillaging?

"Please." Delóren raised his hand, a glib smile in place. "It's just a precaution. The herodons must be *assured* that you will not attack their families—or pillage their homes."

The king's voice was unusually smooth for a humanite. Truly he had charisma. Hrossar crossed his arms, inhaling deeply.

"This is merely a deterrent. An adequate precaution—wouldn't you agree?"

A few nods. Some still seemed unsettled—but they would conform. Hrossar assumed their desire to see the herodons leave would eclipse their qualms.

"Now, if you'll just sign here and deposit the fee beside me..." Delóren unrolled the scroll further—and only then did Hrossar notice the jar beside him. Undoubtedly more were stacked beneath the stage. Efficient.

"I'll sign! Sure!"

"I'll sign it in my blood if I have to!"

"Where do I put my name?"

The fact was, many of these peasants were illiterate. There

"signatures" would comprise nothing more than scribbles at best. Haphazard pledges of loyalty.

Hrossar raised his chin, studying the crowd. Nonetheless, the intention was what mattered.

"It seems to be going well." Father came up beside Hrossar. "Has he informed them of every condition?"

"Not entirely." Hrossar lowered his voice. "It is clear he wishes to reveal certain…fine print after the signatures have been obtained."

"Hm." Father nodded, focusing on Delóren. "We selected him because he's a charismatic speaker and businessman. If anyone can arrange this deal, it's him."

"I don't believe he is having much difficulty," Hrossar noted, arching an eyebrow. "They seem eager to jump off a cliff—if it means our departure."

"Do you blame them?"

Hrossar's brow furrowed. "Pardon?"

"We have disrupted their entire world. We've both heard the complaints, Hrossar. While we lived in Brekh'cha, they could only occasionally hire us. But while we live here, everything revolves around our hire. Can you truly argue that this is where we belong?"

Hrossar narrowed his eyes, keeping his arms crossed. He let out a faint snort. "No."

"Precisely." Father put a hand on his shoulder. "I had hoped, however, that we could find a new realm to inhabit. One which would not require war."

"And would we not be forced to leave there?" Hrossar gestured with one hand. "Are we to be constantly moving? Despised wherever we reside?"

"No." Father studied the crowd. "That would not be optimal."

"Precisely. Perhaps war is inevitable where we are concerned."

Father digested that. He raised his snout, placing his hands behind his back. "Perhaps."

"Thank you!" Delóren was speaking again, waiting for attention. Peasants crowded him, each trying to sign the paper. "Most of your signatures have been acquired. However, I may have forgotten one other detail."

The crowd began grumbling.

Really? A catch?

Are you kidding me?

103

Delóren, stop playing games.

Hrossar arched an eyebrow. Delóren tolerated a significant level of disrespect from non-royalty. Granted, these were not his subjects. But Delóren was unique in that, among the so-called kings of Newílderashe—who were more like feudal warlords—he had influence without belonging to any faction.

A smile tugged at Hrossar's lips. Truly Delóren was a mercenary king.

"Now, now." Delóren raised his hand, quieting the crowd. "It's not so bad. It's only a small provision, in fact."

"How small?" someone in the crowd asked. "Just the shirt off our backs?"

"Oh, it's not monetary." Delóren coughed into his fist, clearing his throat. "It's just a little clause at the end. In the event the herodons fail to conquer their part of Brekh'cha—"

The whole crowd laughed. Delóren blinked at them, holding up the scroll. "I'm serious. In case they should fail to take Brekh'cha—"

"They won't fail!" A lady shook her head, peals of laughter rolling through her. "They're herodons! They're invincible!"

"In the event they succumb to the geolites," Delóren continued, enunciating his words, "you have agreed to give them additional time—upon their return—to find a new homeland."

"Sure!" A man waved dismissively. "Not like it matters. They won't fail."

Nods of assent. No one in the crowd doubted their capabilities.

"Excellent." Delóren inhaled deeply, searching the crowd. "You may continue signing now."

"Well then." Father's voice was low—too low for humanites to detect. "It seems the burden is on us to succeed."

"You assume they will forsake this aspect of the agreement?"

"Perhaps not." Father turned to Hrossar. "But will you take that risk?"

Hrossar uncrossed his arms. Placing them behind his back, he dipped his snout. "I would not."

"Precisely." Father studied Delóren. "We are off to war, Lieutenant Hrossar. And we must not fail."

12 DUTY

5960 OT, 2nd month (two days later)

Father's blades whistled, slicing grass as he rolled ahead of the battalion. Hrossar rolled just behind, ears picking up sonic vibrations to guide him. The whistling veered right...Hrossar veered right, accelerating as grass bowed beneath him.

They'd been rolling for two days. Three stops—two for sustenance, one for sleep.

Now it was night again. And the next stop would be war.

He could hear the geolites ahead. They'd just spotted the herodons—he heard one cup his hands to his mouth. The shout seemed almost distant—its pitch was too high for Hrossar's low sonar—but there could be no doubt.

The first battle was beginning.

Cracking sounds. Two geolites near the crevice burst apart as herodons rammed them. Hrossar wove his way between them, slipping into the crevice. Now he was inside Brekh'cha, bumping along as he sped down an entrance tunnel.

He burst into a cavern. Three herodons followed him, branching off to shatter the incoming geolites. Hrossar selected a corundumite and veered.

He felt the impact before he heard it. His body slammed into the geolite, shockwaves reverberating through his rubber hide. He could sense fractures penetrating the corundumite's body—then the geolite exploded into fragments, shards flying everywhere.

Hrossar uncurled, claws digging into the dirt. He put his hand against a pillar of quartz—what was wrong? What had just happened?

105

His stomach roiled with nausea.

Something struck his side—his body jerked. He fell against the pillar with another blow. He rolled to his feet—then spun as a golden chalcopyrite leapt on him. Blow after blow rained upon his head, and Hrossar lashed out with his claws.

The geolite gasped, pieces of his face torn off. Hrossar threw him aside—then got to his feet.

His skull was throbbing. He put a hand on it, blinking. He could barely concentrate—what was happening? Herodons were shattering geolites, geolites fighting back—no one was paying him mind except this chalcopyrite.

The geolite began spinning, fists out. A standard whirlwind attack. He approached Hrossar, fists a blur.

What was the proper defense? The fists would form a barrier around the geolite—and they were in close quarters, so Hrossar could not build up speed to shatter him with a roll...

Hrossar put his back to the quartz pillar. He dove aside just as the chalcopyrite attacked, rolling to his feet as chunks of quartzite flew from the pillar. The geolite turned to him—but it was too late.

Hrossar descended upon the stone, claws a blur as he struck repeatedly. Chunks of stone flew out with each strike. The geolite stumbled back, growling.

Hrossar could not stop. He kept striking—again and again, leaving jagged craters in his foe's chest. Golden chunks of chalcopyrite glittered in the silver light of the lava river flowing on the ceiling, tumbling down the ridge. The geolite's chest was gone—his face was barely recognizable.

Then the geolite fell on his back. His arms dropped at his sides, and he stopped moving.

Hrossar fell to his knees. His body burned like fire—he could feel bruises along his abdomen and chest. Had the geolite been striking him? Hrossar did not know.

Then he noticed the geolite's expression. The stone's eyes stared into empty space, the lava's light glinting off his glossy pupils. Half of his mouth was missing, replaced by a crater. The rest hung slightly ajar, stony lips parted.

Hrossar felt nausea welling up in him. He wanted to vomit—but no. He had to be composed. Weakness was unacceptable.

He put his hand against the cratered pillar and rose. Inhaling

106

deeply, he stilled his trembling muscles. Searing needles still shot through him—the fire in his veins—but it would subside.

A grinding sound. Hrossar spun as three herodons rolled up. They uncurled before him, scanning the cavern.

One of them was Father. He shifted both kama to one hand and plucked a small whistle from the pouch on his belt. After clearing his throat, he blew on it. Other herodons gathered around him, though a few were limping.

"Excellent work." Father's voice was unusually soft. "In one hour, geolites will be alerted that an invasion occurred here." He looked from herodon to herodon, tucking the whistle into his pouch. "By that point, we will be long gone."

Hrossar put his hands behind his back. He straightened, stifling the nausea.

"But as you know, our real target is Liekhren City—eight miles south of here. We have diverted their forces through this distraction." A corner of Father's lips lifted. "By the time they discover our ruse, it will be too late—as we roll significantly faster than they do."

No one moved. Every herodon stood at attention, though some had bruises on their chest.

"You have done well." Father's eyes settled on Hrossar—and his next words were even softer. "This first strike is a victory for us."

Hrossar swallowed. "Yes, General Feodon."

"Now, I will stay behind to ensure our battalion has exited—but the rest of you must head south to Liekhren."

Hrossar made to curl up—when father raised a hand. "Lieutenant Hrossar will stay behind with me."

Hrossar straightened again. "Yes sir."

"All others are dismissed."

A chorus of "yes sir." Herodons curled up and rolled into the tunnel. For secrecy's sake, they would take the plains.

"It is difficult."

Hrossar focused on Father. The herodon was studying him, one eyebrow arched. "Is it not?"

Hrossar hesitated—then nodded. "If I may speak freely, sir."

"Of course. I am still your father."

"Thank you." Hrossar inhaled deeply, putting his hand against the quartzite pillar again. "This was more difficult than I had anticipated. Why?"

107

"Well, they are geolites. They are not so easy to defeat as humanites."

"That is not what I meant."

"I know what you meant, son." Father knelt down, laying his kama on the ground. Then he approached Hrossar, claws clacking lightly on the stone. "But you have killed before."

"Have I? This is different." Hrossar averted his eyes, claws scratching the pillar. "I was always destroying those who would refuse justice and crush the oppressed. Now—" he swallowed, closing his eyes, "—now I am the villain."

"You are not."

Hrossar felt a hand on his shoulder. He opened his eyes to see Father studying him. Hrossar opened his mouth—then licked his snout, trying to calm himself. "The geolites do not deserve this."

"Correct. They are simply defending their home."

"Then what are we doing here? This is wrong."

"We are supporting our kinsmen." Father raised a finger. "That is of utmost priority."

"And what of the preservation of life?"

"Hrossar…" Father expelled a soft sigh. "There will be moments when our duties conflict with one another." He raised his eyebrows. "And that is difficult—but one duty supersedes the other. Fighting for our kinsmen is the higher duty."

Hrossar shook his head. "Truly?"

"Truly."

Hrossar licked his snout again. He flexed his fingers, closing his eyes. "For a war we should not be fighting."

"Whether we agree with the war or not is irrelevant. This is our duty."

Hrossar opened his eyes. "Duty."

"Yes. We have a duty to love our kinsmen first—and others second. Our consideration for our kinsmen may sometimes override our consideration of others."

"But why?"

"Why else?" Father shrugged, spreading his hands. "Should we value the geolites more than our own brothers and sisters?"

If Father was uncomfortable, he was not showing it. Hrossar opened and closed his fists, averting his eyes. "I suppose not."

"Precisely. They are our family." Father put both hands on

Hrossar's shoulders. "Listen, son. You have a wife. Eventually you may have a child. If you prioritized others above them, who would care for them?"

Hrossar kept his eyes on the ground. This was a fair point. "I suppose no one will."

"That is correct. It is our duty to care for those under our charge." Father indicated himself with a claw—then put his palm on Hrossar's chest. "First our family, then our kinsmen. *Then* the rest of the world."

Hrossar's muscles were tight. He would have preferred to shake his head—but Father was making sense. As usual. "Are you not disturbed by this?"

"Highly." Father stepped back, inhaling deeply. He seemed very weary all of a sudden. "But this is the course our people have chosen. We will not betray them."

Hrossar swallowed. There was nothing else to be said.

"Do you understand, son?"

Hrossar met his father's gaze. There was a great degree of compassion in those eyes…but a fire burned as well. Hrossar was expected to share that determination. His stomach knotted as he dipped his head. "I understand."

☆ ☆ ☆

ONE MONTH LATER

Lava pressed against Kel, searing orange in all directions. He forced one foot in front of the other—one step, another—keeping his lips pressed together. Hiking under lava was a chore.

He was going uphill. He knew that much.

It was as though the lava was thousands of hands pressing upon him—but the heat added to the pressure. Kel didn't know how much more his body would take. How long had he been under the lava?

He kept his grip tight around the hand leading him. That hand belonged to a timekeeper—marking off seconds, calculating angles to turn so they could maneuver without seeing their path.

The top of his head suddenly felt cool. The pressure subsided there. Had he just broken the surface?

Kel took another step—then two, then three—and his eyes broke the surface.

Lava boiled and hissed around him as he emerged. Searing droplets fell from him, hissing on the shore as he took a couple awkward steps. About time.

"Excellent." The pumicite timekeeper released his hand. His voice was barely more than a whisper. "Now don't make a peep. Wait for everyone else to emerge."

Oh—right. Kel had been holding someone else's hand. They'd formed a chain under the lava, and the obsidianite behind Kel was still stepping out of the river. More stepped out behind him, and soon the whole battalion was out. All ten geolites.

"Can everyone hear me?"

They all focused on the timekeeper. A few nodded.

"Perfect." The timekeeper pointed at a massive green lava pillar. "You see how that stretches up into a hole in the ceiling?"

A few whispered aye's.

"You'll be surfing that. A week ago, five timekeepers—including me—maneuvered this river and hid surfboards here. The boards'll be waiting for you in that alcove." He pointed at a crevice near the ceiling. "Just roll up the wall—no special gravity zones."

A few geolites moved—but the timekeeper held up a hand. "Don't be hasty. I need to fill you in on the plan. As you know, we left our hidden stores when we evacuated Liekhren. So surfboards aren't all we've stowed—"

"Isn't time limited?"

Kel turned to the obsidianite beside him. Concern etched the geolite's face. "We're in Liekhren now, no? I recognize this area. The herodons might've spotted us."

"The herodons have lookouts on the *standard* entrance points." The timekeeper raised his eyebrows. "Understand, lads? They're not counting on us to travel under the lava. No one saw us enter—and we're well past their border patrols now."

Ah...Kel nodded. "Great plan, timekeeper."

"Aye. And I apologize for keeping you all in the dark. Better the way of caution, they say—and now, I don't have to repeat myself. So listen closely." He beckoned, and they all moved in. The timekeeper looked from geolite to geolite, grim lines running along his face like cracks on barren ground. "Your lives depend on following these

110

instructions, lads."

☼ ☼ ☼

Kel eyed the green lava pillar. Its heat reflected off his skin, and he hefted the surfboard under one arm. Almost ready.

He scooped up two balls of searing magma and dumped them into his shell. They throbbed like live coals, shedding lava as they rolled.

The timekeeper was sitting meters away, eyes closed. How they knew time was beyond Kel. The stone raised four fingers—and put one down. Then a second went down, and a third—

The timekeeper's pinky fell, forming a fist. Kel placed his board against the pillar and leapt on as gravity shifted.

The current rushed him through the hole in the ceiling, and for a second he was surrounded by darkness. Then white lights sparkled all around him—hematite reflecting silver lava ahead. He plucked the magma balls and squeezed them, red lava dripping between his fingers.

Then he was in the open. His pillar curved into a river, and he spotted three herodons standing guard beside it. He tossed one magma ball—it splattered on the first herodon, lava hissing on his chest. The creature barked, stumbling back. Kel's second magma ball hit the other herodon's face.

Kel picked up the board and, feet planted on it, flew into the third herodon. The creature barked as Kel rolled off him. Kel spun in a whirlwind attack, fists still searing red from being under lava. Each blow connected with the fallen herodon's face, smoke rising from his rubber hide.

The other two herodons were on their knees, trying to wipe off the lava. Kel had heard they could heal by heat—but lava was hot already. There was a limit, he'd been told.

Kel kept his fists swinging, knocking both herodons over. Three down. His eyes darted around the cavern—anyone else?

No. Just the herodons he'd killed.

One herodon was looking at him. Kel leapt back, raising his fists. Then he looked closer.

Lava dripped along the herodon's snout, hissing as smoke rose

111

from it. The herodon's eyes weren't staring at Kel—they were looking past him. Into nothing. The creature's mouth was half-open, his arms and legs splayed.

Kel swallowed. His mouth was dry all of a sudden. What was the matter? These herodons had attacked them. They deserved it.

But he couldn't stop looking at the dead herodon. He backed up a couple steps—and nearly tripped over the first herodon.

Two geolites came surfing down the pillar, arms out to keep their balance. One wobbled as he reached the shore. "You got them, Kel?"

"Aye." Kel felt uneasy. A wee bit nauseous. "I got them."

"Three intruders!"

He spun to see a herodon pointing. The creature cupped his hands to his mouth—and the ground vibrated a little. Six herodons came rolling around the corner to Kel.

Perfect. Kel stood in place, arms out as the other two geolites came beside him. Any moment now—

A sound like crunching rocks met Kel's ears. He dropped to the ground as fragments of magma and rock hurtled toward the herodons. Great timing.

He glanced behind. Two more geolites were throwing balls of molten rock at the far wall—where gravity zones shifted the balls so they would start falling sideways. Now they were plummeting toward the herodons at full speed, coming apart in fiery sparks. The herodons uncurled just in time to be plastered.

Then the green lava river exploded with geolites. The rest of Kel's battalion rose from its banks, dripping with glowing green lava. They rolled toward the dazed herodons, ramming them off their feet.

But some of the herodons in the back had covered their faces in time. Their claws dug into the ground, and they turned sideways as the geolites hit them, letting the stones bounce off their rubber hides.

Kel curled into a ball and rolled full speed. He ricocheted off a herodon, bouncing beside the lava river. He plucked a rock from the bank, dipped it in the lava and hurled it at the herodon. As the herodon blocked, another geolite rammed him.

The herodons were forming a defensive formation—no doubt trying to reclaim their organization. Geolites were pounding at them, fists still searing hot from being under lava for so long. The herodons were striking back, claws tearing out chunks of rock.

"We require reinforcements!" A herodon in back shouted down

the tunnel. "Now!"

That was the signal. Kel tossed a piece of debris up the lava pillar, so it skipped along it like a stone up a stream. Was that enough for the timekeeper to tell?

He turned back just as a herodon struck at him. Pieces of rock dislodged from Kel's shoulder—and as he gasped, more came from his chest. The herodon's fists were a blinding blur. Kel swung blindly, but the herodon did not flinch.

Another geolite rolled in, and the herodon leapt back. The creature circled them, claws gleaming in the lava's light.

Any moment now—what was the timekeeper doing? Kel started spinning, fists out in a whirlwind attack. He only needed to make the herodon back up.

It was working. One by one, herodons were retreating. But the ground was already rumbling as reinforcements arrived. Twenty herodons rolled down the tunnel, rubber balls bumping along the uneven ground—

The ceiling exploded. Charges set in place just before the city had been evacuated blew, courtesy of the timekeeper igniting them. The pumicite stood on the ceiling, fists cracking against each other to make sparks. Another set of charges blew—and rubble rained upon the incoming herodons.

Dust rose in a choking cloud as the first herodons spun to see their colleagues buried. They were cut off.

Kel growled, rolling full force. He rammed one of the remaining herodons, and the other geolites followed. They descended, fists swinging. Blow after blow, landing with cracks and grunts as the herodons stumbled back into the pile of rubble. One dolomite picked up a huge boulder and bashed it over a herodon's head. The herodons were striking back, claws flashing—but they were outnumbered.

Everything had gone according to plan.

☼ ☼ ☼

"And that's it."

Kel sat down, feeling a bit dizzy. He'd lost quite a bit of rock from his chest and arms. "That it is."

113

"Only time will tell if the other ambushes went right," the obsidianite whispered, staring at the lava river. "But if this is any indication, we've retaken Liekhren."

"Aye." Kel followed his gaze. Though it seemed rude, the river had been the final tomb for each herodon. No sense risking that the bodies were only unconscious and might awaken. "This one's a win for us."

The obsidianite swallowed. He was still staring at the river, but his fists were curled. "I just hope we didn't lose too many stones."

Kel felt queasy again. Lose too much mass, and a stone could die. He'd come too close. If his fellow stones had fared poorly…

"At any rate, we did well." The obsidianite took a seat beside Kel, attempting a smile. "That's what matters. Right?"

Something about his tone bugged Kel. "Your name?"

"Doesn't matter." The obsidianite tucked his legs in, using his hands to keep himself from rolling. "I don't want to know—as you might die tomorrow."

Ah. Kel averted his eyes. "I see that."

They were to stand watch as the other geolites touched base. Not that any herodons would be rolling this way for a while.

Kel tucked his legs in, pressing his lips together. He hoped it would be a short war.

13 TARGETING THE TIMEKEEPERS

5961 OT, 3rd month (ten months later)

A breeze stirred the silent plains, tall blades of grass waving beneath a star-speckled sky. Hrossar stood with the other eight herodons, watching Father. Not a muscle moved.

Father's kama gleamed in the moonlight. He studied each of them, letting silence prevail. No doubt assessing their mentality.

At last his mouth opened. "The geolites have made strides in the past several months."

No one spoke. They stared straight ahead, ears alert.

"They have ambushed us from beneath the lava—set charges and utilized a superior knowledge of Brekh'cha's caverns to outwit us."

Hrossar swallowed. Their own battalion had barely escaped the last confrontation.

"However, I have been working with the other generals on a new strategy." Father inhaled deeply, turning to Hrossar. "The geolites are held together by leaders known as timekeepers. They allow them to maneuver under lava—as they must time their turns to navigate."

Hrossar knew this. The discovery had been made only a month ago.

"We believe we can now identify the timekeepers—and eliminate them at the onset of the battle."

Hrossar raised his eyebrows. That would be remarkable advantage.

"The timekeepers are characterized by concentration—they typically close their eyes and wait beside a tunnel. Or even on the ceiling, where charges may have been planted." Father gestured with his kama, moonlight glinting on the scythes. "You are to target them before engaging with any other geolites. Understood?"

"Understood, General Feodon!" came the unified reply.

Hrossar gave a soft snort. Though voices carried on the plains, they were using their low voice. No geolite could hear those—as far as he knew. His eyes darted along the plains, watching for movement.

"Lieutenant Feodon."

Hrossar straightened, staring ahead. "Yes, General."

"All of Brekh'cha rests under the Southwestern Great Plains, correct?"

"Correct."

"And so we may roll anywhere we wish, entering Brekh'cha at any point?"

Father was testing Hrossar. "No sir."

"Why not?"

"Although it is true that Brekh'cha may theoretically be entered from any point on the Southwestern Great Plains, geolite lookouts have been posted. Even our current location may be known to them."

"Correct." Father raised a finger. "Which is why we travel in groups of ten. Can you tell me how that helps us?"

What was the purpose of this test? Hrossar dared not loosen his posture. "By scattering ourselves in groups of ten, we prevent the geolites from knowing where we will strike next—and as we roll faster than they do, we are able to unite those groups to attack one location before they can react."

"Correct. As long as we control the plains above Brekh'cha, they have no perfect defense against us and must spread their forces."

An advantageous strategy, considering the geolites outnumbered the herodons significantly. The Supreme Declarer of Ticora had not been exaggerating about the recent reproductive cycle. The geolites were numerous.

"As it stands, we are preparing to take Kerosohk City. Some of you may have grown up there. Though geolites live there now." Father gave the softest of snorts—or was it a sigh? "We are coordinating with eight other generals to attack the city from different angles. Like ours, their battalions consist of ten herodons each."

One of the herodons cleared his throat.

"Yes?"

"Only eighty herodons, sir?"

116

Father nodded. "Only eighty will be needed. With their timekeepers eliminated, they will be thrown into chaos. As we have superior coordination and combat capabilities, we will prevail."

The herodon nodded. "And they won't be expecting us?"

"The scouts have told them that only eighty herodons are in this area," father explained, arching an eyebrow, "and most of those herodons appear to be near larger groups targeting other cities. They will not expect an assault at this time."

The tactics of war amazed Hrossar. To a child, one soldier fighting another might be sufficient. But in a large war, every detail was paramount.

"Lieutenant Feodon."

Hrossar focused on Father. "Yes, General?"

Father approached him, holding out his kama. "You are to lead this charge."

Hrossar's brow furrowed. "You are a General. Where will you be?"

"Following you." Father dipped his head. "You must have experience leading troops, Lieutenant. Now is as good a time as any."

None of the herodons moved—but Hrossar sensed the discomfort. Was this favoritism based on their familial ties? Hrossar knew Father better than that—but did his troops?

"This is an order. You must prove yourself."

Hrossar stared at the kama. The way they reflected the moonlight almost made them seem as though they were glowing. He took them carefully, holding them in one hand. He tucked both under his shoulder and dipped his head. "Thank you, sir."

"You will also need the whistle." Father unhitched a pouch from his belt and held it out for Hrossar. The silent whistle only herodons could hear—perfect for coordinating troops. "You know the correct whistle lengths and intervals for commands, no?"

"I do." Hrossar accepted the pouch and hooked it on his belt. Swallowing, he tried not to look at the other herodons. "Thank you, General."

☼ ☼ ☼

117

Timing. That was the key to every plan.

Hrossar rolled along the grass, speeding sixty miles an hour as his scythes whistled around him. Blades of grass bowed before him, his battalion following. Somewhere back there was Father, ready to turn when Hrossar turned.

His ears detected an opening in the ground. Two geolites stood by it—this was his entrance. He veered toward it, and his father's troops followed as one.

The geolites cupped their hands to their mouth—the herodons had been spotted! One rolled into the entrance.

Hrossar veered and rammed the other, but the stone only cracked. The geolites had been placing more structurally stable sentries at their entrances lately.

Hrossar's troops rolled past him, rubber hides a blur under the moonlight. Hrossar struck at the cracked geolite, then kicked him. His strike made the crack wider, and the geolite stumbled back.

The stone was no longer a threat. Hrossar dropped the kama—they would be useless once inside—curled up and burst into a roll, tumbling down the entrance. He veered to dodge a massive boulder, nearly crashing into the wall. When had that been placed there? Were the geolites rearranging the terrain to gain an advantage?

Then Hrossar was through the tunnel. Punches echoed throughout the main cavern, herodons barking as geolites assaulted them. Three of his troops were still rolling—but where were the timekeepers?

Hrossar uncurled behind a boulder, using it as cover. Separation was important—the geolites were known to lure groups of herodons to be buried by their hidden explosives. Hrossar peeked around the boulder—then ducked back behind it.

Just as he'd suspected. No timekeepers to be seen.

No matter. They were no doubt under the lava, counting out seconds before they would emerge. In the meantime, Father's troops were outnumbered.

Hrossar pulled out the whistle. He gave it three short blows—scramble formation.

His ears perked as the vibrations changed. His Father's troops were all rolling now, dodging geolites as they wove between boulders. The primary goal was to stall.

Hrossar heard the fist swinging and ducked. Pieces of the boulder dislodged, raining debris on his head. He turned and struck at the geolite attacking him—but his claws bounced off the geolite's ruby skin. Corundumites were easily shattered, but impossible to scratch. Naturally they would be used for close-quarters combat.

This would not go in Hrossar's favor. He rolled past the corundumite, speeding along the lava shoreline. If the timekeepers showed themselves, in all probability they would emerge from here.

Hrossar uncurled only inches from the lava. He turned to see the pursuing corundumite barreling toward him. Hrossar leapt aside as the geolite plunged into the lava river.

Excellent. The corundumite would only be delayed for a few seconds—but it was enough. Hrossar put the whistle to his lips and gave one long blow. A universal summons.

The herodons changed course. They weaved between geolites, dodging fists. In seconds they would reach Hrossar. Geolites rolled after them, pebbles scattering as they tumbled along.

A ball of magma splattered Hrossar's arm. He gasped, flinching as lava seared his skin. His rubber hide was smoking—melting as drops of lava pierced his arm like fiery needles. The smell of burnt flesh met his nostrils.

Another magma ball. Hrossar ducked, then leapt aside as two more splattered the ground beside him. He turned to see geolites tossing magma balls from clefts near the ceiling. One of them was throwing his balls at the far wall—where gravity shifted, causing the debris to hurl sidewise toward Hrossar like shots fired from a cannon. Hrossar crossed his arms to block, but small sparks pelted his face. He squeezed his eyes shut, claws digging in.

A rolling sound. Herodons uncurled around him, claws digging into the dirt.

Then the river exploded. Geolites leapt from it, bodies throbbing red like a live coal. They spun in a whirlwind attack, rushing the herodons.

Perfect. Hrossar pointed with his good hand. "Focus on the one who rose first!"

The geolites had risen in a line—and the first to rise was most likely the timekeeper. Father's troops descended on that geolite, ignoring the others.

Hrossar's arm was still smoking. He couldn't roll while lava covered it. He ran from the geolites, leaping to dodge a fist. He tucked the whistle in his pouch—then plucked a rock from the ground and wiped the lava with it. Heat seared his fingers, and he winced.

A shattering sound. He spun as the timekeeper exploded in fragments.

One down. He wiped more of the lava, letting it splatter the ground with a fiery hiss.

A geolite rolled toward him. He twisted to let the assailant bounce off his rubber hide, then tried a final wipe. His fingers burned, but most of the lava was gone. Only scattered pinpricks of fiery liquid remained, glowing like sparks. That would be sufficient.

The herodons were brawling. Claws dug in, squaring themselves so their rubber hides deflected each strike. Two geolites descended on a herodon, each grabbing a leg. They pulled him up from the ground, then tossed him in the lava. The herodon barked—then made a gurgling sound, hissing as smoke rose from him. Lava enveloped his body as his mouth opened in a silent scream.

A searing fist sent Hrossar stumbling back. He spun to the geolite and struck with both claws, aiming for the eyes. Blow after blinding blow, tearing chunks of rock out. This was only a dolomite—easily chipped.

But they were outnumbered. Geolites were rolling in, tightening a line around them. When would the other seven herodon detachments arrive?

There. Twenty herodons rolled in—ten from either direction—shattering geolites. Another battalion poured in from the back of the cavern, each soldier coming from a different entrance. The geolites had long left their clefts—and now they were surrounded themselves.

But the stones were clever. They had a plan—what was it?

Hrossar pulled out his whistle and gave it three short blows. His herodons scrambled, and he tucked the whistle away. Where were the other timekeepers?

Then magma balls came hailing down upon the herodons. Flaming debris hurled sideways toward them like stones from a slingshot. Herodons crashed into boulders, magma plastering their smoking hides.

Hrossar ducked behind a boulder. Where was the next timekeeper? These attacks were too carefully timed to be a coincidence.

His eyes darted across the cavern, ears alert. Around him geolites and herodons rammed each other, fists swinging, claws striking,

120

magma balls flying, lava spattering—but he watched. The timekeeper would be perfectly still, counting off seconds.

There. In a cleft hanging over the river's far side. The geolite was an apatite—almost perfectly camouflaged with the red rocks surrounding him. Only the glint of lava in his crystalline structure gave him away. That, and his quartz-like fingers were moving—marking off seconds, then motioning to unseen geolites.

Yet how could he be reached? Hrossar searched the ridges beside him. Loose stones along a far wall—an indicator of a shifted gravity zone. That was his way up.

The others were occupied. Hrossar aimed for a hill by the lava river and rolled.

In two seconds he'd accelerated to twenty miles an hour. He zoomed up the hill—and for one second, he was flying over the lava river, heat singeing his ears. Then he landed on the other side, pebbles scattering and dust rising. He rolled onto the wall, gravity shifting as he picked up speed, vibrations from the apatite's fingers guiding him.

In three seconds Hrossar was there. The apatite turned in time to be shattered.

Hrossar burst out of his roll, watching the geolite's pieces tumble to the lava below. Only one shard remained, and the eye on it stared into empty space. Hrossar kicked it over the edge, swallowing. No time to dwell.

He took a step toward the ledge—and winced. A bruise was forming on his stomach. Why wasn't he healing quickly? Though fire burned through his veins, jabbing at him like white-hot needles, the only healing was in his arm. The rubber hide there was growing back—did his body consider that a higher priority?

He surveyed the battlefield. The geolites were in chaos. Some were glancing his way, and Hrossar could read their panic as they noticed the apatite's absence. Two down.

But wouldn't there be more? Hrossar scanned the ceiling. Near the far wall, a topazite was marking off time on his fingers. A third timekeeper!

Hrossar pulled the whistle from his pouch—and gave two short blows. Herodons turned in his direction as he thrust a finger at the ceiling. "Move!"

The rubble beside the topazite exploded as the stone struck his fists together. Several herodons rolled away just in time, a cloud of dust rising behind them. Several more were buried. The topazite rolled over to another pile of rocks.

Ten herodons rolled up the wall, joining other troops pouring in from crevices by the surface. One of them bounced onto the ceiling and shattered the topazite, the timekeeper's shards flying to the ground like glimmering spears. The herodon uncurled and dug into the soil as geolites surrounded him.

Three geolites rushed him. One of them rammed him against the wall, uncurled and glanced down at the timekeeper's remains. He struck his fists together.

Another explosion. But only three herodons were buried this time.

The geolites were losing their organization. Hrossar could sense it—their patterns were jumbled, chaotic. Herodons were gaining the upper hand.

He took a seat, concentrating on the fire rushing through him. He let his legs dangle over the edge, leaning so his elbows were on them. Inhaling deeply, he kept his eyes on the battle.

He fingered the whistle in one hand. With this small device, he'd beaten the timekeepers.

☼ ☼ ☼

"I believe that is the last body." Hrossar watched as a herodon tossed the cratered carcass of a halite into the lava. It sunk slowly, face down as the bright orange lava swallowed it. "Any further resistance?"

"The remaining geolites fled."

"Interesting." Hrossar raised his snout, eyes narrowed. "So they cannot fight without their timekeepers."

"Not successfully." Father came up beside Hrossar, placing a hand on his shoulder. "Though you certainly did."

Hrossar dipped his head. "I did no more than what I was taught."

"And you were taught well." Father handed him the kama. "I retrieved these from the surface after the fight was over. I see you prefer to use your claws."

Hrossar accepted the kama, brow furrowed. "Should I not return them to you?"

"Not yet." Father placed his hands behind his back, raising his chin. "You have done well—and I would like to give you more practice."

Hrossar studied the kama—watching the way the lava glinted off the blades. A sudden weariness came over him. "Father?"

"Yes?"

Every herodon was watching. They'd witnessed Hrossar's leadership—no more doubts of favoritism would cloud their loyalty. But Hrossar could not reveal any weakness before them.

"Lieutenant Hrossar." Father placed a hand on his shoulder again. He looked into Hrossar's eyes. There was a sort of weariness there too. After a few seconds, he gave a small nod. "You did well."

Hrossar tightened his grip around the kama. Then his muscles loosened—and he dipped his head. "As you say."

14 THE BATTLE OF NICOTA

5962 OT, 5th month (sixteen months later)

The grass was still in bloom, rising to Hrossar's knees. It swayed with a gentle breeze, glowing golden in the evening sun.

Father stood before the battalion, kama in hand. He looked from herodon to herodon, jaw firm. No one moved a muscle.

"So we have come to this," Father whispered, voice almost indistinguishable from the breeze. "To attacking Nicota."

Hrossar could sense the discomfort of his colleagues. No one dared to object—but this was not their goal. Nicota had never been occupied by herodons.

"You know the reasoning." Father inhaled deeply, waving his kama. "The geolites have placed all their forces in Eastern Brekh'cha—the cities they know we will attack. They feel no threat to the cities we have no interest in."

If anyone disagreed, they gave no indication. Another breeze rustled the grass—and Father stepped up to Hrossar, handing him the kama and whistle pouch. "At this time I will have Major Feodon elucidate the situation further."

Hrossar accepted the kama and pouch, dipping his head. "Thank you, General Feodon." He made his way to the head of the battalion, hooking the pouch on his belt. "The geolites outnumber us considerably," he began, looking from herodon to herodon, "but their disadvantage is the sheer expanse of territory they must defend."

One of the herodons swallowed. Otherwise, not a muscle twitched.

"We must force the issue. By attacking Nicota, we declare that all

124

territories are fair game—and compel them to spread their forces thin. Seeing as we control the plains and roll faster, we can strike anywhere." Hrossar pointed past their battalion with a kama. "Clearly we are more concerned with the eastern cities than Nicota. Nonetheless, forcing them to spread themselves thin will give us an advantage."

Were the herodons convinced? Hrossar could not tell. However, believing in each battle's cause was mandatory if they were to succeed. "Furthermore, some of our tactical experts believe Nicota is a mobilization point for timekeepers. It would be advantageous to eliminate them here." He lowered his kama. "Think of it as a system of guerrilla warfare. We may strike anywhere, keeping them constantly on guard and demoralized."

One of the herodons gave a small nod. Perhaps they were understanding.

"Today we modify the fundamental parameters of the war—declaring that all of Brekh'cha is our battlefield. Though we are only conquering Eastern Brekh'cha, the geolites must be forced to defend the whole of their territory." He arched an eyebrow, surveying the battalion. "Understood?"

"Yes sir," came the unified reply. One of them cleared his throat. "Sir?"

"Yes?"

"The geolites have not militarized Nicota. There will be non-combatants there."

Hrossar's stomach knotted. He swallowed. "Correct."

"How do we tell the difference between non-combatants and soldiers? It is not as though they wear armor."

Hrossar raised his snout, considering. "The ones fighting you will be combatants. But if the civilians should flee—" his next words were softer than ever, "let them leave."

The herodon dipped his head. "Understood."

"Excellent." Hrossar turned, raising the kama. They gleamed in the evening sun's light—flashing as he turned them to the right position. Then he curled up and burst into a roll.

Nicota was only an hour away.

✧ ✧ ✧

125

"I've loved your visit, Kel. I hope you get on leave again soon." Mom laced her fingers through his, studying him. "You hear me? Your mom wants to see you again in one piece."

Kel grinned. "I'll wager that can be arranged."

"Good." Mom held his hand, hiking along the eastern exit of Nicota. "Come back safe."

"Mom—" Kel chuckled, shaking his head. "I can take care of myself."

"I realize that." Mom glanced at him, fiery streaks dancing through her opal skin. "I'm just worried. Every mom has a right to be, you know."

"I know."

They walked along in silence for a few seconds, eyes ahead. Then, "Kel, have you thought about what I said? About doing something after the war."

Kel tried not to roll his eyes. "Aye."

"It doesn't have to be showcasing your contraptions. You could ask Kharema out." Her voice was low. "But do at least one."

"I know."

"Do you?" Mom turned to Kel. "I care for you, Kel. And I want to see you use your wonderful talents for something. Or find happiness."

"I know. And I promised—"

A shout echoed down the cavern. "Herodons!"

Herodons? "Really?"

Another shout. "Three battalions! Attacking Nicota!"

Mom's brow furrowed. "Why would they attack Nicota?"

"Doesn't matter." Kel grabbed her arms. "Roll to the lava docks, Mom. I'll fight them off. My leave's over anyway."

"You can't hold them off by yourself!"

The ground was already rolling as geolites sped toward them. Kel half-smiled. "We've got a detachment here. You just go on."

Mom studied him, lower lip trembling. "Be safe, Kel."

Then she turned and rolled off, opal skin flashing in the firelight.

Kel balled his fists, watching her disappear down a side tunnel. Whatever the herodons were planning—they'd get no farther than here.

✧ ✧ ✧

Hrossar burst into the cavern, vibrations informing him of the situation. Two herodon battalions had joined them, shattering geolites left and right. But stones were rolling in from every direction, swarming them.

Hrossar uncurled behind a boulder, claws digging into the dirt. Had Nicota been prepared for this? Perhaps the fact that they mobilized timekeepers warranted precautions.

Two massive black geolites flew along the cavern's ceiling, each large enough for three herodons to ride on their back. Magnetites.

Hrossar gave an impatient snort. The magnetites had been weaponized for a year now, and a counter had yet to be found. Those geolites could use their electromagnetism to glide along magnetic rock, zooming along the ceiling and pillars while tossing balls of magma. Catching them was impossible unless one knew their trajectory.

A magma ball exploded beside Hrossar, splattering his leg. He winced, smoke rising from his rubber shins. Moving would be optimal.

But where was a timekeeper? Hrossar's eyes darted around the cavern. There—at the top of a ridge. Surprisingly accessible. Could he be a decoy?

Hrossar burst into a roll as more magma balls splattered around him. He swerved between boulders, bumping along rocks as he accelerated up the ridge. The timekeeper's fingers were moving— counting out seconds.

Something was wrong. The fingers were moving erratically. This timekeeper couldn't tell time.

Hrossar uncurled two meters from the geolite, claws sliding in the loose pebbles. The geolite struck his fists together.

An ear-piercing explosion. Hrossar's body shook—and he leapt back as the ground beneath the geolite exploded. Hrossar landed on his back, sliding down the ridge with his legs in the air. Some geolites could survive explosions—while herodons certainly could not. A useful trap.

But now rocks were tumbling off the newly formed pile, bounding down the ridge toward him. Hrossar flipped himself so he was sliding on his knees, then crossed his arms to block the debris. Fiery pebbles bounced off his forehead, and he gritted his teeth. Then he turned and burst into a roll, barely dodging a boulder as he sped into an alcove. Such diversionary tactics were becoming more common.

Pebbles scattered. Geolites were rolling up to Hrossar—he was cornered!

Hrossar burst from the alcove in a roll, but a fist glanced him. He crashed into a boulder, vibrations shaking his limbs. He uncurled to find a geolite advancing on him, fists raised.

Hrossar tried to stand straight, blinking. His rubber hide had absorbed most of the impact—but crashing was disorienting.

Fists pounded his abdomen in a whirlwind attack. He stumbled back, flinching. He needed to plant his feet! His claws dug into the dirt, and he angled himself so the fists bounced harmlessly off his hide. He returned with a quick thrust, claws flashing in the red light of a lava river winding along the wall.

The geolite gasped as one eye was torn out. Hrossar thrust with furious speed, chunks flying from the geolite in a blur. Then he rolled past the geolite, bumping over small rocks. He uncurled behind a boulder as magma balls exploded beside him.

Where were the timekeepers? The geolites seemed chaotic—disorganized at best. Though they outnumbered the herodons, they were throwing out attacks and magma balls in frantic patterns. Were they without a plan?

Hrossar narrowed his eyes. "But a plan will not function without timekeepers," he whispered, searching the cavern. No such timekeepers were present.

He plucked the whistle from his pouch and put it to his lips. One short blow. The nearest herodon would find him and ask for directions.

Hrossar's ears perked—and he ducked as a magma ball sailed overhead. Another one hurled past his face, heat singeing his snout. Two more magnetites flew past, throwing magma balls at random.

Then a herodon uncurled beside Hrossar. "Sir!"

"The Nicota Docks," Hrossar began, voice soft. "They're evacuating the timekeepers. If we do not head for the docks, all the timekeepers will escape."

"Understood."

"Make for the docks. The others will follow."

"Yes sir!"

Hrossar watched the herodon roll off. Then he gave two blows—the first long, the second short—on his whistle. The signal to follow the herodon who'd just spoken to him. The other herodons would have been tracking his progress through vibrations after the first whistle.

Hrossar tucked the whistle into his pouch, raising his snout. He would watch the exits to coordinate reinforcements.

☼ ☼ ☼

Kel pounded at the herodon, fists spinning in a whirlwind attack. The creature stumbled back, caught off guard. Kel pulled at his legs, flipping him onto his back. Perfect.

The ground rumbled. Kel looked up as twenty or thirty herodons rolled his way. He dove aside, nearly crashing into the wall. They sped past, dust rising in a choking cloud. Kel's teeth shook as he watched.

"Now where could they be going?" He searched the ground for the herodon he'd been attacking—but the creature had rolled off with the herd. Was it the docks they were aiming for?

If so, more than the timekeepers were in trouble. Kel rolled off, determined to follow their dust.

☼ ☼ ☼

Hrossar uncurled behind a new boulder, magma balls sailing past. He'd directed the new reinforcements—but their situation was poor. The geolites were following his troops to the lava docks of Nicota. Any battle beside great swaths of lava easily favored the geolites.

Soon they would need to retreat. But would Hrossar's whistle carry that far?

High ground close to the tunnels. That would be optimal for whistle blows. Hrossar aimed for a ridge and rolled. He was nearly at the top when a magnetite landed before him. Hrossar bounced off, cracking the magnetite's abdomen.

Another magnetite landed behind him, the ground shaking. Hrossar could not hope to contend with such massive geolites. He dove between the first magnetite's legs, pebbles scattering as he came to his feet. He turned—

The magnetite whirled around with a swing. Hrossar was knocked off his feet. He slid on his back just as the magnetite seized his leg. Then the stone ran, dragging Hrossar behind him—and leapt off the ridge, magnetism pulling him to the ceiling.

Hrossar twisted his head around, looking ahead. They were flying toward a river of lava.

Hrossar kicked at the magnetite's hand, clawed toes digging into the fingers. The stone's grip loosened—and Hrossar kicked again, grunting. The magnetite released him—and for one perilous second Hrossar was hurtling through the air, curling into a ball. Then he collided with a pillar, debris exploding. Even with his rubber hide, the impact jolted his bones.

Gravity shifted. He was tumbling down the pillar as though it were a hill, chunks of magma hurtling past. The collision had destabilized the lava above the pillar—and pieces were flying toward him like balls from a cannon.

He dug his claws into the pillar, slowing himself as specks of lava hissed on his hide. Then he leapt off, tucking his limbs in. He bounced on the floor, rolling to a stop by the lava river.

Fire ran through his veins as he uncurled, searing his limbs like white-hot needles. He fell to one knee, then tried to stand up—but coughed blood, wincing.

Where were the others? Hrossar struggled to his feet, coughing. Blood dribbled from his lips, the world spinning around him. He clenched his muscles, chest heaving. Fire burning through him, each nerve alive with heat. Had the other herodons made it?

☼ ☼ ☼

Kel rolled full speed, ricocheting off boulders at every turn. He burst into a cavern with massive stone pillars rising up into a ceiling of lava. Magma dragonflies buzzed around each pillar, and on the ceiling helenboats floated as geolites of all shades boarded them.

The evacuation party.

Herodons were already rolling up the pillars toward the sea, barreling full speed at the geolites. Why would they attack noncombatants?

Kel rolled up a pillar, gravity shifting around him. They must've been after the timekeepers.

He reached the lava docks in seconds, where herodons tore at the dock guards. Pieces were flying from their chests and face as they stumbled back, gasping.

Kel swung at the first herodon. The creature stumbled back, and Kel took another swing. Then he pulled the herodon's legs out and threw him off the pillar's edge. The creature gave a high-pitched bark—then the lava swallowed him as he twitched, smoke rising.

Mom—where was mom? Kel swung around, fists out. There—on the pillar next to him. But that was ten meters out, and there was no way over—not without boarding a boat. Precious little time for that.

A herodon struck at Kel's arm. He winced, grabbing the herodon's claws before he could strike again. Kel shoved the creature back, then seized both arms in a vice grip. He forced the herodon to back up, growling. The soldier dug in, toes sliding in the pillar's soil, muscles bulging, chest heaving as he contested Kel.

But geolites were strong. Kel forced him to back up a step—then another. Toward the lava. The red sea's light glinted off the herodon's claws. The creature's eyes flashed in rage, fangs bared.

In his peripheral vision Kel spotted Mom. She was swinging her fists—striking herodons as they tried to get past her. Fiery streaks danced in her opal skin with each blow, flashing orange and red through the blue hues. Timekeepers boarded the boats behind her, kicking off into the Nicota River.

She was stalling the herodons—but it wasn't safe! And she didn't know how to fight! "Mom!"

The herodon pushed Kel a step back. He needed to focus! He tightened his muscles, growling. The herodon stepped back again, and his eyes darted over to Mom.

He saw it in an instant. A herodon was rolling up the pillar, rubber hide gleaming in the light of magma dragonflies. Mom was swinging her fists wildly, shouting as herodons struck at her. She didn't notice the rolling soldier—

The herodon collided with her, and she shattered. Shards of opal scattered across the pillar, fire twinkling in them.

"MOM!" Kel roared at the top of his lungs, giving a mighty shove. The herodon before him stumbled back, arms out to keep his balance.

Kel burst into a roll, aiming for the base of his pillar. Tears formed in his eyes as he rolled, and he gritted his teeth. No!

☼ ☼ ☼

Hrossar staggered onto the top of the ridge, pulling the whistle from his pouch. He gave it three long blows—retreat. If the herodons hadn't destroyed the timekeepers by now, it would be too late. Any longer and they would be cornered at the lava docks by geolite reinforcements. Victory for the geolites would be a matter of throwing the herodons off each pillar, as the dirt was too loose for any real traction.

His ears detected rumbling. If the herodons were returning, they would encounter the incoming geolites. There would be a skirmish— but on more optimal terrain.

Hrossar's eyes darted across the cavern. There—a nearby exit. He took a step, flinching as pain sliced through his ribs. The healing was not complete. He coughed—but no blood this time. He licked his snout, placing a hand on his side.

Securing an exit was the priority at this time. Hrossar would be the best candidate.

He tucked the whistle into his pouch—then tightened his muscles, preparing to roll. Fire burned in his abdomen and ribs as he inhaled sharply. He could not delay.

Yet he had one task still to perform. He dipped his head, closing his eyes. He crossed his fists over his chest—for all the herodons and geolites who had fallen.

Then he opened his eyes, charted a course to the exit—and burst into a roll.

☼ ☼ ☼

Kel reached the dock's end just as herodons rolled past him. They were retreating, no doubt—though many timekeepers still remained— but Kel had one goal.

He uncurled by the shards of his mother, feet skidding in the soil.

This was where—

No. He swallowed, kneeling beside the pieces. Tears blurred his vision—and he reached out, plucking a piece of opal from the ground. The lava's light glinted off its sky-blue contour, fiery streaks dancing through it for the last time.

He spotted an opal hand resting a couple feet from him. He walked over, clutching the first shard. He picked up the hand, staring at the glossy blue fingers.

A tear rolled down his cheek as he put the fingers to his chest. They would never hug him again.

15 FURY

5962 OT, 6th month (three weeks later)

Kel clenched his fists, glaring at the tunnel's exit. Soon they'd be on the plains. Every muscle in him twitched, eager to be out there.

"Now most of you may find this unusual." Their commander faced them, hands by her side. "Attacking herodons on the plains, where we have no advantage."

A few geolites grimaced. The thoughts had crossed their minds.

"But we've got little choice. What with timekeepers being spread too thin, herodons attacking us left and right—" she sighed. "As long as they control the plains, they control the war."

They knew this. Couldn't she just skip past the refresher?

"As we have no interest in Newílderashe, we have two choices: attempt to defend a hopelessly vast swath of land," she counted off the options on her fingers, "or take away their means of attacking that land by going for the plains."

Still no one spoke. One geolite cleared his throat.

"Now we haven't gone for the plains before now because we have a terrible disadvantage up there. They roll faster, hit harder—and no charges or lava. We know the terrain in Brekh'cha better than they do—but on the plains, all knowledge is equal."

"Aye." One of the geolites finally spoke up. "Just a flat plateau, isn't it?"

"More or less." The leader blinked. "Any questions?"

Kel raised his hand. "When do we begin?"

"When? Seeing as you all know the plan..." The commander looked from geolite to geolite, eyes narrowed. "As soon as we signal the timekeepers."

☼ ☼ ☼

Kel rolled along the moonlit plains, grass swishing beneath him. He could see the herodons in small glimpses, though they were only pinpricks for now. Hateful creatures, milling in a group. No doubt planning another assault.

Kel sped up, gritting his teeth.

This part of the plan was simple. Edge them in on all but one side. The other geolites came in from Kel's periphery, surrounding the herodons. The creatures barked, striking defensive poses. But Kel doubted they had a plan.

And they were about to be surrounded.

In seconds Kel was in the fray. He rammed a herodon, bouncing off the creature's rubber hide. He rolled away and circled back, grass swishing furiously beneath him. His legs popped out, skidding in the grass as he let his arms come out. He curled his fists and began swinging.

The first blows bounced off the rubber hide. Kel angled his whirlwind attack higher—there! The herodon's jaw cracked with another blow. The creature lashed at him, claws flashing in the moonlight.

Chunks flew from Kel's chest, nauseating pain slicing through him. He roared, leaping on the herodon. His fists pounded down on the creature's chest, barks escaping the herodon's mouth.

Grass swishing all around him. More herodons were rolling in.

That was fine. Kel leapt off and began spinning his fists. Herodons swerved to dodge, but more were rolling in. No doubt the lead herodon had used that silent "whistle" of theirs to summon them—though its pitch was too low for any ear to pick up. Unless they were a herodon.

Kel hissed through clenched teeth. Hateful creatures, all of them.

Stone fists burst out of the ground. Geolites lifted themselves from new holes in the plains—like bursting out of lava. Twenty of them, exploding from hidden tunnels just beneath the grass. The herodons backed up, striking defensive poses. They were hemmed in.

On all but one side, of course. The leader noticed and blew on his silent whistle. The herodons turned and rolled after him, hides gleaming under the moonlight.

The cowards were running! Kel rolled after them. Not that he could keep up with them—but they'd have a nasty surprise coming.

Geolites exploded from the ground far ahead, grass flying. Every ounce of this attack was planned—timekeepers motioning, hidden geolites attacking. This was the final phase.

Kel uncurled before the herodons—about forty of the beasts remained—and began pounding. Swinging, fists bearing down, screaming—rage coursing through him like fire. He leapt on a herodon, plowing him into the grass. His fists came down—blow after blow, pounding like a hammer.

Chunks of stone flew from Kel's arm. A herodon was striking him! No matter. He would keep pounding until—

An explosion clapped Kel's ears. His teeth rattled as the ground shook. Just beneath the plains, charges had blown. The plains collapsed beneath them—and every soldier, geolite and herodon went plunging through the broken ground.

Kel was still atop the herodon as they fell, chunks of grass and dirt plummeting around them. Far beneath them a vast sea of lava glowed orange, so bright it hurt his eyes. They'd herded the herodons to this spot on the plains for a reason.

Kel grabbed the herodon's throat and raised his fists. He brought it down, cracking the herodon's jaw. He raised his fist again, stony muscles gleaming dark green in the red lava's light—

They hit the lava. The herodon yelped, eyes widening. His mouth opened as lava swallowed his arms. Kel kept pounding—pounding, swinging, hammering. He growled as he delivered each blow, clenching his teeth. The herodon gurgled, twitching as the lava consumed his head.

Then Kel was sinking. Orange lava enveloped him—but he could still feel the herodon's throat between his fingers. He squeezed harder, crushing the melting throat. He kept his eyes open, though he could no longer see past the orange lava pressing in on him. Its heat pushed at every muscle in his body.

The throat was gone. Kel could hear a sound like hissing—was that the rubber hide?

Then his feet touched the bottom. He fell to his knees, lava swirling around him. Where was the herodon's corpse? Could Kel even punch under lava?

I'm worried, Kel.

Mom's words. Kel blinked. Why was he thinking of her?

You're empty inside.

He blinked again. This...this wasn't him. None of this.

Another hiss. A tear was forming in one eye—but it instantly evaporated in the lava.

Kel swallowed, eyes searching the endless orange. Was that how all his tears would go? Would he stop making them eventually?

His fists loosened, and he let his arms hang by his side. Would this be who he became?

I care for you, Kel.

Another tear—another hiss. The orange darkened as his tears evaporated. Why was he crying? What was this feeling in his chest?

The herodons deserved it. Beasts, they were. Every blow landed an inch too shallow as far as he was concerned. One fist curled again.

Then his muscles loosened. No. This wasn't him.

This. Wasn't. Kel.

He put his hands over his eyes, closing them. Lava pressed in on his eyelids, and even through them orange enveloped his vision. What was this war?

He choked back a sob. More tears hissed from his eyes. Madness, all of it.

Kel withdrew his legs, sinking to the lava sea's floor. Tears hissed, sobs shaking his body. He tried to keep his lips closed. The lava pressed in on him, closing over his arms like a vice.

He could rejoin his battalion later.

16 THE OATH

5963 OT, 9th month (fifteen months later)

Hrossar gripped the kama, sweat beading his snout. His clawed toes dug into the loose soil, pebbles sliding down the ridge behind them. Silver lava coiled toward the ceiling in thin pillars around him, heat washing across his face. Silver dragonflies buzzed here and there, fiery stingers dripping magma.

Behind him nine herodons trudged. Father was among them—guarding the rear, naturally—while Hrossar led the way.

He paused at the top. A massive cavern greeted him, tunnels opening into it from the ceiling and walls. Herodons poured out of them, rolling along every angle. They shifted gravity zones, tumbling along as pebbles scattered after them.

Here was the rally point. Hrossar turned as his battalion reached the ridge's peak. He handed the kama to his father, who dipped his head.

Silence. Three thousand herodons uncurled as Father, now the Chief General of this operation, surveyed them. Father's eyes met Hrossar's—then he inhaled deeply, turning to his troops. He shifted the kama to one hand. "So we are here."

No one moved. It seemed no one even breathed—muscles tense, snouts raised. Hrossar stood beside Father, eyes fixed ahead.

"For the last two days, you have rolled carefully in small battalions through the nether regions of Western Brekh'cha." Father's voice was a little hoarse—but otherwise, soft as ever. "You circled around the plains to avoid geolite scouts…and entered secretly by crevices near Old Ticora—risking an encounter with what is known as

138

'the Flame Dragon.'"

A few herodons shifted their footing. That creature which had long been thought to be myth. Thankfully Hrossar had never encountered it—but in the last five months, some had not been so fortunate.

"You all know why we're here. Our scouts discovered the dragon—and found that we could not inhabit Western Brekh'cha. We would conquer our territory in the East or be forced back to Newílderashe." Father licked his snout, as if his lips were dry. "But the war has not been kind. We have been challenged for the plains—and without adequate knowledge of where geolite charges are planted, many have fallen."

The soldiers knew this already. Though offering a review was mandatory before each assault, Hrossar gave an impatient snort. The longer they delayed, the greater their risk of being discovered.

"We realized at the outset that this war would be one of attrition," Father continued, placing his hands behind his back. "Give and take. Systematic strikes meant to demoralize and maximize casualties. But with the plains under threat, we are losing too many herodons."

Hrossar swallowed. That they would be brought to this point was unthinkable. Even a year ago.

"Though we adapt to them, they adapt to us. The war drags on. And thousands are dead." Father pointed at the silver lava, its light glinting off his claws. "Our brothers' tombs rest in the lava blanketing Brekh'cha—the crucible of the land for which they fought. And we will surely follow if we do not end the war soon."

A dragonfly buzzed above Hrossar. He shifted his footing, ignoring it.

"Though we are confident that we would eventually win, we are also certain that too many casualties would be sustained in the process. And so the other generals and I have devised this sneak attack to end the war swiftly. Otherwise, no one will be left—herodon or geolite—to inhabit Brekh'cha." Father scanned his troops, eyes burning. He bared his fangs. "This is our last stand."

Still no one dared speak. Father was speaking at too low a frequency to be heard by geolites—but precaution was paramount.

"No geolite is aware of our presence at this time. So far as we know, we are on the border of Ticora, famed capital of the geolites, without their knowledge. We have crept and rolled under the plains in

139

secrecy, avoiding their scouts to infiltrate this area." Father reached into his pouch, pulling out a golden whistle. "And if we capture their capital with a force strong enough to defend it, we can hold it for ransom. Ask for our lands in return. End the war."

Some herodons nodded. Others averted their eyes, arms stiff by their sides.

"But for this to succeed, we *must* suffer no more than minimal casualties." Father enunciated his next words. "Victory must be both swift *and* efficient."

Hrossar's eyes settled on the golden whistle. Its frequency was slightly different from others—enough to be recognized as the Chief Whistle.

"We could not spare more than three thousand herodons for this assault without arousing suspicion. Our other troops have been attacking Eastern Brekh'cha at a higher rate than usual—to distract the geolites from our true intentions." Chief General Feodon pointed at the ground. "And so we have been given this golden moment with their blood. We must. Not. Fail."

Every herodon's gaze was on Father. Hrossar turned to the general, giving a soft snort. Was the speech over?

"The next time we speak, we will be regrouping at the center of Ticora—or the war will be lost." Father surveyed his troops, eyebrows rising. "Understood?"

The herodons crossed their fists over their chest. No speech was necessary.

Father raised his kama in one hand, glancing toward the tunnels on Hrossar's right. Among the sounds of Brekh'cha—the hiss of lava, the buzzing of dragonflies—Father's soft voice rose. "Let us proceed."

☆ ☆ ☆

Vibrations guided Hrossar as he rolled up the tunnel. Around him the ground shook as three thousand herodons burst into rolls. The geolites would hear them now—but in seconds it would not matter.

Hrossar burst from the tunnel, sailing through empty space. He uncurled, spreading his legs as he landed on a slope. He slid down it, claws digging in as pebbles skittered after him. Hundreds of herodons

140

uncurled around him, some brandishing kama. Others pulled whistles from their pouches—each a different frequency to prevent confusion—and began blowing out orders.

Hrossar had his own whistle. He plucked it from his pouch and gave two long blows—follow the whistle blower. Only his battalion would respond to this frequency.

He glanced back to see nine herodons rolling toward him. Excellent. He burst into a roll, tumbling down the ridge as they followed.

Geolites were already emerging from their alcoves. Orders were being shouted, no doubt—Hrossar could sense some cupping their hands to their mouth—but it mattered little. The outer guard on Ticora's western side was of no consequence.

He rolled past a pair of geolites, shifting zones to the wall of a tunnel. Time was crucial. They needed to penetrate inner Ticora in approximately thirty seconds or geolites would reinforce its defenses. His battalion rolled after him, ignoring the geolites.

More whistles blew ahead of him. Some herodons had already reached the interior. That was according to plan as well—separate periods of arrival created chaos for the geolites. Whistles mingled with shouts of war.

Hrossar entered a new cavern, picking up speed. Now he was going sixty-one miles an hour—and the vibrations confirmed his location. A long cavern, like the inside of a monolithic cylinder, with a central pillar running through its middle. Smaller pillars jutted out from the central pillar, giving the effect of spokes on a wheel. The entire tunnel was lined with these spokes—this was Hrossar's destination. Many living quarters would be here.

Hrossar aimed for a geolite and shattered him. He uncurled, lashing out at two more stone soldiers. Then he curled again and sped past them before they could retaliate. Sowing chaos was essential to destabilizing any defense.

So far the plan was effective. Hrossar rolled up a "spoke," gravity shifting around him. He bumped along windows, weaved between alcoves and made his way toward the central pillar.

Then he heard it. A high trumpet, echoing throughout the cavern. No doubt a geolite signal—but for what?

The spoke beneath him shook, rattling his bones. He uncurled at the central pillar, the geolites around him a blur. Why was everything shaking so much?

His eyes darted around the spokes. Hundreds of other herodons were battling on them, claws flashing in the green light of lava globules bobbing up and down. Each globule hovered in clusters between spokes, like jade constellations in a clouded sky. Yet even they were shaking.

"Behind you!"

One of the herodons was pointing past Hrossar. He spun to gaze down the cylindrical cavern—

Hrossar crossed his arms over his head, letting the debris bounce off his rubber hide. It was flying sideways at him, as if he were standing on a wall and the debris coming from the ceiling. Chunks of flaming rock flew past him, and he leapt aside. More debris—he lowered his head, letting it bounce off his forehead and arms.

What was occurring? Still more debris rained upon him, falling in green fiery chunks. Hrossar got down on one knee to stabilize his position—arms crossed, eyes closed. Such a massive explosion must have required hundreds of charges. Was Ticora booby-trapped?

He opened his eyes. The spoke was still trembling—but only a little. He got to his feet as light filled the end of the cylinder.

Where was that coming from? Was a tide of lava rushing their way?

No…Hrossar's eyes widened. At the far end of the cylindrical cavern, a sea of red lava rested. But the explosion, severe as it was, had destabilized its gravity. Now lava was falling from the sea toward them, as if the sea was no longer on the floor but the ceiling. Everything in this giant cylinder would be swallowed—

Hrossar put the whistle to his lips. Three short blows—scramble. No time for more.

Then he tucked the whistle into his pouch and dove off the spoke, curling into a ball.

He fell for five seconds before crashing into a boulder. His whole body shook—and he ricocheted into another boulder, then bounced into a crevice. Gravity shifted around him, and he tumbled down the hole.

The vibrations told him this crevice had no floor. Hrossar uncurled, hands and feet digging into the wall. He bared his fangs, growling as his claws slid in the dirt. Gravity shift—he required a gravity shift!

142

He detected lose pebbles just feet away. He reached out with one hand, grabbing a pebble—and gravity shifted. He tumbled onto the new "floor," darkness shrouding him. He got to his knees, trying to catch his breath—then spat out blood, fire running through his ribs.

Heat washed across his face. A wall of lava flew past his crevice, rushing as though falling from a waterfall. He was only ten meters away.

He tried getting to his feet—then flinched, coughing more blood. How many troops had survived? The geolites could survive being buried in lava—but the herodons would be dead almost instantly. An effective trap.

He stumbled forward, flinching as more heat swept across his chest. The lavafall was still falling, rushing past his crevice's opening. In the distance he heard barks, almost muted in the heat. The first wave of herodons was no doubt retreating.

Where could he go? Hrossar scanned the crevice. A small opening, just feet away—optimal. Hrossar dove in, ignoring the pain slicing his ribs. He would recover in minutes.

He crawled through the tunnel for a few seconds, trying not to wince as his chest dragged along the jagged floor—then pulled himself out on the other side with a grunt. A singular red lava globule floated just over the floor. Otherwise, this chamber was dark.

His legs felt chilled. Hrossar looked down to see purple mist covering them. He gave a soft snort, backing up to the wall.

Whispers. His ears perked as voices filled the cavern. The lava globule darkened while mist flowed over it, glowing blood red. As the mist swirled around it, odd shadows danced on the wall.

The hairs on his arms were standing. This was dragon mist—and though he knew little of it, he knew what it heralded. Whether in person or in essence, the dragon would not be far behind. That the mist could float much farther than the dragon could ever roam—as far as Ticora, or Nicota in small wisps—was irrelevant. Leaving was imperative.

"Animals!"

He jerked his head around to see an old woman glaring at him. She seemed quite similar to a female he'd met in Newílderashe just three years ago. She thrust a trembling finger at him, screaming at the top of her lungs. "You don't deserve to breed here!"

"We know what you're up to." A pearly dolomite rose from the mist, crossing his arms. "No more heckling, you rogues."

A man shook his fist at Hrossar. "Our world, you filthy animal!"

Hrossar inhaled deeply, closing his eyes—then took a step forward. His arms trembled as he took another…and another. The voices grew louder—but no matter. He would ignore them. That was the way of the mist.

At the sound of sobbing he opened his eyes. Before him Holshe rose from the mist, crying with her cracked porcelain armor. His muscles tightened, and he blinked.

No. He stepped through her, raising his snout. No time to be distracted. From what little he knew, the dragon used this mist to devour its victims' souls.

"Look at them in their wedding garb!" The sound of windows shattering. Hrossar winced. "Animals!"

A small boy with red hair and freckles rose from the mist, fists balled. "You and your kind are always getting in the way!"

Hrossar waved him aside, stepping through as his image dissolved. Inconsequential memories.

The chamber exited into a tunnel. He took a few steps down it, trying to ignore the voices.

"Thieves!"

"Animals!"

"Rogues!"

And then the weeping. Soft at first. But as the other voices were fading, Hrossar could hear Holshe's weeping. It was as though a great symphony were surrounding him, each note designed to pluck at his emotions.

Hrossar willed his muscles to relax, exhaling slowly. These tricks would not distract him—the dragon must not prevail!

He turned a corner in the tunnel—and all went silent. Hrossar stopped.

There before him stood himself. Beside the dim, blood red light of a mist-clouded lava river running along the lower wall. Standing straight, hands by his sides. The mirror image dipped his head. "Greetings, Hrossar."

Hrossar arched an eyebrow. "You are hardly a distracting thought."

"Yes, about that." The image chuckled in a way that was most unlike Hrossar. "You know, Hrossar, you're a difficult one."

144

Hrossar should continue walking. But this was most unlike the mist. "How so?"

"Most creatures would be trapped in this mist in the first five seconds or so." The mirror Hrossar grinned—though with the way his fangs were bared, it was more of a snarl. "Yet you seem to have ignored everything."

Not without difficulty. Hrossar's muscles tensed. "Perhaps I am not like other creatures."

"*All* creatures have bitterness." The mirror Hrossar's voice seemed distorted somehow. Not quite soft in the way of Hrossar's voice, but more in the way the crackling of flames might be heard as soft. "And I don't introduce any special drug to trap you in the mist. I only introduce you to your most bitter thoughts. I find that is enough to occupy most."

"I have been taught not to be consumed by my bitterness." Hrossar raised his chin. "Therein lies your challenge."

"Ah, ah, ah," the mist Hrossar waved his finger with each "ah." "But you are more vulnerable than you know. Though I admit—it took me some time to discern where."

Hrossar blinked. Something was very wrong. The mirror Hrossar seemed almost…hungry. Its eyes burned with sparks of purple.

"You may have been taught not to hold bitterness against others—but you failed to remember the most obvious target of bitterness." The image placed a hand on its own chest. "Yourself."

Hrossar gave an impatient snort. He should be leaving. Should be walking through this creature—yet its claim was too ridiculous. He had to debate it. "I am not bitter at myself."

"Are you not?" The creature chuckled—and now Hrossar could hear it clearly. The soft hiss of flames with each chuckle. "After all, much of this is your fault."

"Much of what?"

Images rose from the mist. Herodons sinking in lava, yelping and gurgling. Geolites shattering into pieces. "All things you could have stopped. But instead, you were part of the problem."

Hrossar's stomach knotted. He curled his fists, raising his chin. "I did try—"

"Oh, I know you did." The other Hrossar cupped his snout in his hands, as if faking compassion. "I know you tried your very, very hardest. But here we are—lives being destroyed, one thing leading to another—and you couldn't stop it."

Hrossar blinked. He averted his eyes, attempting to conjure counter-arguments. "The herodons made their own decisions. Father and I argued—"

"Argued! Oh, how adorable!" Now the other Hrossar gave a very odd laugh. Again, like the crackling of flames. "Tell that to your friends and comrades who were just buried under several tons of searing lava."

Hrossar swallowed. "My statement makes sense—"

"Oh, of course it makes sense! Logically." Images of smoldering herodons rose from the mist. Smoke was rising from their rubber hides, their mouths open in a silent scream as their skin and bones melted before Hrossar's eyes. "I'm sure such logic will make them feel much better."

"They chose to give up their lives!" Hrossar snarled, raising a fist. "You cannot tell me this is my fault!"

"Oh, but I can." The image spread his hand toward another piece of mist. As it formed, Hrossar recognized himself standing before the other herodons at the council in Newílderashe. His mouth was moving, but no words were coming out. The mirror Hrossar shrugged. "That's about all the impact you had on determining whether this war would happen or not. You didn't really say much at all."

"I said enough."

"What is 'enough'?" The other Hrossar approached Hrossar, grinning. "To the stubborn who will never be convinced, Hrossar Feodon, what will ever be enough?"

Hrossar felt weak. The more he stared into the image's purple eyes, the more strength fled him. The mist was right—he'd been weak. "It was my duty to follow."

"And I suppose duty…" The image came up to him so their snouts were inches apart, enunciating each word, "is all that matters."

Hrossar swung his fist. To his surprise, it collided with the image's snout—and the other Hrossar stumbled back. But then the mirror image leapt upon him, claws a blur. Hrossar staggered backward, gasping as blood pooled on his chest. How was the mist tangible now? Weren't the images simply illusions?

No. His eyes widened, nausea rippling through him. The image could only touch him after Hrossar had longed to touch the image. *He* had given this creature power.

Many pairs of arms grabbed his legs. The old lady, the boy with freckles—even Holshe—were trying to drag him back into the chamber. Hrossar growled at them. "Leave me!"

"It wasn't a simple matter to trap you," continued the image Hrossar, hands behind his back, "as I assumed the moment I obtained any leverage you would immediately catch on to what was occurring. But you were, in the end, compliant—" he grinned again, fangs bared, "—as all creatures are."

This was the dragon speaking. The mist was simply its avatar. Hrossar roared. "Release me!"

"Make me."

Hrossar shook his head. He had to deprive the mist of reality. Withdraw the power he had granted it. But how?

The many hands yanked his legs out from under him. He dug his clawed fingers into the dirt—but somehow, they were stronger! He felt himself being dragged back into the chamber. Inch by inch—foot by perilous foot.

He inhaled deeply, closing his eyes. Debate…he had to win this debate. If he blamed himself for the war…

There. His eyes flew open. "You."

The misty Hrossar's brow furrowed. "What?"

"You orchestrated the war."

The hands were still pulling at Hrossar's legs—but they weren't as strong. Hrossar kept his claws firmly entrenched in the dirt. "You drove the geolites eastward by your fiery presence—until they crowded our territory and forced us to leave or face conflict."

"Correct."

"And by the memories you searched with your mist, you knew Newílderashe would be no home either. In fact, I sincerely doubt there is a location suitable for our whole race."

The image arched an eyebrow. "And why's that?"

"Because we are mercenaries. We will always alter the economic infrastructure of wherever we live. You knew this."

Was a smile tugging at the misty Hrossar's lips? "Perhaps."

"You created war simply by existing in the bowels of Western Brekh'cha." Hrossar hissed through clenched teeth, getting to his knees. The hands were no longer holding his legs. "You caused everything."

"But you could have stopped it."

Hrossar felt hands grasping his legs again. He shook his head. "*You* did it."

"But you could have *stopped* it!" The other Hrossar raised more images of geolites shattering. He created an image of a herodon mother standing before her home. Another herodon was telling her something. She began weeping, covering her eyes as her body shook. "Imagine how many homes no longer have men in them because of *your* failures."

"No." Hrossar found his feet. He stared straight ahead—past the images, to a faint light at the tunnel's end. "You are irrelevant."

"I *am* you!" The image roared—though now it seemed more like the roaring of flames. "I am your failures personified! *Heed* me!"

"I will not." Hrossar took one step—then another. He dared not look into the misty creature's eyes. "I am Hrossar Feodon. I am on a mission from Father to conquer Ticora in order to hold it for ransom and reclaim our lands."

"A mission that will extinguish more lives!" The other Hrossar was looking less and less like a herodon now. Parts of his body were burning with purple flame. "Like kindling for the bonfire, so my soul is fed by every death in my realm. It is sweet music to me."

Hrossar kept walking, stepping past the image. There was no purpose in responding.

"So go, music-maker! Kindle my fire!" A cackling. "Kindle it until it burns the entire world down!"

Hrossar burst into a roll. He did not know the terrain—but he could resist no longer. If he did not exit now, he would turn and assault the image with all his strength.

He sped up—tumbling, bouncing. He had no choice but to proceed.

☆ ☆ ☆

Chaos. Balls of magma exploded as herodons dodged. Geolites stumbled back, fragments of rock flying from their faces as claws dug into them.

Hrossar uncurled from his roll by the bottom of a ridge, fiery rocks tumbling past him. Heat swept his face as lava globules flew

148

past. These explosions were destabilizing the gravity of Ticora. Pools of lava were now deadly clouds.

Hrossar blinked, eyes tearing from the heat, raising an arm to shield himself as more lava sailed past him. Where was Father?

There. High up in an alcove near the ceiling. Watching the battle, fingers on the pouch at his waist. The golden whistle rested within that pouch—but it would only be used for emergencies. Father trusted the herodons to coordinate their own groups.

Hrossar curled his fists. His own group was lost—buried in lava.

No matter. He would report to General Feodon and be assigned a new detachment. It was that simple. The dead would be mourned later.

Hrossar curled into a ball—then sped off, bouncing up the ridge and angling for his father's alcove.

☼ ☼ ☼

Hrossar uncurled beneath the alcove. It was ten meters above him—a well-situated lookout point. He dug his claws into the soft rock—small chips in the rock indicated his father had used this method to climb as well—and began making his way up the cliff's face.

A ball of magma exploded on the wall beside him. Of course. Geolites were seeking easy targets to pick off. He craned his neck around and spotted some geolites hurling magma balls from a cleft in the ceiling.

He accelerated his pace. Another magma ball exploded below his feet, but he kept climbing. At this distance they could not aim accurately. Even if one ball found its mark, his rubber hide would absorb the impact.

He reached the top in seconds, throwing his legs over the edge. Rolling to his feet, he found General Feodon four meters away—engaged with three geolites. Hrossar advanced, claws extended—

A geolite. Rolling toward Hrossar from the ceiling.

Hrossar leapt aside as the geolite sped past him. The corundumite slammed the alcove's back wall. The stone soldier uncurled, landing on the ground with his hands out. A spear flew into them, thrown by a geolite standing on the ceiling. The corundumite hefted his new spear—then squared his feet, facing Hrossar.

149

Hrossar's eyes settled on the weapon. It was red-hot, as though it had just been taken from the furnace. Such metal could be pounded at on an anvil. One thrust would have the same effect on his organs as lava. It was a recent development in the war to counteract the herodons' healing capabilities even more.

Father would have to wait. Hrossar held out his hands, fingers spread, clawed toes digging into the dirt.

The geolite thrust his spear—and Hrossar dodged, batting away the spear with a backhand. Then Hrossar rushed in, kicking at the geolite. Corundumite could not be chipped—but as it shattered easily, pushing this geolite off the cliff would suffice.

The corundumite stumbled back, then thrust again. Hrossar dodged, batted the spear and kicked him. The soldier stumbled over the edge—but as he fell he shouted, hurling his spear at the geolites fighting Father. One of them turned and caught it.

Hrossar's eyes widened. Father's back was turned—he was tearing at the other two soldiers! He couldn't see—

"Father!" Hrossar rushed forward, claws reaching for the geolite. The soldier thrust his spear just as General Feodon turned.

The molten metal plunged through Father's abdomen, bursting out the back of his hide with a smoking hiss. A sharp bark escaped Father's lips—and he dropped to his knees.

Hrossar flew into the geolite with a kick. The creature tumbled off the cliff, and Hrossar spun to the other geolites. They were on the ground, craters riddling their still bodies.

Another bark. Father clutched at the molten red spear with one hand, smoke enveloping his fingers. "Son," he gasped, blood trickling out his lips. His other hand dug into the wall to keep him from falling further.

This could not be real. Hrossar's pulse pounded in his temple— and he dashed over to his father. He got to his knees, glancing behind them. The geolites on the ceiling were distracted with other herodons. Not that they would strike a wounded target anyway—they possessed at least some honor. Hrossar refocused on Father, clutching the general's shoulders. "I am here, Father."

"Son." Another sharp bark. Father shoved the spear into himself, spitting blood. The spear's barbed tip made withdrawal impossible— the sole method of removing it was to push it all the way through until it exited the body. "Help me—" his voice was a hoarse, choked whisper, "help me with this weapon."

Hrossar gripped Father's forearm—handling the heated steel would be unwise—then shoved. The spear passed all the way through, tumbling out the other side. It clattered to the ground as Father gasped.

"Thank you." Father's clawed fingers slid down the wall—and his other hand, still smoking, hit the floor. Blood dribbled out his lips, his eyes half lidded. "My son."

"Father!" Hrossar clenched his teeth, fangs bared. "Those who did this—"

"Are fighting for their homeland." Father fell against the wall, sliding down it so he was facing the battle. "Just like you and me."

Hrossar growled. "This is unacceptable!"

"You just noticed?" Father spat out more blood. "Or does it matter more because it's someone related to you?"

Hrossar clutched Father's shoulders, his stomach roiling. "You can recover," his voice was a trembling whisper, "you *will* recover."

Father's eyes were half closed. He took in a deep, shaky breath. "Perhaps. But it—it would take hours. With a wound this hot."

"And?"

"And my healing capabilities will boil me alive long before then."

Hrossar's clawed fingers dug into his father's rubber hide. "No...no. You cannot mean that, Father."

"If I concentrate, I can slow down my healing properties..." Father's words came out slowly, syllable by syllable, with a light wheezing between sentences. "But then the wound will stay. Even if I survive, I will be crippled—likely never able to fight again."

"Yes." Hrossar nodded. "Yes, slow it down. Then it won't burn you up."

"And that is if I survive." Father's eyes were nearly closed. "Which is unlikely."

"Father!" Hrossar growled. "Do not lose consciousness!"

"Son..." The general gave the smallest shake of his head. "Listen to your father."

Hrossar swallowed, claws tight around his father's shoulders. "I am listening, Father."

"You must...you must promise me something."

"Anything, Father."

"Don't do it, son." Father raised a trembling hand and set it on Hrossar's chest. "Don't be paid to debate. Don't become like them."

Hrossar's brow furrowed. "Father. I must—"

"Don't do it, Hrossar." Father swallowed, blood trickling from the edges of his mouth. "You must not join in a line of work that has only a dishonest future."

"And what am I to do? Be a mercenary?"

Father gave a barely perceptible nod, swallowing. "You must fight for truth," he coughed blood, "for justice. Defend the oppressed."

"Father…"

"I know." A smile tilted at Father's lips. "You have never liked battling, Hrossar. But nor would you like debate—despite your sentiments otherwise. It is a different kind of battling."

Hrossar waited as Father took a deep, trembling breath. The General spat more blood, eyes squeezed shut as he coughed. "Son…I know you were never meant to fight like this."

Hrossar blinked. "What do you mean?"

"I can see it in your eyes. You're a philosopher. And in another age, herodons might have been philosophers too. But we are sophists and mercenaries now—bound to strife."

"I can fight, Father." Hrossar shook his head. "I'm no coward."

"I agree. Which is why…despite your nature, you will be a mercenary. Swear to me."

Hrossar's shoulders fell. He could not hold the General's stare. "Father…"

"Swear to me." Father's claws dug into Hrossar's chest, and he bared his fangs. Sweat lined his snout, his eyelids fluttering. "You think debating would be good for you. But there are so many details. And I have found—" he coughed, squeezing his eyes shut, "—I have found that it is too easy to get caught up in the details and lose sight of the big picture."

Hrossar swallowed. "As this war has done."

"Precisely. I do not wish for that to fall upon you in debate."

"It won't, Father. I am strong."

"Are you? Then prove it to me by being a mercenary." Father held up his other hand, three fingers displayed. "Give me three by three years—nine in all—as a mercenary. Then if you still wish to become a debater, you may do so."

"Father…" Hrossar averted his eyes. His father could not control his life decisions. Yet how else could Hrossar honor his father but to heed his wishes? "Nine years. No more."

152

"Swear to me on oath."

"On oath." Hrossar put his palm on Father's chest. He clenched his jaw. "I will give you nine more years as a mercenary."

"Thank you." Father reached into his pouch. Fingers trembling, he held up the golden whistle. "This is yours now, son."

Hrossar stared at the whistle, his stomach knotting. "Is it."

"Take it now." Father's voice barely rose above a whisper. "Take it!"

Hrossar took the whistle. He turned it in his fingers, letting the distant lava's light glint off its surface. This did not feel real.

"Now watch the battle. Tell me what you see."

"I will not leave you, Father."

"You need only stand by my side. *Tell me* what you see."

Hrossar stood and turned to the battle. Herodons were shattering geolites, rushing in from unseen corners. But magma balls were flying at them, and countless geolites were rolling in from a tunnel near the back of the cavern. "We appear to be winning—but only by a small margin."

"Small indeed."

Hrossar turned back to see Father's eyes closing. The General swallowed. "You see it, don't you."

See what? Hrossar's brow furrowed. "Pardon?"

"I have never been wrong in my tactical assessments." Father expelled a trembling breath, arms resting by his sides. "I have been told it is like I can see the future."

"Indeed." Hrossar nodded. The herodon's tactical prowess was well-known. "And you agree that we are winning?"

"Yes." Father swallowed, licking his snout. "But only barely. And that is the problem."

Hrossar turned back to the fray. "Because in order to hold Ticora, we must suffer only minimal casualties."

"Correct."

"And now it will be taken from us."

Silence. Hrossar turned to Father. The general was still upright—but his mouth was slightly ajar, his eyes still closed. "Father!"

Father's eyes fluttered open. "I apologize. I...I cannot retain consciousness for much longer, Hrossar. You must listen."

"I am listening, Father."

"In order to win this war, we had to conquer Ticora with minimal

153

casualties. At the rate we are proceeding, Ticora will be ours...with too few soldiers to keep it." Father coughed more blood. "The geolites will retreat to retake Ticora, granting us the advantage on the plains."

Hrossar nodded. "I understand that."

"Then you know what will occur? We will use the plains to conquer our cities...for a time." A sardonic smile pulled at Father's lips. "And the war will essentially restart...but with more violent devices and increasingly devastating tactics."

Hrossar knelt to his father's level. He put his hands on the General's shoulders—why were his arms trembling? "Perhaps, Father."

"You *know* that I am correct." Father's eyes burned as he studied Hrossar. "You know what will occur."

"The war will stretch on."

"And on, and on, like a flame on the plains. Burning, devouring all it touches. Until it is a roaring fire, and no one knows where it is going or where it came from. Or how to stop it." Father clutched Hrossar's arms, blood flying from his lips. "It will never end, Hrossar!"

Hrossar felt pinpricks of pain on his arms. Blood was pooling where his father's claws dug into them. "I see."

"No victory is worth this! Do you understand?"

"I do."

"I lack the physical strength to blow that whistle."

Hrossar's brow furrowed. Was Father—? "I am not sure I'm hearing you correctly."

"The soldiers trust that whistle, Hrossar. Three short blows and every battalion will retreat, thinking the battle is lost."

Hrossar blinked, his mouth hanging open. "You cannot mean this."

"They can't see the battle from their vantage point—they do not know that we're winning—and if we retreat, all will be forced to admit that we have lost the war. A peace treaty will be forged."

Hrossar glanced at the golden whistle in his hand. "That would be dishonest."

"Is a war won when no one is left to claim victory? Because that is the alternative." Father clutched Hrossar's shoulders, craning his neck so his snout was close to Hrossar's. "Do you understand?"

"I—"

154

"Hrossar." Father's next words were a hoarse whisper, each syllable forced out between clenched teeth. "End. This. War!"

Then Father's chin dipped to his chest—and his eyes shut, his grip loosening. He expelled a trembling breath, and his arms slipped from Hrossar's shoulders. Hrossar put his finger to Father's neck—a pulse was still there. Faint at best.

Hrossar got to his feet clumsily. He shook his head, swallowing. "No," he whispered, turning to the fray. Herodons tore at geolites, barking as lava splatted across their chests. Spears stabbed them, red-hot and smoking. Geolites shattered into countless shards.

End this war.

Hrossar studied the golden whistle in his hands. With this device, he could end the war that had plagued them all these years…in failure.

All they had fought for…

A herodon struck at a geolite, his claws flashing. A spear pierced his chest, and he was shoved into a river of lava.

Every battle, gone to waste…

A geolite struck repeatedly at another herodon. A third herodon rolled in and shattered him.

The lava would bury his kinsmen forever, their efforts useless…

It will never end, Hrossar!

Hrossar raised the golden whistle with trembling fingers, eyes on the battle. His arms felt numb. *All* of him felt numb. Was he going to do this? Was he truly going to blow this whistle? *Could* he do this?

So go, music-maker! Kindle my fire! The dragon's words echoed in his mind. Kindle it until it burns the entire world down!

Hrossar blinked. Father was right. This would never end. It would burn forever, until no one was alive to be declared victor…

He put the whistle to his lips, inhaled deeply—and gave three short blows.

The herodons stopped. They began rolling his direction, heading for the tunnels below Hrossar. Tunnels that exited Ticora. Blindly they trusted his whistle. Blindly they'd accepted the lie that Ticora could not be taken.

But perhaps, in the end, they were not so blind. Perhaps Ticora could not truly be taken—or at least not held. Perhaps they truly had lost regardless.

Or perhaps Hrossar was rationalizing. Hrossar tucked the whistle into the pouch containing his captain's whistle, turning to Father. His

155

body was tingling, his heart pounding hard. Rationalizing or not, it no longer mattered.

Hrossar went over to his father's unconscious figure, hoisted the General's body over his shoulders—and began plotting his course down the cliff to exit Ticora.

17 THE HERODON ACCORDS

5964 OT, 2nd month (five months later)

"The War Council has reached a conclusion."

Hrossar's muscles tightened. He looked up at Derofon, jaw firm. The Major General stood behind a raised podium, claws clacking the wooden surface. Hrossar dipped his head. "We will accept the council's conclusion."

"As you are here representing your father, who is still in recovery…" Derofon inhaled deeply, letting his words trail off. "We believe the wounds General Feodon has received are significant compensation for his breach of protocol."

Angry murmurs. Many of the herodons glared at Derofon.

"This is—" The elderly herodon raised a hand—and all went silent. "This is the majority decision. The anonymous voting has been tallied. And I agree with this conclusion." Derofon leaned forward. "Your father acted in the best interests of the herodon race—for which I applaud him. His actions may have been uncouth, but they yielded a favorable result."

More angry murmurs. Clearly many disagreed.

Hrossar blinked. Was he truly hearing this? Derofon had been in favor of reclaiming their cities in Brekh'cha. Now he was agreeing with Father?

"Furthermore…" Derofon raised his hand again. "You are absolved of all responsibility, as you were following General Teros Feodon's orders. We cannot punish herodons for obeying the orders of their superior, as the chain of command would break down."

Murmurs of assent. At least the herodons could agree on that.

157

"Therefore, his battalion will be assigned to you, and you are personally acquitted of all charges, potential or proven."

Hrossar dipped his head. "Understood."

"If any wish to voice their objections, they may do so in writing." Derofon rapped his claws on the wood. "Council dismissed."

☆ ☆ ☆

ONE WEEK LATER

"These are the terms for peace." The geolite handed Derofon a scroll. "I know you'll find them acceptable."

Not that Derofon had much room for negotiation. Hrossar watched from the crowd, arms crossed as he leaned against a pillar. Liekhren was the perfect neutral ground for these accords. The war began here—it was fitting that it should find its end in these granite halls.

"Our kinsmen are remarkably quiet."

Hrossar turned to Father. The former general was bound to a wheelchair—courtesy of the geolites. They were as merciful in victory as they were shrewd in battle. Hrossar cleared his throat. "Our kinsmen are most likely plotting to murder us."

"As the humanite saying goes, blood is thicker than water." Father's voice was softer than usual. Too soft for the geolites to hear. He arched an eyebrow. "And besides that, many agree with my actions."

"Clearly." Hrossar glanced at the other herodons. Some were glaring at him—others cast him a warm glance. Most were staring ahead, watching Derofon negotiate with the Supreme Declarer of the Ticora council. "You would have been charged with sabotage otherwise."

"Even if I had not been exonerated by Derofon, it is important that they laid the responsibility on me." Father took a deep, rattling breath—then coughed into his fist. "After all, I was in a position of authority over you—both as your father and as the campaign's Chief General."

"Naturally."

158

"But what do you think?" Father turned to him, setting his arms in his lap. "What will become of the herodons?"

Hrossar surveyed the crowd. "I am not certain."

"It is obvious what will occur. Don't you see it?"

"As usual, I lack your particular foresight." Hrossar furrowed his brow. "But I think I could make a conjecture."

"Continue."

Hrossar inhaled deeply, uncrossing his arms. "The herodons are without identity. They have no purpose."

"No purpose. Yet the psyche, like nature, abhors a vacuum."

Hrossar nodded. "Correct."

"Then do you know what will become of us?"

Father was testing him. All these years of lessons in psychology…

"Son?"

Hrossar swallowed. "Where optimism fails, discontent creeps in. With nothing to do, we will become restless. And the restless are easy to manipulate."

"Correct." Father raised a finger. "While the war was occurring, we devoted ourselves fully to it. We believed in the dream of our homeland." He coughed into his fist again. "But now all that is lost. We are without a dream, without a purpose, without identity. Shattered. And that makes us easy to manipulate."

Hrossar put his hands behind his back, shifting his footing—eyes on Derofon. A familiar proverb echoed in his mind. "Without vision, it is easy to stumble."

"Then you understand me." Father leaned forward in his chair, giving a hacking cough. "Who will manipulate us, Hrossar? Who will ford the muddied river of our discontent and turn it toward his own ends? We are fair game for the unscrupulous."

Hrossar closed his eyes, fingers closing into a fist behind his back. "Because we no longer believe in anything."

☆ ☆ ☆

Kel sat hunched in a corner, back against the wall. Eyes squeezed shut, fists curled. In the cavern outside, herodons and geolites were speaking. Arranging a peace treaty.

159

He slammed the ground with one fist. No! He couldn't accept it! The herodons should've kept fighting—they certainly had enough strength in them—but for efficiency's sake and to save their own blood, they'd given up.

Cowards. Kel gritted his teeth.

I care for you, Kel.

Mom's voice echoed in his head. Kel opened his eyes, a tear escaping one. This wasn't him. He couldn't hold a grudge like this.

But he couldn't forgive, either. He couldn't move on—but he couldn't keep looking back. His arms shook as he growled.

I want to see you use your wonderful talents for something.

Was that the solution? Bury himself in his contraptions…maybe show them off at a convention in Newílderashe…

Or find happiness.

And there was Kharema. Kel had nearly died on many occasions—wasn't that cause enough to ask her out? If she'd even waited this long.

I'm just worried.

Of course she'd been worried. And now Kel was falling apart. He had to do *something*.

But if he went to Newílderashe, the herodons would be there. They'd be looking at his contraptions too. Running their claws over it.

Kel shook his head fiercely. The herodons would *not* control his life! His mother wanted him to do something with his talents—and by great stones, he would. It didn't matter who was watching.

But—what of Kharema?

Kel opened his right hand. In it was nestled a shard of opal. It still gleamed—if you tilted it just right in the firelight. "For you, mom," he whispered, another tear sliding down his cheek. "I'll try to make something of myself."

☼ ☼ ☼

"Simply accept those counter-terms and we will be on our way." Derofon stood before the head geolite, arms crossed. "Is it agreed?"

The chief geolite adjusted his spectacles, pouring over the scroll. "Not quite. There is still one matter to discuss."

That the herodons could offer counter-terms at all was remarkable. Hrossar gave a soft snort. Apparently the geolites were still intimidated by the prospect of battling the herodons.

"Which one?" Derofon squared himself off against the head geolite. "Your analysts certainly found the terms agreeable. Do you not?"

"It's a good compromise. We'd accept it..." The head geolite let his voice trail off. "But we found a wee little technicality." He rolled up the scroll into a cylinder. "It seems you're allowed to attack us still."

"Yes—but not for loot."

"Aye, but that's the problem. We want no more war with you, under any circumstances."

Derofon gave an impatient snort. "These accords forbid us from raiding you for supplies and such—"

"But not raiding us to kidnap people."

"Precisely. What if you are harboring an individual of interest to us?" Derofon waved his arm, as though it would explain the obvious. "We must be able to claim that individual."

"That's still raiding us though."

"Do you want peace or not? These are our terms. Herodons are hired for many reasons, and if word spreads that people can simply hide in Brekh'cha to evade us—well, that might be problematic." He held the geolite's gaze. "For both of us, as you will be overrun with refugees."

"Perhaps." The Supreme Declarer rubbed his chin, grimacing. "But we want no raiding."

"Then this will be perfect for you." Derofon crossed his arms, raising his chin. "Unless you are harboring someone of interest to us, we will never raid you. You will have no cause for concern."

A fair deal, considering it came with no true hostility. But did the herodons have enough leverage for it?

The head geolite turned from Derofon. The stone ruler listened as his analysts whispered into his ears—then he whispered back.

"What do you think will happen if they reject this offer?"

Hrossar turned to Father. The wounded herodon had his claws in his lap, eyes pointed ahead. "Will the war resume, Hrossar?"

"No." Hrossar inhaled deeply, hands behind his back. "For they will not reject the terms."

"And why is that?"

"Because they are as desperate as we are for peace."

"Correct." Father closed his eyes. "But I suppose they must wrestle with the treaty—for dignity's sake."

The declarer turned to the herodons, eyes wandering over the crowd. He pressed his lips together. Then—

"Agreed." The stone offered his hand, and Derofon shook it. "Now begone."

"As you wish." Derofon bowed, turned—and made his way into the crowd of herodons. No applause followed him—no cheers, no whistles. Just a silence like death.

The herodons turned and, one by one, began making their way to the exit.

18 THE VOICE IN THE HOLLOWS

5964 OT, 4th month (two months later)

Kel stood before the door, fist raised. Just one little knock. Not too difficult, right?

He lowered his fist. For other stones, maybe.

He turned from the door, pacing. Bah! Why was this so difficult! Any ounce of bravery and he'd be rapping at the door like it was nothing. But no. He was a hesitant stone at times.

He cast a glance at the door. Polished feldspar, with neat little letters inscribed near the top.

The Office of the Jadess
Chief Assistant to the Supreme Declarer of the Ticora Council
And Current Head of the Northwestern Guard

He suspected she'd carved the title herself. The second line was much bigger than the third—no one would have to guess as to her ambitions.

A corner of his lips lifted. Still the same determined stone.

He approached the door again—and this time gave a timid rap. There. No backing down now.

"Come in."

The door slid open—and Kel stepped through.

Everything was perfectly polished. Desk perpendicular to the walls, shelves lined neatly with books, file cabinets that gleamed in the torchlight burning from porticos on either side of the Jadess's chair…

163

And there. Square center sat the jade stone herself, writing something with a quill. She didn't even bother looking up. "What's your business?"

"I, eh…" Where should he begin? Kel ambled up to the desk, mind racing. He hadn't thought of what to say! Somehow he thought he'd have more time. "I'm a surf scout in the army."

"M-hm."

She still wasn't looking at him. Her pen scribbled fiercely, glasses reflecting firelight from the porticoes behind Kel. Four porticoes in one office. And that with polished, reflective floors and walls. No doubt she was tired of faint light.

The Jadess herself wasn't a spot different. Her spectacles seemed new, but otherwise…just the same as three centuries ago. Kel supposed he'd changed his appearance a little, what with all the smelting he'd needed from getting his chest torn out. Great stones, he'd probably replaced half his body from the war alone.

"Well?" She expelled a soft sigh, scribbling some more. "I am listening, you know. Please continue."

The "please" seemed as robotic as ever. Barely believable, if that. A corner of Kel's lips lifted. "As you can verify—talk with Captain Jakon—I was a brave stone. A real fighter in the war."

"Wonderful."

Could a voice drip with more sarcasm? Kel swallowed. "But seeing as the war's over—I'm more useful here. I know Western Brekh'cha like few other stones. I'm taking this moment to request…" his mouth was very dry now. He tried licking his lips. "Eh, I'm hoping to transfer to a scout team for Western Brekh'cha."

"Well that's unusual." The Jadess adjusted her spectacles, as they'd been slipping down her bump of a nose with each scribble. "Curse these glasses. Slippery as the last pair. I'm sorry, you were saying?"

"I'd like to be on a scout team in Western Brekh'cha. To keep on the lookout for the dragon."

"I see. That's very unusual." The Jadess opened a drawer—and pulled out a blank sheet of paper. "Well, I'll write up a form to fill out. I don't question your bravery—and I know you're no deserter seeking to abandon the Eastern Guard. If you were a coward," here she gave a wry smile, still focused on the paper, "you'd go anywhere but here."

Kel waited as she filled out some lines on the paper. Did she not recognize his voice? It had been about three centuries…

"There you go." The Jadess slid the paper toward him, expelling a sigh. "Truth be told, we do need another pair of eyes. There's been something…curious in the Northwestern Hollows."

Curious? Kel cleared his throat. "How so?"

"A voice." She adjusted her spectacles, putting her quill on the other paper. "A teenage boy from the voice, scouts report. Though no one's seen him."

"A herodon?"

"Regalite. Or humanite—no one knows." She scribbled something, then arched an eyebrow. "You know how voices echo in the Hollows—no one has a notion where he is. But they say he's crying out for help."

That seemed mighty odd. "When can I go?"

"First thing in the morning." The Jadess scribbled another sentence—then shoved the paper aside. Pulling open her drawer, she plucked another page with her chisel-tipped fingers. The tips of her fingers seemed quite smooth, like they were honed regularly.

"Anything else, scout?"

Kel nearly jumped. "Eh, well…" he pressed his lips together, debating. Should he say it? Kharema was no doubt part of the Western Guard…he could request to be in her detachment.

"Well?"

But what would that do? Would Kharema still talk to him—after all his stalling? Could he look her in the eyes? He'd sputter, no doubt.

"I'm sorry—" the Jadess looked at him for the first time, "do I know you, lad?"

"Ehm…" So she didn't recognize him. Time and smelting did change appearance, if nothing else. "Aye. My name is—"

"Don't tell me." She waved dismissively. "I've far too many names to keep track of as it is. I'll forward your form to our scout assigner and you'll be in. Agreed?"

Kel nodded, swallowing. "Agreed."

The Jadess gave him a nod, putting her quill to the new page. "Wonderful."

☆ ☆ ☆

The silver lava bubbled and hissed before Kel, meandering along the ridge. If he stepped onto the ridge, gravity would shift around him—and it would become the floor. As it was, he was standing on an incline. He took a seat, using his hands to prevent himself from rolling.

His eyes darted around the cavern. The way the dragonflies flitted about near the ceiling, heads tilting as they considered each rock, almost made him forget their vicious nature. One of them plucked a rock from the wall and buzzed off, sparks flying from its silver molten body.

A rolling noise. Kel glanced back. "There ya are!"

Grekham uncurled beside him, grinning. "Sorry I'm late. When I heard you'd been accepted in the guard, I came fast as I could."

"You know anything about my assignment?"

"I'm the one leading your group." The ilmenite pointed a thumb at himself. "Never guessed I'd be a responsible leader, eh?"

"Still wouldn't, truth be told."

"Oh—" Grekham put a hand on his chest, "now that's just cold."

"No more than you deserve."

Grekham barked a laugh—then took a seat beside Kel. "Now what's got you motivated to join us? Besides the surfing."

Kel shrugged. "Surfing's enough."

"But you didn't apply during the war. What's the drive?"

Kel hesitated. He pressed his lips together, eyes on the ridge.

"Is it Kharema?"

"No!" The words blurted out of his mouth. "I mean, ehm…alright—maybe. More or less."

"Aye." Grekham shrugged. "I thought so."

"Eh…" Grekham had the read of things, as usual. Kel gave a soft sigh. "I was hoping to run into her, perhaps."

"Right. That's understandable." Grekham scratched his chin, the yellow speckles on his knuckles flashing in the silver lava's light. "That might happen, you know."

Kel felt queasy again. His arms felt weak all of a sudden. "I know."

"You gonna ask her out then?"

"I…" Now came the hard part. "Maybe."

"Maybe?" Grekham gave Kel a look. "Why now, lad? What's really motivated this change of career?"

Kel put his legs out so he could move his hands. He tried gesturing

166

with them, but just waved them up and down. How could he phrase it? What about Kharema? You have so much to do, Kel.

Mom's words. Kel licked his lips. "Heat and pressure, Grekham. They change a stone."

"Ah...too much wandering under lava then? I thought you looked shorter."

"No." Kel swallowed, curling and uncurling his fists. He focused on the lava river. "I mean in my personality, Grekham. I picked up some wisdom over time, you know—and I figured something."

"What's that?"

"A stone doesn't change without motivation. You need heat and pressure."

"Oh—I see. The war got to you? Many stones had trauma."

"Eh...a little bit of the war." Kel hesitated. His mouth was feeling very dry. "I, eh...I've had chunks torn from my chest many a time. Each time, it felt worse. Staring at the dead soldiers..."

What if your time runs out?

And there was Mom. But—after all this time, he still couldn't speak of it. "It's just heat and pressure."

"Ah." Grekham nodded, though Kel doubted he had any real understanding of Kel's situation. To be captain of the Western Guard, Grekham probably would've been here when the war started. No combat experience. Grekham cleared his throat. "So it got to you inch by inch."

"Aye. Just as no single bit of heat or pressure can change a stone, no single event did it. It was the whole of time and heated pressure."

Promise me you'll try something after the war is over.

Kel's muscles were tight. Why couldn't he mention Mom? "That's my lay of it, anyway."

"Not bad. You're no klutz at thinking."

"I peer into people at times. Got it from my mother." Kel shrugged again. "Suppose I should peer into myself more."

"Greetings, geolites."

They both turned to see a humanite approaching them. Metal armor that gleamed in the lava's light, a utility belt—and a bald head with no helmet. But more than that, narrowed eyes and a sneer on his face. Pebbles crunched beneath his feet with each step, and he paused before a small boulder. Who was this?

"My name is Titanius Liege." He studied them, jaw set. "I assume you have heard of me."

Grekham clenched his jaw. Apparently he had.

"Your cooperation is necessary." Titanius put his foot on the boulder, then leaned on his knee with one elbow. His other hand gestured lucidly. "You see, I'm new to the area. The Northwestern Wilds are a menagerie to me."

"And what're you doing here, hunter?" Grekham balled his fists, getting to his feet. "Here to whip someone?"

"Not quite." Titanius's lips curled as he focused on Grekham. "No whipping is necessary at this time."

Now Kel spotted the whip. It hung on Titanius's utility belt, curled tightly.

"I'm actually hunting a small target—a boy." Titanius took his foot off the boulder. He approached them step by step, keeping his eyes on Grekham. "He seems to be lost in the molten wilds of Northwestern Brekh'cha."

"And are you aware that the Flame Dragon prowls these grounds?"

"Only past the blocked tunnels." Titanius's lips barely parted. "Which you are aware of. So why mislead me?"

Grekham didn't answer. Some of his yellow speckles turned orange—he must've been furious. But why?

"It matters little. I will have your cooperation." Titanius smiled—though again, it was more of a sneer. "You see, I have already discussed this with the Council of Ticora. They have assured me that you will assist me."

"Where's your proof?" Grekham raised his chin, fists still clenched. "Or are you just making it up?"

Titanius reached into a pouch, keeping his eyes on them. He slipped out a small scroll, a corner of his lips tilting. "And of course you'll want to read it."

"Give it to me."

Titanius handed him the scroll, the lava's light glinting off his gauntlet. "You may satisfy your curiosity."

Grekham pulled the string off—and unrolled the scroll. Kel peered over his shoulder, studying the tiny parchment.

168

This document states that the hunter Titanius Liege has acquired full permissions and cooperations for the explicit purpose of hunting an undisclosed regalite in the Northwestern Wilds of Brekh'cha. He is to be granted full expediency through its tunnels, with no individual impeding him.

Any knowledge he requires will also be granted him regarding the layout of the Wilds, provided it is not confidential.

From Kehron
Supreme Declarer of the Council of Ticora

Below was the geolite's personal seal.

Well—that was fancy. Kel inhaled deeply, nodding to Titanius. How had the hunter pulled it off? And anyway, what would he want with a regalite boy? "You're a big man then. What're your connections?"

"He's considered the best hunter in the world," Grekham spat, rolling up the scroll. He glared at Titanius. "Though not the kindest."

"Cruelty is necessary at times." Titanius held out a hand. "Why should I refrain from means which would further my purpose?"

Grekham picked up the string—and slipped it back on the rolled scroll. "Animal," he whispered, handed the scroll back. "You've got no moral compass."

"On the contrary," Titanius snapped, lips curling. "*You* have no integrity. You would fail in your task simply to indulge your weaknesses."

"Compassion is not weak."

"It is the rot of fallen empires." Titanius raised his eyebrows. "And can you really prove it's effective for any cause?"

"It's what's keeping me from pummeling you right now."

"Is it?" Titanius's next words barely rose above a whisper. "Try it."

This was pointless. Kel stepped toward the Hunter. "I don't want to debate—you've got your opinion, we've got ours. But we'll get you a map."

"When?"

"Now, as you please." Kel glanced at Grekham—the ilmenite nodded. Kel took a few steps toward Titanius, but the hunter wasn't moving. "You coming with me, hunter?"

169

Titanius shook his head. "You may fetch it. Though I won't require your assistance as soon as I have the map. I shall travel the wilds in solitude."

"Very well." And Kel would no doubt be better off for it. "I'll roll then."

A corner of Titanius's lips tilted. He turned from them to survey the cavern, armor flashing as a dragonfly zoomed overhead. "Naturally."

☼ ☼ ☼

Twenty minutes and they'd meet up with Kharema. Twenty minutes and Kel still had no plan.

He'd tried rehearsing the conversation in his head. That never went well.

Kharema: So you have something to ask me, Kel?

—Kel: Eh, yes. What would you think of taking a stroll together?

We used to stroll all the time, lad.

—I mean as…ehm, as more of a date.

Oh really? And it took you three centuries to ask. Why's that?

—Because I eh…I didn't…

That was where everything fell apart. Would *anyone* wait that long?

Kharema's a good stone. Mom's words echoed in his head. Firm but patient.

Mom had only met the rhodochrosite a handful of times, but here she was telling Kel Kharema's deepest secrets. Kel shook his head.

You've got to take initiative, though. Kel, I'm worried.

Not that he doubted Mom's lay of Kharema. He just wasn't sure…

He clenched his fists, hiking along the shore. What could he even say? How could he phrase it? Lasses were hard to talk to.

Well, not always. His muscles loosened. Kharema was easy most of the time. No one else was. But she was easy to be around.

He rolled his eyes. At least, when he wasn't trying to ask her out.

Hello?

A voice. Like that of a regalite boy.

"Hear that?"

170

Kel glanced at Grekham. "You think I'm deaf? 'Course I hear it."

Anyone there?

The voice again. The way it echoed made Kel wonder how far away the boy was. "Over here!"

Who are you?

"Geolites!" He cupped his hands to his mouth. "Who are *you*?"

You guys know Titanius?

Kel stiffened. This boy knew he was being hunted! What was going on here? "We do."

He probably made you look for me, huh?

The boy's voice seemed more distant now. Grekham cupped his hands to his mouth. "We were searching for you before then! We're just curious."

Yeah, right. I'm going to the Ticora Council. Seeking asylum.

Would he even get asylum? Kel stopped walking. "You sure you can get it?"

Might as well try. Wouldn't you?

This kid was unusually confident. "Do you know the way?"

I'm still figuring it out. And trying to avoid Titanius on the way.

Kel and Grekham exchanged glances. "Of course he would be," Grekham whispered, glancing down the cavern. The voice could be coming from anywhere.

I figure you guys are bound by some contract or something to help him. Am I right?

This whole situation was mighty odd. Kel's brow furrowed. "Mind telling us what's going on? Why are you being hunted?"

I'm not actually sure. But Titanius isn't the nicest guy. So could you do me one and roll on past this point? I think I need to cross the river. Am I right?

He seemed so casual. Not exactly what you'd expect from a regalite stuck in Brekh'cha without parents.

Guys? It would be nice.

Something was very wrong. Kel shook his head. "Listen, do you have any parents?"

Oh, yeah—definitely. They're coming for me. Might take a while, though.

Why would it take a while? "Did you wander here yourself?"

Um… The voice finally showed some sign of uncertainty. Not exactly. It's kind of a long story. You know what I mean?

171

"We have no idea what you mean," Grekham shouted, hands cupped. "Come on, lad! You're not being forward!"

Yeah...sorry about that. Not sure who I can tell what. You hear me?

"Hearing is not the problem! You're making no sense!"

Yeah, well... Kel could have been imagining it, but he thought he heard muttering. Was the kid talking to himself? *Sorry, buddy. I just need you to move on. Okay?*

Kel glanced at Grekham. Grekham shrugged—neither of them had a clue. "It might not hurt if we let him get to Ticora," the ilmenite whispered, looking back the way they came. "It might—you know—not count as impeding Titanius."

"Isn't helping the hunter's quarry impeding him?" Kel raised a hand before Grekham could speak. "Eh. You know what? I don't care." He cupped his hands to his mouth and shouted, "Go past the river and down the middle tunnel. Right at the fork, left, right, right. Then follow the green dragonflies a bit. Got it?"

No response. Maybe the regalite was wondering if Kel was leading him into a trap?

"You'll just have to follow geolites from there—without being seen, of course."

Still no response. A magma dragonfly zoomed over the river, buzzing as fiery sparks fled its wings. Bubbles formed and popped slowly on the lava.

Then, Okay, thanks!

Did the kid even believe them? Kel couldn't tell from his tone. Grekham arched an eyebrow—and Kel shrugged. "Hey, I can't make him believe me."

You guys gonna roll on or what?

So the kid could see them. Kel cleared his throat. "We're moving on now!"

Thanks. Really appreciate this!

Kel glanced at Grekham—and they both nodded. Then they withdrew their limbs and burst into a roll. One side tunnel, another...In seconds they were past the cavern.

Kel gritted his teeth, veering perfectly along the tunnel. The whole thing was mighty odd.

"So this is where we'll meet her."

Kel shifted his footing, eyes darting around the cavern. He felt very aware of himself suddenly. "Aye."

"You ready?"

He shook his head stiffly. "No."

"There you are. And on time—incredible." They turned as Kharema finished uncurling from her roll. "And I see you have a new colleague—" her eyes went wide. Her mouth dropped a little—then she recovered, blinking and clearing her throat. "Kel."

Kel just stared at her, mouth hanging open. Grekham nudged him, and he jumped. "Hey, Kharema."

"Long time no see."

"Aye." Kel just stood there blinking, arms hanging by his side. "Long time."

"Oo! You know what?" Grekham pointed down the way they'd come. "I realize I forgot to scout a side tunnel. Be right back—then we'll report what we found."

Kharema did not take her eyes off Kel. "Proceed."

Grekham rolled off. Kel could've sworn he'd never seen the ilmenite move faster.

"So."

Kel turned back to Kharema. Her arms were crossed, eyes narrowed. "You joined the Western Guard."

Kel swallowed. "Aye."

She arched an eyebrow. "Any particular reason?"

Kel averted his eyes. This was the hard part. He could feel his fists tightening. No! He had to follow through! "I...wanted to see you."

"Really?" Kharema's eyebrows went up—then she cleared her throat, and her tone flattened. "What for?"

"I, eh..." Kel was looking everywhere but Kharema. He forced his eyes to her feet—then lifted them so their gaze met. "You're...well, you're my friend, Kharema."

"Is that all?"

She knew. She was waiting for it. But why? To reject him—or go out with him? "I, ehm...aye. For now, that's all."

Her muscles loosened. Was it disappointment or resignation? "I see."

That statement felt wrong. Kel needed to say something—reassure her somehow! But how? He couldn't make himself say it. "Aye."

Kharema turned from him, frowning. "Well then. That's—" her voice cut off, and she swallowed, "—that's great that you're my friend."

It's so obvious.

Mom's words again. Kel pressed his lips together.

"So I guess we'll keep looking for the regalite?"

Was that statement supposed to mean something else? Kel answered with what he hoped was the right answer. "For now."

Kharema gave a nod. "Right. For now."

Kel felt weak…every muscle in his body felt tired. He could say something—*should* say something. What was wrong with him?

"Stones won't wait forever, you know."

His eyes met hers as she turned to him. Those sapphire irises, twinkling in the red light of suspended lava globules bobbing up and down above them. Had she just said that? "I know."

"'Course you do." She turned from him again, looking down the tunnel she'd rolled through. "You know more than you give yourself credit for."

That was it. Mom was right. Mom was really right! Kel could ask her out now. She'd say yes, right?

He opened his mouth—and nothing came out.

What was wrong with him? Why couldn't he just ask the question? Why was he so shy!

"See you later, Kel." She withdrew her limbs and rolled off.

Kel reached out, opening his mouth—then squeezed his eyes shut. She was disappearing down a side tunnel! No doubt she could still hear him—but he had nothing he could say.

His strength had failed him. Again.

Kel sat on the cavern's floor, withdrawing his legs. He glanced up at the floating lava globules. They never worried about any drama or asking people out. They had no life and breath to them. Content to bob up and down for untold eons, they'd shed light for any passerby. And they never felt alone.

He let out a soft, trembling sigh. More than alone—he felt weak.

19 ASYLUM

5964 OT, 4th month (almost a week later)

The regalite boy stood before the Council of Ticora, chin raised. They'd been deliberating for most of the day. From what he could tell, he was about a hair away from being turned over to Titanius.

Lovely.

The glassy marble floor sloped up like a bowl—and he was standing in its center, looking up at the high benches. The seats spread out from the central podium like wings, with the Supreme Declarer— a grainy ebon geolite—shuffling his notes behind it.

Most of the murmurs were fading. The geolites had no doubt decided exactly what would happen to him.

"Mr. Sai..." The declarer heaved a sigh, adjusting his spectacles. "You realize what a position you've put us in."

"It's a question of compassion. You can't fork me over to Titanius."

"Yes. But—" the Supreme Declarer rested his forehead on his fingers, pressing his lips together. "We already promised him our full cooperation."

"So? That was based on location. I eavesdropped when I was out there." Sai grinned. "You'd help him in what you call the Northwestern Wilds. Technically you can still offer me asylum in Ticora—right?"

"Technically." The Supreme Declarer peered down at Sai. "However, it would be a mite dishonest. After promising our help, we protect the one he's hunting?"

"Oh come on." Sai crossed his arms. "You can't really make an

175

argument from morality here. Which is worse—dishonesty or hanging a kid out to dry?"

"We don't know who you are or what you've done." The geolite arched an eyebrow. "For all we know, he's hunting you for good reason."

"He's hunting me because someone hired him to." Sai leaned forward, eyes widening. "It's that simple. I didn't do anything wrong, so it's their problem."

"Well..." The Supreme Declarer leaned back as geolites began murmuring. He drummed the table, stone fingers clacking on the marble. "You are just a child..."

The murmurs grew louder. Many geolites exchanged glances. Kind of odd for them to be alarmed, since they'd already reached their conclusion—right?

"Sai." The declarer studied him, eyes narrowed. It was like he was peering into Sai's heart—and the way he leaned forward made it look as though he was concentrating pretty hard. Quite unlike his behavior up to this point.

Sai uncrossed his arms, brow furrowing. "Yes?"

Another sigh. The declarer shook his head—then withdrew it into his body. "No." His voice was barely a whisper. "I can't do this."

The murmurs stilled. Every eye was on the declarer.

"I, Kehron—" he cut himself off, squeezing his eyes shut, "I, Kehron, exercise my annual judicial authority as Supreme Declarer of Ticora to not simply declare, but overrule the decision of the council."

Gasps. Some geolites placed their palms on their chests. Kehron inhaled deeply, drumming the podium. "I am hereby granting the regalite Sai asylum in Ticora. Let it be shown in the record—both in the flames and the papers—that I have taken this action of my own accord." He seemed weary all of a sudden. "No one else is responsible for this decision."

Silence. No one dared speak.

Kehron plucked a gavel from the podium—then slammed the marble with it. "My word is final. This council is adjourned."

They could do that, huh. Just like that. One moment it was a council of elders—but apparently the head honcho got to cancel the vote once a year. Sai arched an eyebrow. "Thanks."

"Don't mention it." Kehron clenched his jaw. "I mean it—keep this a secret. No one outside this room can know what transpired here."

Sai dipped his head, a smile tugging at his lips. "Will do."

☼ ☼ ☼

Sai's footsteps had long faded, leaving only silence. Every eye was on Kehron, waiting for him to speak. He opened his lips—then swallowed. "There are times where difficult decisions must be made."

"This is Titanius!" The complaints came rushing in like a tide. "You want to endanger our relations with the Coalition of Hunters? With his employers?"

Kehron set his gavel down. "His employers may understand."

"We don't even know who they are!"

"Aye! What if they're the herodons!"

"What if they take this as an act of war and—"

"And what if this was an innocent child, and we were condemning him to death?!" Kehron's voice rose above the council. "What then! What blood would you have on your hands!"

Silence. Some in the council averted their eyes. But others still glared at him.

"I did this for our sake," Kehron continued, eyes darting from member to member, "to keep blood from our stony fingers. And this is precisely why the annual overruling exists."

"You could've endangered us all, Kehron."

"I could've. But you don't know that."

"Aye. And you don't know whether he was innocent."

"I studied him." Kehron surveyed the council, lips pressed together. "I'm a good judge of character—as many of you know—and I saw innocence. The lad is no criminal."

"But you don't know what this'll do! Brekh'cha may make enemies for it!"

Kehron raised his hand to silence them. "I know what it *won't* do."

Their voices stilled. Some leaned back, arms crossed.

"And that's enough to keep me sleeping at night."

"But see now, Kehron." An elderly goethite—Ekhere, a good friend—held out his dark crystalline hands, pleading. "We need some insurance. Brekh'cha cannot take the heat for this."

177

"Which is why I'm resigning."

Gasps. Murmurs rose, and many shook their heads.

"I know you agree with me. The blame rests squarely on my shoulders—and as I resign, Brekh'cha cannot be held culpable for my actions." Kehron raised a hand again. "Courtesy of the International Treaty of 4720. Leaders take responsibility for most decisions, and upon retirement blame is shifted from the state to their person."

A few nods. Some eyebrows shot up. "But we—who will replace you, Kehron? You're a mighty fine leader."

"Thank you, Ekhere. I appreciate the compliment." Kehron gave a long, drawn out sigh. "But I've been thinking about this for a while. Since the war, really. What I could've done to prevent it—and what I didn't do."

"The herodons were the ones who started it. They came for—"

"I know. And they also ended it." Kehron looked from councilmember to councilmember, sorrow lining his features like cracks in barren ground. "Maybe we could have ended it too. Maybe we could've done *something*. But we didn't even try."

No response. A few geolites looked down at their desks. Most still glared at him.

"We were so eager to have the herodons off our land, we didn't consider the cost." Kehron gave a small chuckle. "And we won. Some victory."

"We were able to preserve our lands."

"That we did. Shame we lost so many of the stones who live on those lands. Not to mention blowing up our own homes."

"You..." Ekhere shook his head. "Now see here, Kehron. This isn't like you."

"I'm tired of it, Ekhere. Having all the big decisions to make. Knowing people die for those decisions. I want to—" Kehron licked his lips. "I *need* to retire to a nice alcove in the Western Hollows. Keep some time to myself."

"Hm." Ekhere crossed his arms, leaning back against his seat. The green flames' light glinted off his face as he narrowed his eyes. "People will always die, Kehron."

"But not today." Kehron indicated the entrance with his finger. "Today, one regalite will live."

"One possibly guilty regalite."

"Something's got to live." Kehron pleaded with his hands, fingers

178

clutching at the air. "Don't you see, Ekhere? Doesn't *any* stone see? Something's got to live."

A few council members cleared their throats. Others exchanged glances.

"We've had so many deaths. I can't—I can't let one more happen. In all this war, in all this bloodshed..." Now his voice was a whisper, mingling with the crackling of the flames. "Something's got to live."

"Then who will replace you?" Another geolite gestured, palm up. "As Ekhere pointed out, you're a good leader. We can't be without a Supreme Declarer."

"No. And you won't be." Kehron cleared his throat, raising his chin. His eyes swept the council room—and he swallowed. "I am hereby exercising my right to appoint a successor—by appointing my chief assistant, a jadeite who refers to herself as the Jadess, to the position of Supreme Declarer."

No gasps this time. Most would approve of this choice.

"Should there be any objections, they may be submitted to me in writing." Kehron inhaled deeply, leaning back in his chair. He closed his eyes. "You have three months to complain—as after that, she will replace me."

20 STANDARDS

"Thank you for coming." The humanite stood on the castle ramparts, hands behind his back. Black hair slicked back, his skin a pale white. "I realize I'm new to these parts."

Hrossar stood behind him, surveying the battle ramparts. An impressive castle—but he had seen better. "I believe your letter mentioned a job."

"Of course." The humanite turned to him. "And I apologize for not introducing myself earlier. The name's Cisera." He extended a hand, which Hrossar took. "And yes, I have a job for you."

"Excellent." Hrossar inhaled deeply, keeping a firm posture. "You must know, however, that I brief my employers before accepting tasks from them."

"Of course." Cisera dipped his head, hands behind his back again. "You need to know if you can trust me."

"More than that." Hrossar set his hand on a merlon. "I need to know if you are a virtuous employer with a just assignment."

"Just?" Cisera snorted, waving dismissively. "Come now. Such antiquated language serves no one. You must be more enlightened than that."

Hrossar arched an eyebrow. "Enlightened."

"Without a doubt. Come with me." Cisera beckoned, and Hrossar followed him into a tower connected to the battlements. A torch burned by the stairs, sparks flying as it crackled. "Up the stairs, if you please."

If you please. Hrossar narrowed his eyes, a muscle in his neck twitching. Something about the humanite's tone was almost too polite. "Very well."

"You mustn't be preoccupied by outdated conventions, you know. We stand on the crest of the seventh millennium. Why should we live in the past?"

Hrossar was not sure if he appreciated this kind of language. "I agree that clinging to the past can be detrimental…"

"Precisely. Now I have something to show you." Cisera opened the door at the top of the stairs, sweeping his palm out. "Well, not some 'thing' exactly. It is a vision of the future."

Hrossar's stomach knotted. Something felt wrong here. He stepped across the threshold—then stiffened as Cisera closed the door. The humanite was still smiling—but something seemed amiss in his eyes. Yet what was it?

"Well then," Cisera inhaled deeply, rubbing his hands together, "you'll find this interesting." He stepped over to a bookshelf, slipped out a green book and slapped it onto the desk. "An isomorphic book."

Hrossar studied the object. Its embossed gold lettering seemed to glow—and as Cisera opened it, the pages exploded with light. Shapes and images danced across the room, as if Hrossar had been transported into the book's pages. Images of herodons bickering.

"Your people." Cisera took a bow. "Hrossar—tell me about them."

"Splintered. We have been unable to find a new homeland." Hrossar raised his chin. "Though we still have some loyalty to one another."

"The way I understand it, the end of the war was quite controversial among your people. Some would say it caused a rift."

"That is correct."

"And many herodons, including you and your father, would prefer your kinsmen to be more…unified."

How would Cisera know this if he was new to Newílderashe? Hrossar inhaled deeply, chest rising—then expelled his breath, muscles tense. "You have the sum of the situation."

"Thank you. And I realize this is uncomfortable for you." Cisera raised a hand as if apologizing. "I really mean you no discomfort."

Hrossar arched an eyebrow. "Undoubtedly."

"But you must understand, I've been studying your plight for quite some time. And after a year of research and thought—well, it's

181

time to act. I moved into Newílderashe, and I've been introducing myself to all the herodons."

"I appreciate your concern." Hrossar tried to keep his tone neutral. "However, I doubt there is much you can do to assist us."

"Ah." Cisera raised a finger, then put it on his own lips. "But that's where you're wrong. You see—the question is one of purpose. Your people are purposeless."

What was the goal of this conversation? "You stated you had a job for me."

"Of course, of course. And we'll get to that." Cisera tapped the book, and the images shifted. Now herodons marched in unison, waving an inscrutable banner. "You see, my vision is that of a unified herodon nation."

Hrossar arched an eyebrow. "That is extremely ambitious."

"But it's also quite doable. The thing is," here he grinned, "I have something the herodons lack. I have a dream."

It sounded more like a delusion. "You believe you can convince every herodon to march under your banner."

"Not *my* banner." Cisera leaned in, lowering his voice. "A banner for a land of great vision. Vision enough to provide purpose to every creature under the sun. The end of sorrow, poverty, ideological conflict. Peace."

"Naturally." A smile tugged at Hrossar's lips. "But in order to achieve this vision, you require force."

"Don't be so crude." Cisera placed his hands behind his back, pacing around the table. "Every great movement in history requires some level of strength. But this only serves to provide purpose to your race."

"And if we decline?"

"Well..." Cisera cocked his head, grimacing. "I'm afraid you'd be denying your countrymen the opportunity to be one people again."

Hrossar gave a soft snort. The way this man spoke...why did it disturb him? "One people."

"Imagine." Cisera tapped the book again, and the images morphed. Now herodons were toasting glasses, patting each other on the shoulder, laughing under a sunrise. "A bright future, filled with camaraderie and fellowship. One people. One purpose. And most of all, no more shame."

Hrossar inhaled deeply, brow furrowing. That did sound

excellent…

"How long, Hrossar?" Cisera placed his palms on the table, voice a shrill whisper. "How long's it been since you looked in the mirror and saw something other than a failure? Something you could be *proud* of?" He clutched at the air, then curled his fist. "There is no pride in your people. Only the shame of *defeat*. Your spirits are crushed."

"That is our business."

"But I can help you." Cisera reached out to him, fingers splayed. "You will be one people, filled with power and purpose once more. You will never have to sorrow or feel shame again."

"This is appealing." Hrossar swallowed. His fists were curled— though he did not understand why. "You are a persuasive humanite."

"Thank you. I really have your best interests at heart."

"Yet all you have are words."

"For now." Cisera raised a finger. "But with your endorsement, many herodons will join me. After all, you are in a position of some influence among your people."

Hrossar did wield considerable influence as Teros Feodon's son. Hrossar lowered his snout, considering. "And the justice of your 'land of great vision'?"

"Justice. There's that word again." Cisera shook his head, smiling. "I repeat, you mustn't use terminology like that. It's simply outmoded."

"How so?"

"Well, Hrossar…" Cisera chuckled, as if this was obvious. "Look around you. Everyone strives for their version of what is just. Where does it get them? What does it achieve?"

"Justice is its own end."

"Says who?" Cisera leaned in again. "That sounds like the exact kind of talk which holds people back from achieving their true potential. Rules, regulations…" Cisera waved dismissively. "Purpose does not need a set of antiquated notions to work."

"On the contrary." Hrossar arched an eyebrow, placing his hands behind his back. "Without traditional notions of right and wrong, purpose cannot be evaluated. You may, for instance, be assigned the purpose of murdering the innocent. What will stop you when—"

"The innocent? Who are they?" Cisera spread his hands. "These are all relative terms to justice. Products of being conditioned by

183

outdated conventions."

This was feeling more like a debate every second. "It is you who have decided they are outdated."

"They clearly don't work! Again, look around you!" Cisera lowered his voice. "The purpose of such notions is to create a better tomorrow. But all 'right' and 'wrong' have done is create an ideology which brings tension between different peoples. Conflict." He pinched air between his thumb and forefinger. "We're this close to peace. If we just surrender our notion of 'justice.'"

"You mean our standards." Hrossar raised his chin. "And yet these standards are precisely what give us purpose. For my own part, I accept or reject jobs based upon my standards. They *define* my purpose."

"Ah, but they don't *have* to." Cisera held up his finger. "I knew this might be difficult. After all, it requires a certain...*vision* to see the picture I'm painting. One of perfect peace and harmony. All that's required is—"

"Amorality. Sociopathy." Hrossar gave an impatient snort. "Sugarcoating it won't change the reality of your proposition."

"But justice is self-defeating! Don't you see? It fails to bring about the world it promises."

"Your proposition here relies upon two assumptions." This was now a debate. And Hrossar would not shrink back. Adrenaline surged through him, fire burning in his veins. "First, it relies upon the assumption that the aim of justice is to create a better world."

"Well—" Cisera stepped back, "—that seems natural enough."

"This indicates a fundamental misunderstanding of justice, which exists to serve its own ends. Second," he raised a clawed finger to cut Cisera off, "second, it relies upon the assumption that creating peace is the ultimate 'good'—a difficult proposition to defend when 'good' and 'evil' are proposed to be relative terms."

"Well, 'good' isn't exactly the term I'd use. Perhaps 'beneficial'..."

"And why should we do something beneficial to society? You describe the *effects* of the action, but have not told us *why* we should strive to achieve those effects. Why should we help anyone?"

"Because—" Cisera chuckled. "Because you should! You should create a better tomorrow!"

"'Should'? What is morality, Cisera?" Hrossar leaned in. "Simply

184

put, it is a list of things that ought and ought not be done from a higher perspective. It is a 'vision,' as you like to say, of what we 'ought' to do and what we 'ought not' to do. You are proposing that we *ought* to do that which benefits society." Hrossar arched an eyebrow. "Without morality, there is no necessary reason for me to do this other than that you *feel* it should be done."

"But—" Cisera rolled his eyes. "Come now, Hrossar! I know you believe in creating a better tomorrow as well."

"Because I believe it is just to help society." Hrossar held his palms out. "You see, to motivate your position you must have some kind of obligation behind it. That we *ought* to create a better society. That we *ought* to abandon 'antiquated notions,' that we *ought* to stop fighting one another. That what you refer to as harmony is 'good,' while what we see as justice is 'bad.' But all of these 'oughts' are by nature moral statements, as any first-year student of philosophy knows."

Cisera clenched his jaw. His eyes seemed darker all of a sudden. "And you disagree with these 'oughts'?"

"No. But I have a reason to believe them."

"And what is that?"

"I believe in justice. It is a force greater than any in existence. It discerns, it vindicates, it condemns. It sweeps across the land, bringing purpose and order—true harmony—to society." Hrossar put a clawed finger in Cisera's chest. "What's your reason, humanite?"

Cisera stared at him. Then a snort of laughter escaped his closed lips. His body jerked as he gave another snort. Then he burst into laughter. "Ah, Hrossar. Hrossar! Putting up a good debate as always. Like your father."

"Your point?"

Cisera shrugged. "Well, it seems to me that you don't have much choice. I've heard about your 'standards,' Hrossar. You barely let anyone hire you."

"There are very few honorable people *left* to hire me." Hrossar bared his fangs, eyes narrowed. "And you are not one of them."

"So what will you do, then?" Cisera adopted a kinder tone. "I imagine it must be difficult, telling your herodons day after day—the whole army you are in charge of—that they'll have to scrounge for themselves or starve."

Hrossar swallowed. He could not betray weakness.

185

"And I'll imagine it's even more difficult when you get home, and your children run up to you holding their hands out. 'Daddy, daddy!' they say, pleading with their eyes. Your wife appears around the corner, watching you." Cisera frowned, eyes settling on the book. "But you have nothing to give them."

Hrossar's fists curled, his heart pounding. "I will provide, as always."

"No, you won't. Not at this rate." Cisera put a hand on Hrossar's shoulder. "You're going to have to compromise your silly ideals *sometime*, Hrossar. That or starve—along with your wife and children."

Hrossar's muscles were tingling. He took Cisera's hand—and lifted it from his shoulder, exhaling slowly. "I believe that is my business."

Cisera hesitated, waiting as Hrossar released his arm. Then he shrugged. "Well, it's going to happen sometime. So why not join me now? Your fellow herodons are."

"And that is their business."

"But you believe they're wrong."

"Correct. As *I* would be wrong to accept your offer." Hrossar turned to the door. "So manifest your vision with other fools."

Silence. Hrossar reached the door, then opened it with a creak.

"You'll give in."

Hrossar glanced back at Cisera. "You do not know me."

Cisera laughed—it was more like a giggle. "I don't have to. You need to feed your family. And I know you want what I have to offer."

"Enough to sacrifice everything?" Hrossar shook his head, turning to the stairway. "I would sooner die."

"Then you will. Along with your family—dead from starvation because you failed them. How does *that* align with your morality?"

Hrossar did not respond. He began descending the steps, fists balled.

"You'll have to compromise eventually!" Cisera's voice echoed in the stairwell. "You can't stand on your supposed 'high ground' forever!"

Hrossar swallowed, focusing on the steps. He would not respond. He could suffer, he could beg for food. He could be humiliated.

But he would not yield.

186

21 CONTRAPTIONS ON DISPLAY

5969 OT, 1st month (three years later)

Kel stood straight, hands flat by his sides. Humanites milled beside his contraptions—a catapult, ten surfboards and a wagon—chatting with one another. To them it was just another engineering convention. Contraptions on display, spread across the market square. As ordinary a show as the next.

Kel shifted his footing, swallowing. But how could a geolite's throat feel so dry? And his heart…it was pounding at his chest like an anvil. He could barely focus.

He glanced back at his horseless wagon. Not a particularly impressive piece of machinery. Probably could've left it at home, truth be told. Now it was just an eyesore.

Kel winced. All the other engineers had impressive contraptions. Better catapults, mighty siege craft—and he was sitting here with naught but a few tokens.

Kel pressed his lips together. He should pack up. Go home.

I want to see you use your wonderful talents for something.

Mom's voice. Kel squeezed his eyes shut, teeth clenched. She was why he was showcasing his contraptions in Newilderashe—and he wouldn't be a coward! This was for Mom.

"Now this is something."

Kel nearly jumped. He jerked his head to see a middle-aged man in robes approaching him. The blonde humanite had a large bird perched on one arm. The creature's eyes were covered by a blind, which was slipping a wee bit onto its hooked beak.

"Oh yes, *quite* something." The man grinned, rubbing his chin

187

with his free hand. "Now don't tell me you're the creator."

Kel blinked. Creator. He was being asked a question. "Of what?"

"Well this, of course." The humanite extended his fingers toward the horseless wagon. "It seems just like an ordinary wagon—but I notice a device like a pump in the middle. It looks like an impressive piece of architecture."

Impressive? The man liked it? "Eh—sure."

"Your sanding is immaculate as well. You must have put days into this."

Kel's cheeks were warming. Probably turning a darker shade of green. "That's mighty kind of you to say."

"And the design's execution..."

Kel cleared his throat. "It's a design I found after a bit of research, actually. That's how all my contraptions are. I don't come up with anything, I just..." That didn't sound good. "Eh..."

"You're more of a manufacturer than an inventor?" The humanite arched an eyebrow, and the bird shifted footing on his arm. He clicked his tongue, glancing at the creature. "Steady, now."

"Ehm..." Kel couldn't blow it. But what was there to say? This was going better than he'd hoped. "Who are you?"

"Delóren. King Delóren." The man offered his hand—and only then did Kel notice the thin golden band resting on his forehead. The king's eyebrows rose expectantly. "And you are?"

"Kel." That was poor form—giving a nickname. "Kelmor Ketarn. A geolite from Brekh'cha."

"Wonderful! It's so rare to see a geolite in these parts." The man's voice was a mite smoother than Kel was used to. And the way he drew out certain words had a soothing feel to it. "Here for the business?"

"Eh..." How much should Kel say? "I'm really only visiting for the convention, truth be told."

"Then I hope you stay a while! There's no need to be reserved." Delóren put a hand on Kel's shoulder. "We have excellent accommodations for stones like you. Just a few days at my castle and you'll feel polished as marble."

For a modest fee, no doubt. Kel had heard stories of Delóren's shrewd business tactics. "I'll pass, thank you."

"Oh, don't be wary!" Delóren chuckled, waving dismissively. "This stay will be on me. Consider it a sample of my hospitality."

"Alright then." What was the king up to? "So you wanted me to explain the wagon's propulsion contraption to you?"

"If you don't mind." Delóren glanced at his bird, which was shifting its claws on his arm again. "Oh, and this is my new eagle. The old one just died, and I'm getting this one accustomed to me so he can be my eyes in the sky. Name's Laramie." Delóren winked. "He's quite the charmer."

Laramie made a screeching noise. Kel flinched.

"Don't mind his manners. He's also a bit new." Delóren cupped one hand to his mouth and whispered, "Still thinks he rules the roost."

"Aye." Kel half-smiled. This humanite had a charm to him. "I suppose creatures can be like that."

"Not just creatures." Delóren grimaced. "I get a bit big for my britches at times too."

What? Kel's brow furrowed. "You're a king, aren't you?"

"Ah, but 'king' is such a relative title." Delóren waved his free hand, indicating the marketplace. "Over what do I rule? The people could buck me if they wanted. They put up with me because I bring money into the economy. And that's it."

"Well—don't you have an army?"

"My castle has guards, of course. But an army? Whenever I need muscle, I just hire some herodons. And since I have the most money..." He let his voice trail off, as if the conclusion was obvious. "Well? You know the ways of Newílderashe. He who handles the herodons handles the land. Or stays in power, in my case."

Why was Delóren telling Kel this? The man was either a wee bit too glib or trying to get Kel to relax. Kel suspected the latter. "Do you need something?"

"I do. And I'm glad you asked." Delóren's brow creased, highlighting his wrinkles. "I can see you're a business-minded geolite. I respect that. So I won't waste your time anymore."

"Aye." Too late for that. Kel was a friendly enough stone, but not when he'd been warned about someone. "What's your need?"

"I'm looking for sufficient transportation for a large number of supplies on my trade routes." Delóren straightened, raising his chin. "And I'm afraid I don't have enough horses to drive it. But it looks like this wagon of yours might just do the trick...?"

"Well, it's not properly my design—"

"But if it works, it's better than the last one I tried."

"The—" Kel blinked. "The last one?"

189

Delóren gave a small laugh—more like a puff of air. "What? You didn't think this was the first time I'd seen one of these, did you?"

This humanite could change attitudes instantly. The man was a natural born actor if Kel had ever seen one. Kel cleared his throat. "Truth be told, I'd assumed you were new to the horseless wagon market when you asked me how it worked."

"Oh, I was just making small talk. But I'm looking for expert manufacturers. And I've heard geolites, when they build, are very reliable." He extended a hand palm up toward Kel, cocking an eyebrow. "Am I right?"

Kel felt his face warming. That flattery again. But it seemed genuine enough—didn't it? Why else would Delóren be seeking his contraptions? "You're not wrong."

"Of course I'm not." Delóren grinned again. Then he bit his lip, as if excited. "So will you consider a price and get back to me?"

A couple of herodons. Entering the vending gallery near the back of the crowd. Kel glanced at them—then blinked and refocused on Delóren. "Aye. Why not."

"Excellent. Be seeing you." Delóren turned, hefting his eagle. The creature squawked, and Delóren shushed it. "Come now, Laramie. You must have better manners than that."

What an eccentric king. Kel shrugged, turning back to his wagon.

A herodon was standing beside it.

The creature was running one finger along the wagon's edge—claw clicking as it bumped along each ridge. The herodon inhaled deeply, chest rising.

"What're you doing?"

The herodon glanced at him. "Examining the handiwork, of course."

"That's *my* handiwork. And you've no need to examine it with your dirty fingers."

"It is a wagon." The herodon's eyebrows went up. "It will get dirty regardless."

"Not from you."

"Pardon?"

Great. Kel was offending potential customers. Kel tried loosening his fists—but they wouldn't obey. "I don't want to make a scene. Just step back, please."

The herodon took a step backward. He dipped his head, closing his eyes. "As you wish."

As you wish? Kel wanted to spit at the creature's feet. But that wouldn't pass here in Newílderashe. He'd heard cruelty against herodons was practically against the law.

"What is its price?"

"Eh—what?" Kel narrowed his eyes. "You want to purchase it, herodon?"

"Correct."

Kel took a deep breath, crossing his arms. He squared his legs apart. "It's too much for the likes of you."

"Is it?" The herodon arched an eyebrow. "I am quite wealthy."

"I'm sure you are." Kel pressed his lips together. "With your mercenary trade."

"I myself am a debater. Though I have several friends who are mercenaries."

"Do you?" Kel was running out of things to say. This creature clearly had no hostility toward him. But he didn't care. "That's great. I'm sure you skip off together, thinking of how many people's lives you can ruin."

The herodons eyebrows creased—and he gave a soft snort. "I mean no ill will towards you. I merely wish to purchase your horseless wagon."

"Aye. The way you meant no ill will when you lived in Brekh'cha. Or when you rolled in and—" Kel swallowed suddenly, heart pounding in his chest. He couldn't do this. He couldn't have a civil conversation. Not right now. "The answer's no, herodon."

The herodon studied him, unblinking. Then he dipped his head. "Very well."

The sound of a catapult being launched made Kel jump. He whirled around to see a black-haired regalite in a cloak standing beside Kel's catapult. "Nice!" The regalite whistled, hands on his hips as he squinted into the distance. "That went far."

Kel followed the regalite's gaze as a pouch sailed past the town tower. "What do ya think you're doing, regalite?"

"Testing out your catapult. Which happens to be pretty well-built, by the way."

"What—but you—" Kel tightened his fists again. Was it normal to just test out the equipment? "So you like my contraption—eh, lad?"

"Yeah, it's not bad. For using my design, anyway." The regalite

191

began cranking the catapult again. "You've really brought out the potential. How did you make it so precise?"

"Eh…" Clearly no apology was coming. "It's your design?"

"M-hm. About a month ago I put this on paper and sold it to Delóren's archives. He must've leased it to public commons to pay some bills." He chuckled. "Didn't think anyone would build it so proficiently, though."

Kel's cheeks were tingling again. He shrugged. "I'm a precise stone."

"Obviously." The man stood back, rubbing his chin. He set his other hand on his hip, cocking his head. "Seriously, how *did* you get it so precise?"

"Eh, I've some experience building and sanding surfboards." Kel indicated the surfboards with his chin. "Micro differences in their curvature meant the difference between catching a wave and flipping over."

"So you had to be exact…but how can you spot the micro differences?"

"I got a feel for it over time." Kel shrugged again. "Been doing this for centuries, y'know."

"Centuries?" The regalite's eyebrows flew up. "Okay. That's pretty impressive."

"Aye." Kel was beginning to feel more confident. He rolled his shoulders, a smile twisting his lips. "That it is."

The man hesitated—then thrust out his hand. "Name's Siege. I'm the big techno-mercenary around these parts. You may have heard of me—or not, if you're as far away as Brekh'cha."

Kel took the hand—and Siege shook it vigorously. "Afraid I know nothing of you."

"Well, I figured." Siege turned to the market square. His eyes wandered across the contraptions, darting between merchants. He rubbed his chin again, lips parted. "Tell you what."

Kel grinned. A proposition was coming—he could sense it. "Shoot."

"Whatever anyone else has offered you—I'll double it."

"Aye. But you'd better be careful about that." Kel was getting in the mood things. He crossed his arms. "One of my customers is King Delóren himself."

"Delóren? I work with him." Siege muttered something under his

192

breath, rolling his eyes. "Should've known he'd go for you. Geolite craftsmanship is rare around here."

"It's in demand, eh?"

"Right. And I need a good manufacturer." Siege stuck out his hand again. "So? Will you work for me?"

Kel shrugged. Should he negotiate for more? Double seemed reasonable. "Seeing as I'm using your designs..."

"Exactly. I'll keep you supplied with blueprints for the best products. You just produce them." Siege cocked his head. "Is it a deal or not?"

Kel rubbed his chin with a thumb and forefinger. Why not? He hadn't a scratch of negotiating savvy anyhow. And this was his first real offer!

"Well?"

Kel took the hand, his heart beating. This whole displaying contraptions thing might work after all. "Aye."

☼ ☼ ☼

ONE YEAR LATER (5970, 5TH MONTH)

"So there I was, trying to fix a wonky catapult. You've no idea the trouble it was causing." Kel leaned over the smooth marble table, hands spread. "One time the wheels fell off as it was firing. Rolling, clattering along the cobblestone! The vibrations were too much," he could barely keep from laughing, "poor thing couldn't throw a pebble!"

Siege chuckled. "Needed your magic touch."

"That's right. I went to work—and in no time it was perfect."

"Of course it was." Siege shook his head, leaning back in his seat. "Your last batch was excellent, by the way. I haven't had a single complaint."

"Great." Kel glanced at the bar. Even in what dim light the flames burning in porticos cast, he could still see the bartender arguing with a couple guests. Had their order been forgotten? "I've been experimenting with a new sanding technique too. What do you think?"

"It's good." Siege leaned in, putting his elbows on the table. "By

193

the way, anything new or strange going on in Brekh'cha? Just curious."

That was a random question. Kel rubbed his chin. "Well, now that you mention it…aye. There's something mighty odd in the Northwestern Hollows."

"Is there?"

Kel pressed his lips together. How much should he say? "Now this is really geolite business…"

"Of course. But I have a healthy curiosity in this realm— particularly in the Hollows."

How had this never come up? "I hadn't noticed."

"That's because I've never asked you about it before. I've been feeling a bit more comfortable around you lately." Siege gave a light shrug with his shoulders. "Guess you got on my good side."

Kel grinned. "Aye."

"I mean, it's not like I would be meeting you in a Nicota pub otherwise—now would I?" A smile tugged at Siege's lips. "This is a bit of a ways from Newílderashe."

Kel suspected this straightforwardness was more significant than he knew. How many people did Siege trust, really?

"So…" Siege drew out the word, his smile fading. "What's odd? Isn't that where the dragon roams?"

Kel cleared his throat. "Funny you should mention that. As many stones believe the dragon's involved."

"Really?" Siege blew out his breath. "Lovely. What's going on?"

"It's a young lad, actually. A black-haired regalite, like you—but younger."

Now Siege's eyebrows went even higher. "*Really.*"

"Aye. Now we spotted a regalite like him six years ago, you understand…" Kel gestured with one hand, averting his eyes. "We didn't really know what to do with him—and truth be told, I don't know what became of him."

"Except now he's back."

"Aye." Kel swallowed, glancing at the other tables. No one was paying them any mind. He lowered his voice anyway. "You understand, we were tasked with helping a hunter named Titanius hunt the boy. And it didn't sit well with many geolites."

"Oo. I'll bet it wouldn't." Siege grimaced. "What happened?"

"No one knows. At least, no one *says* they know. There are

194

rumors of a deal made with the council—but rumors are rumors, you know?"

Siege nodded. "About as reliable as that catapult you were telling me about."

"Right. So I'm leaning toward another answer. One whispered rather than spoken."

"And that is?"

Kel kept his voice low. "I think it's a ghost."

"A ghost?" Siege gave a "hm." "That seems random."

"Not when you consider our actions. We practically turned him over to Titanius—gave the hunter a map so he could maneuver the Northwestern Hollows—so we're guilty of the regalite's blood as much as he."

"But you don't know if Titanius caught him." Siege put his fingers together, leaning forward. "Or even if he was killed."

"Eh, but come on." Kel leaned back, cocking his head. "What d'ya *think* happened?"

"I don't know." Siege laced his fingers, then set his chin on them. "But it seems a bit far-fetched to call him a ghost."

"Think about it. He's back to haunt us for helping Titanius. And there's more." Now Kel's voice was a whisper. "People say he's leading unwary travelers to the Flame Dragon's lair."

"They—" Siege cut himself off, swallowing. "Do they have evidence? That also seems far-fetched."

"That it does. But it's mighty strange." Kel put two fingers on the table, moving them like they were legs walking. "People follow this boy for a few days and never come back. Last report sees them going northwest. Toward Old Ticora."

"Okay…" Siege swallowed, narrowing his eyes. "The dragon."

"Aye." Kel spread his hands. "So that's it. The boy's haunting us. Some're calling him 'the guide.' And we're warning foreigners to steer clear of the Northwestern Hollows."

"Makes sense." Siege was a wee bit subdued. "I guess it's a theory."

"That it is." The techno-mercenary's behavior was mighty odd. Kel narrowed his eyes. "What about you? Why're you so interested in Brekh'cha?"

"Well…" Siege inhaled deeply, leaning back. He let one palm slide across the table as he brought it back to himself. "That's a fair question, I suppose."

"Aye."

"And…" Siege licked his lips. He put his fingers together, his thumbs spinning around each other. "Yeah, I should probably tell someone. And you're about the best candidate, I guess. No one's going to question you, since you live in Brekh'cha—right?"

Who would question Kel about Siege? "Alright then."

"And I need to tell someone my identity in case I die…" Siege blew out his breath, looking past Kel. "I trust you. So yeah, why not."

Siege was telling him his identity? "I knew 'Siege' wasn't your real name."

"Yep. It's a title I got for my antics. Once laid siege to a castle by myself, you know." Siege arched an eyebrow. "That was a pain in the butt."

"I know. People have been telling me about you."

"Right. Then you know my real identity is a secret."

"Aye." Kel shifted in his seat, swallowing. "But you're telling me now?"

Siege raised his finger. His eyes darted around the bar—and he lowered his voice. "I'm telling *only* you." He leaned in, enunciating his next words. "Understood?"

"Understood." Kel put his hands on the table, palms down. Why did this seem so important? "Your secret's safe with me, lad."

"Yep. I know." Siege hesitated, mouth open—then licked his lips. "And anyway, I have to tell *someone*."

Kel nodded. "Fire away then."

Siege nodded—probably more to himself than Kel. Kel had rarely seen him so nervous. The techno-mercenary held his hands out, as if they could explain for him. "Now my past is a bit complicated…"

22 DESPERATION

A breeze rustled the plains, tugging at the ears of impatient herodons. The army snorted, some clawing at the ground with their feet.

Hrossar stood before them—hands behind his back, chin raised. "I empathize with your complaints. We all have families to feed. And money is essential for that."

No response. Most still stood at attention, but a few were murmuring to each other.

"I desire to erase your concerns. To inform you that we have a new employer." Hrossar inhaled deeply, closing and opening his fists. "Unfortunately, I cannot."

The murmurs grew. These were Hrossar's soldiers—but every division had its limits. Now some of his herodons were shaking their heads.

"I realize many of you are operating off the last of your savings. So I would not blame any soldier if you join another company." Though Hrossar's voice carried, it was soft enough to blend with the wind. "I would not burden you with my standards."

"We will die with you!" One of the herodons stepped forward. "You and your father have led us through every battle! Our loyalty will never fade."

Murmurs rippled through the army. It seemed others were not so certain.

"If I cannot find a job in a month's time..." Hrossar cleared his throat, and the murmurs stilled, "If I do not find us a job that will

197

replenish our savings, I will dismiss those who wish to leave. There will be no shame in your exit."

Silence. A few herodons exchanged glances.

"However, it is my understanding that most of you would wish to continue with me. Therefore," Hrossar raised a clawed finger, "I will redouble my efforts at finding a paying assignment for us. One that aligns with justice."

"And if you cannot?"

Another herodon had stepped forward. He fixed his fierce eyes on Hrossar, fists curled. "We will not watch you and your family starve."

Hrossar inhaled deeply. "My family is my concern."

"No, General." The soldier straightened, crossing his arms over his chest in a salute. "We will not abandon you."

"I appreciate the sentiment." Hrossar replaced his hands behind his back. He gave a slight shake of his head. "These are difficult times, my friends. The correct path is not always clear."

"We will stand by you—whatever you decide."

"No. I will not force you to starve for me. Consider this—" Hrossar swallowed suddenly, closing his eyes. He could not betray weakness. He'd even rehearsed this speech. "Consider this your one month's notice. Assuming I do not find a job from an honorable employer, I am dismissing all of you."

A few jaws dropped. But no gasps—this had not been difficult to see coming. Some herodons shifted their footing.

"It is the least I owe you." Hrossar dipped his head—then crossed his arms over his chest. "Thank you for fighting by my side for so long."

☆ ☆ ☆

Moonlight poured in from the window, gleaming on Father's snout. He sat in the armchair, eyes reflecting the firelight. "And that is all you told them."

"Correct."

Father studied him, expressionless. The fire crackled, sending sparks beside them. "You are a bold one."

"I have little choice." Hrossar spread his hands. "They cannot

198

starve—nor would I expect them to."

"Indeed." Father rubbed his chin with his thumb and forefinger. "But how will you survive?"

"I am not certain. Even if you were to allow me to shift to paid debate, there are few honorable employers left."

A smile tugged at Father's lips. "So you *have* been investigating that avenue."

"Mildly. It will not help me." Hrossar expelled a sigh, eyes on the fireplace. "I am trapped, Father."

"Trapped by what?"

Hrossar's brow furrowed. "Pardon?"

"What traps you, my son?"

Hrossar indicated the window with his hand. "Newílderashe. The humanites on the plains. They only pay for their selfish ends."

"And why does that trap you?"

"Because…" What was Father getting at? "When you left debates to take up mercenary work, you told me we would fight for the oppressed. Defend the helpless." Hrossar leaned forward in his chair, baring his fangs. "That we would be heroes for justice."

"I did."

"And here we are. The land can hardly wait to be rid of us—and most of us could care less about justice. Only a few have such conviction."

"And?"

"Certainly, the humanites are upholding their end of the contract and not attacking our dwellings. But for how much longer?" Hrossar sat back in his chair, heaving a sigh. "The war expired years ago. And here we are, having far outstayed our welcome."

"So what traps you?"

Hrossar opened his mouth—then hesitated. *What.* His father was attempting to teach him something. "I suppose it is not a set of circumstances so much as a mentality."

"Or," Father raised his finger, "a lack of one."

Hrossar's brow furrowed. "Explain."

"Imagine your kinsmen were all as honorable as you. They would only accept jobs in alignment with justice."

"Correct."

"What would become of the dishonorable kings in this land?"

Hrossar scratched his snout. This was an excellent point. "They would be inferior militarily."

"Precisely. And being unable to properly defend themselves, they would fail where the just kings succeeded. Injustice requires strength to prevail."

"As does justice." Hrossar nodded, eyes on the fire. "But our kinsmen are not honorable."

"And so wickedness prevails. For we have no *vision* of justice."

Vision. Hrossar gave a soft snort. "Some time ago I was approached by a humanite who claims to have vision."

"Ah, yes. Cisera. He approached me as well—no doubt hoping I could influence your decision." Father chuckled. "I informed him that his vision was no better than the mud which occasionally sticks to my clawed toes."

"And roughly as clear." Hrossar shook his head. "But you were saying?"

"We have no vision. And others manipulate us for it. Therefore only the dishonest thrive," Father clutched at the air with his fingers, the firelight glinting off his claws, "and our race slowly corrupts itself—until all that is left are greed and discontent."

Hrossar tapped one armrest with his claw, staring into the fire. "And that will make us clay in the hands of opportunists."

"Precisely. So what traps you?"

Hrossar met Father's gaze. "Lack of vision. My kinsmen are blind."

Father dipped his head. "And what can be done to ameliorate the situation?"

Hrossar shrugged. "I suppose—" he shook his head, baring his fangs. "I don't believe anything can be done, Father."

"Anything?"

"No."

Father stared at him, hands on his armrests. The older herodon inhaled deeply, chest rising. "Perhaps."

Hrossar growled, his fists curling. "What does one do? Against the wicked and stubborn of the land. They rise up like a tide, threatening to engulf the plains and crush all against them."

"Against *them*?" Father shook his head. "The true battle is against an idea. We must give them vision. We must—"

"How?" Hrossar threw up his hands. "How, Father? When you won't even allow me to debate? Not that it would help—I would face the same corruption—but what am I to do?"

Father stared at him. Hrossar had never cut him off like this. The former general clenched his jaw, eyes on Hrossar. "You must lead by example."

"And what is that accomplishing?" Hrossar pointed out the window, where a few stars shone through the clouds. "If I and my family starve for our vision, what will that tell others?"

"And what will it tell them if you compromise?" Father leaned forward, lacing his fingers. "You would feed fuel to their fire."

"I would *live!*" Hrossar clutched at the air with both hands, snarling. His voice was hoarse, like crunching gravel. "I would live, father! And my family would have something to eat! As would you."

"But at what cost?" Father shook his head. "This is not how I taught you to live, my son. Not without vision."

"Perhaps." Hrossar sat back, averting his eyes. Of course Father was right. And Hrossar would sooner die than compromise. "But what of my family? I have a duty to them, do I not?"

"You do. And—" Father hesitated, jaws parted. "I do not have a full answer, Hrossar. This must be your choice. But remember how you impact society."

"I also provide for you, Father."

"Not anymore."

Hrossar's eyebrows went up. "Pardon?"

"Yes, I—" Father sighed. "I meant to tell you sooner. The doctor informed me earlier today that my wounds have sufficiently healed for mobility." He put a hand on his stomach, his face softening. "I can roll again."

"Excellent." Hrossar scratched his snout. "However, would you not still be under my care? I doubt you can engage in combat yet."

"I am joining the New Homeland Scout Team."

Hrossar's jaw dropped. That meant—"You are departing from Newílderashe."

"Indefinitely. I will be searching the world for a new homeland for the herodons."

"And your application has been accepted?"

"A month ago. They were waiting for my health to improve."

Hrossar's muscles tightened. "A month ago. Why did you not inform me of this?"

"That is a difficult question." Father put his hands on his lap,

201

leaning forward. His eyes fell to Hrossar's feet. "I did mean to tell you earlier, son. But we have been together our whole life." his voice dropped so low, Hrossar could barely hear it over the crackling of the flames. "This is…difficult."

Hrossar swallowed. This was not like Father. "I will be strong, Father."

"I know you will. I am confident in you. Nonetheless…" Father laced his fingers, glancing at the door. "You will have difficult decisions, Hrossar. I do not believe things will improve. And if you abandon your post…"

Abandon? "I must provide, Father. And I will not compromise."

"And who will fight for justice?" Father held out his hands, palms up. "These are your decisions to make. I understand you must care for your family, but…" he sighed. "I cannot dictate your course. What you will do, you will do."

That was remarkably resigned. Hrossar's eyebrows rose. "And you?"

"I will be scouting for a new homeland. Tonight, of course." Father got up stiffly, hands leaning on the armrests. "They wish for me to leave as soon as possible."

"Naturally."

"I had hoped…" Father licked his snout, eyes on the door. "I had hoped I could return to a better land. But I do not know what will I find when I come back."

Hrossar stood, then made his way to the door. "That is not something I may be able to control." He opened it, keeping his eyes on Father. "Though I will not disappoint you, Father."

Father stared at him, jaws slightly open. His voice was barely a whisper. "I know, son."

Then Teros Feodon, former general of legions, curled into a ball—and burst into a roll, speeding out the door and through the dry grass as moonlight gleamed on his rubber hide.

☼ ☼ ☼

202

"Father!" The herodon girl ran to Hrossar, and he plucked her into his arms. He grinned, spinning her around in a circle, then set her on the couch. She hopped up and down, pleading with clasped fingers. "Father, any treats?"

"Not this time, Nhera." Hrossar's smile faltered. "I have been busy searching for a job. I will attempt to secure some treats on my next outing."

"Look out! I'll tackle you!" A herodon boy ran up to Hrossar, tackling his stomach. "Got you!"

"Agh!" Hrossar tumbled to the floor, voice a hoarse whisper. "I have fallen. Victim to the strength of a mighty warrior."

"And a savvy diplomat." The son raised his chin, making a flourish with one hand. "Only the most sophisticated of debaters challenge me."

"Indeed. Simply arranging your bedtime each night is a challenge, Shoran." A smile tugged at Hrossar's lips as he got to his feet. "Though I hope you have not been troubling your mother in the last two weeks."

"Not overly." Shoran shrugged. "Well, *I* don't think so."

"You've been troubling *me*, brother!" Nhera pointed at him. "Don't deny it! Tell Father you've been picking fights again!"

Shoran gave another shrug. "Possibly."

Hrossar gave a snort. He could not humor such behavior. "Fights should not be needlessly 'picked.'"

"I know." Shoran averted his eyes, murmuring, "I'll behave better."

"Will you be gone as long next time, Father?" Nhera licked her snout, wrapping her claws around his arm. "It's been almost three weeks since we last saw you."

"Your father must work for food," Hrossar explained, voice softening. "You know this, Nhera. Our savings have been depleted."

"And if you don't find a job, we starve." Shoran lay on the ground, eyes closed as if he was dead. His croaking gurgle was fairly convincing.

"Except you always find a job—so we're not worried." Nhera took a seat on the couch, looking up at Hrossar. "You're the best, Father."

203

Hrossar's cheeks warmed. "I appreciate that, Nhera."

"It's true." Nhera cocked her head. "So how long will you be gone?"

Hrossar spotted Holshe peering at him from behind the corner. She was cleaning a pot, and her eyes searched his. He gave a small shake of his head.

"Father?"

Hrossar sighed, closing one fist. "I am not certain."

"Maybe you'll find a job that only takes a few days." Nhera clasped her hands again. "That might still pay a lot, right?"

Hrossar took a seat beside her. This was difficult to explain. "Nhera..."

"Your father is stressed, Nhera." Holshe stepped around the corner, drying her hands with a towel. "Give him some time to himself."

"And by time to himself," Shoran sprang to his feet, "you mean time with you, correct?"

Holshe half-smiled. "Correct."

A knock on the door. Hrossar arched an eyebrow. "Were you expecting company, Holshe?"

She shook her head. "Not that I recall."

A second knock—harder this time. "I am here to see Hrossar Feodon!"

A male humanite voice. Curious.

"I have a job offer!"

Holshe's eyes widened. Hrossar turned to the door. "Please enter."

The door opened—and in walked a bald humanite in shining metal armor. Middle-aged or younger, as far as Hrossar could tell. The man fixed his gaze on Hrossar, lips pursed.

"You are?"

"Titanius Liege," the man took a small bow, "a Hunter. Here with a job offer—assuming you're still searching for one."

Hrossar glanced at Holshe. She gave a barely perceptible nod. Hrossar cleared his throat. "Children, follow your mother to the kitchen."

Titanius grinned—though it made Hrossar less comfortable for some reason. "Thank you for giving me your time."

Hrossar inhaled deeply, waiting as Titanius took a seat in the chair opposite him. Holshe and the children moved into the kitchen—although he had little doubt they would be eavesdropping.

"My understanding is you've been searching for a job." Titanius set his elbows on his knees, leaning forward. "Not only that, but you're an honorable herodon."

Hrossar dipped his head. "That is correct."

"Excellent. I am willing to pay you and your herodons enough to sustain each of you for a year."

Hrossar's eyebrows went up. "I have quite a sizable army at my disposal. Where would you acquire these funds?"

"My employer." Titanius raised his hand. "Whose identity is confidential. What you need to know is that you would be well compensated."

This was highly suspicious. "For what?"

"A brief excursion to Brekh'cha."

Hrossar stiffened. His nerves tingled, and he swallowed. "That is impossible. We have a treaty with them."

"Which you will not be violating." Titanius leaned forward again, his lips curling. "I've studied the pathetically vague treaty between your people and the geolites. It clearly allows raiding for the purposes of acquiring any non-geolite individual of interest."

"Yet we would be fighting geolites." Hrossar inhaled deeply, closing his eyes. "No."

"Think carefully, Hrossar."

Hrossar kept his eyes closed. Could he really return to Brekh'cha? After all these years? His stomach knotted at the thought. What would Father say?

"Your army—your family—would not have to worry about food for quite some time."

"And if you lie?" Hrossar's eyes opened, and he clenched his jaw. "That is a great deal of money."

Titanius plucked a small pouch hanging on his belt. He tossed it to Hrossar, then crossed his arms. Leaning back, he lowered his voice. "An advance. To prove the fidelity of my employer."

Hrossar pulled the strings open, trying to keep his fingers steady. Gold coins glittered inside, and he blinked. Enough to cover the next month. For every one of his herodons.

He glanced at the doorway to the kitchen. Nhera's eyes and snout poked out from behind it. She gasped and disappeared into the kitchen.

Hrossar turned back to the hunter. "How long?"

"Only a few days—at most. Assuming you are as competent as is claimed." The hunter's lips curled again. "Which I assume is the case."

"Naturally. However—" Hrossar closed his eyes. Could he not simply accept the task? Just this one instance—ignore the possibility of a dishonorable cause. It would be so simple to say yes...

Hrossar's eyes flew open. No. The simple way led to destruction for a reason. "What is the identity of your quarry?"

"I cannot divulge their identity. Suffice to say the individual is worthy of my pursuit."

"That is not enough information."

"Irrelevant." Titanius crossed his arms, metal armor gleaming in the sunlight filtering through their windows. "Assist me or reject my offer."

Something did not seem right. "If you cannot tell me who the quarry is, how do I know you are just?"

"Just? You want to know if—" spittle flew from Titanius's lips, and he slammed the armrest with a fist. "I am defined by justice."

Defined? Hrossar arched an eyebrow. "Indeed?"

"Every ounce of my being," Titanius enunciated his words between clenched teeth, "every fiber of will in the marrow of my skeletal structure—is devoted to the implementation of justice." He formed a fist. "Where there are fools who believe they will escape justice, I am there—in their nightmares, plaguing their steps. Where there are the lax, the incompetent, the pathetic, I will be their shadow—calling them to account." His face reddened with rage. "I—am—Titanius!"

Incredible. Hrossar had rarely seen such passion. "Fascinating."

"You doubt me?" A vein was bulging in Titanius's temple, and he thrust a finger at Hrossar. "Proceed to question those who have worked for me. Question them and see! Though I am loathed by the unjust, even they will testify. I do not lie!" He slammed the armrest again. "Ever!"

"Very well." Hrossar arched an eyebrow. If this was a deception, it was a bold one. "But is your cause just?"

"It is of the greatest justice." Titanius leaned in, pinching air between his thumb and forefinger. "Of an individual who escaped justice by a hair ten years ago. He must pay. He must not be allowed to walk free."

"And you are assigned to his case?"

"Absolutely."

"By whom?"

Titanius straightened, hands on his legs. "As I stated previously, I cannot divulge that information. You must trust me."

Trust a humanite Hrossar had never met before. "You realize I can investigate your reputation."

"I welcome it." Titanius raised his chin. "Investigate away."

Curious. The Hunter truly seemed as though he had nothing to hide. If he could not divulge several key details…was that simply the preference of his employer?

"Do you still doubt me?"

Hrossar gazed into the hunter's eyes. A great deal of cruelty lay there…but not dishonesty. This man truly believed he fought for justice.

"Well?"

Hrossar shifted in his seat, closing his fists. His family would not starve—his herodons would be provided for. And the hunter claimed it would only require a few days in Brekh'cha…

"Time is of the essence, Hrossar. Will you work for me or not?"

Hrossar swallowed hard—then opened one fist, claws glinting in the sunlight. "When do I begin?"

THREE DAYS LATER (5970, 10TH MONTH, 1ST WEEK, 4TH DAY)

Siege squinted through the magnifying glass, raising the tripwire circle and metal line so they were aligned. Such tricky little pieces—especially at this scale. But they were important for his arm-mounted crossbow.

He shifted in his wooden chair, and it creaked. That thing needed to be replaced. The desk was a little wobbly too. Funny that he was making loads of money, but he couldn't bother replacing his own instruments. Ridiculous, actually.

"It's on the to-do list," he murmured, poking the metal thread through his tripwire circle. Almost perfect—

A knock at the door. He jumped—and the wire slipped out of the circular frame.

207

Great. Siege slammed the hook and line on the table. Was there no respect for privacy around here? "A bit busy."

"I have an urgent message from King Delóren."

Urgent? Really. Siege shook his head, rolling his eyes. "How urgent?"

"He says it deals with requested information."

Requested information. Siege's lips parted, his brow furrowing. What would—oh. *That* information.

"Shall I slide it under the door?"

That seemed like a good option. Blowing out his breath, Siege ran a hand through his hair. "Sure. Why not."

A white envelope slipped under the door. The king's seal gleamed on it in sunlight streaming from the polished windows.

Well—no sense putting it off. Siege got up, his chair creaking. Yeah, he needed a new one. He stepped over to the letter, bent down and retrieved it. Was this about—?

He took it over to his desk and sat, unfolding it. If this was another dead end…

Siege,

As I recall, you've requested constant updates on any unusual activities in or pertaining to the realm of Brekh'cha. And I have just received word that an army of herodons, led by General Hrossar Feodon, is rolling its way to Brekh'cha. Peculiar, no?

What's particularly interesting is that General Feodon objected to the war—the one the herodons waged against the geolites. As you probably know, it concluded six and a half years ago. No herodon has been seen near Brekh'cha since. Until now, of course.

I don't believe General Feodon is picking a fight. He objected to the war in the first place—why would he kindle a new one? No, it is my suspicion something else is going on. But it is beyond me to speculate what.

Assuming you find this information useful, I'll expect another of your designs within the month. As always, it is my sincere pleasure doing business.

King Franz Delóren

One ruler over Dovrenol of Newílderashe

Siege folded up the note and set it on his desk. Well. That was unusual indeed.

He set his chin on his thumb and forefinger, staring out the window. This was not what he'd been looking for...or was it?

He blinked. What if—no. Could it?

Best not to get his hopes up. He stood up quickly, his chair creaking. Striding over to the closet, he cleared his throat. Nope. He was being too optimistic. It was optimal to investigate. See what was going on. That's all.

He pulled his black cloak from the rack, twirling it around and tying its cords to his tunic. He donned the hood, eyes on the ceiling as he considered. What would he need?

Food would be unnecessary. He knew where to find some. His cloak already had the necessary money and traveling supplies—

The barbed hook. That was important—if he ran into Titanius. He strode over to the desk and jerked open the bottom drawer. Digging through metal objects, he plucked the small silver hook he'd designed from the back of the drawer. Perfect.

Siege tucked it into the inside of his cloak, straightening. What else? The crossbow?

He glanced at the arm-mounted crossbow laying on his desk. Nah, too much trouble to get it fixed in time. He needed to be there *now* if he wanted to beat the herodons.

He blew out his breath, running a hand through his hair. The sticks?

Yep. They were perfect. Siege turned to the closet, yanking it open again. He pulled out a pair of long sticks tucked into an x-shaped sheath. He slipped the sheath's straps over his cloak, narrowing his eyes. Anything else?

The stone. Couldn't forget that. How else was he getting there?

Siege knelt down and peeled a floorboard up. Beneath the floorboard lay a small box. He took it out and set it beside the floorboard—then undid its latches with unsteady fingers. It had been so long...

Inside was a ruby no bigger than his palm. Siege pulled out the stone, turning it in his fingers. Sunlight glittered in its crystalline depths, and he noticed the "B" inscribed on it. "Brekh'cha," he whispered, "here I come."

MORE FROM IAN VROON

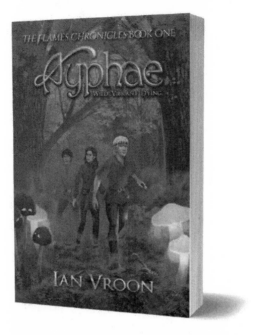

THE FLAMES CHRONICLES, BOOK ONE

Reisor woke up seven years ago with no memory. He found himself in a land of glowing flowers, mushroom houses and psychedelic spores. No one can enter or leave Ayphae—so Reisor is stuck here. He has to cope, and he has to care for his siblings...who also have no memory. They have only dreams, flashbacks—fragments of thoughts they can't explain.

But now the land is withering. Mushrooms are crumbling to ash, trees turning to mush—and no one knows why.

Enter the aiethepa spore. This fungus grows fast and thick throughout Ayphae. No one knows what it does, and no one can open it. Some blame it for the withering—others think it will breathe life into the land.

Ayphae is all they know. But if they can't crack this mystery, it may be the last thing they remember.

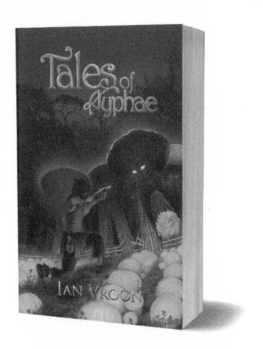

THE FLAMES CHRONICLES, PREQUEL TO BOOK ONE

Mushrooms that fly, spin, or stomp in a beat. Flowers that light up in ripples. A land where farming is the highest occupation and caterers are celebrities. Welcome to Ayphae.

All events and characters in *Ayphae* find their beginnings here. Joven Marshalltoe, a responsible farmer whose path will take him places he could have never dreamed. Nickolar Elegard, the sensitive ranger whose convictions will change his path. And May Evelar, the exuberant field scientist—whose goals are to discover more of Ayphae's secrets while maintaining respectability. All three paths will cross in time.

This compilation of short stories can be read before or after *Ayphae*—and though both stand alone, *Tales of Ayphae* is a great introduction to *Ayphae*.

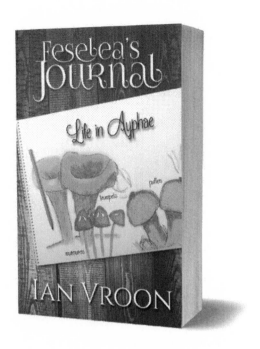

THE FLAMES CHRONICLES, THE WORLD OF AYPHAE

Seven years ago Feselea woke up with no memory of her past. Determined to understand the mystical mushroom-filled world around her, she picked up a journal at a convenience store and began writing. From her loneliness to her relationships, from thieves to getting lost, from scientific inquiries to investigations into the sentience of mushrooms, Feselea's Journal records her seven years in this new world.

More than a story—imagine discovering what day-to-day life would be like in Ayphae through the eyes of Feselea. What would you smell, what you would taste and touch? You'd try your best to adjust to the new life, but you'd need to figure out what to do and what not to do.

This is what makes a fantasy world real—experiencing life in a strange land through the eyes of the character…until the land is less strange and just a little more like home to us. Until we can reach out and touch it. Close our eyes and imagine ourselves standing there. It's what fantasy is all about. Total immersion in the created world.

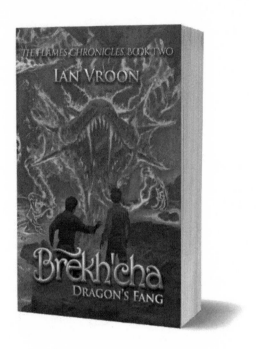

THE FLAMES CHRONICLES, BOOK TWO

Deep in Brekh'cha's chambers of shifting gravity and magma, through winding tunnels of metal and flame, roams a dragon. But this is no ordinary dragon. It is made of fire, its breath a purple mist that becomes the bitter thoughts of those who inhale it.

Wandering through Brekh'cha are the three siblings—Reisor, Feselea and Dane—on their way to Caltswahn. They seek refuge, their lost parents—and answers to their unknown past.

But they are not alone.

The hunter Titanius is here, prowling the caverns of Brekh'cha in search of them. He knows their past, their weaknesses—and he has hired an army of mercenaries to help him. Even the residents of Brekh'cha—stone creatures called geolites—are wary of him.

Enter Siege, the techno-mercenary who laid siege to an entire castle by himself. He has an interest in the siblings and their hunter—but for what? Who is he, really? No one knows—but his actions could influence the chase. In fact, he could change everything

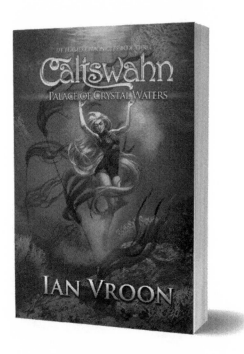

THE FLAMES CHRONICLES, BOOK THREE

Reisor is supposed to be a hero—but he doesn't even know what that is! All he knows is the desperation he feels—protecting his siblings, trying not to let everyone down—fear drives his actions. What's the difference between desperation and heroism?

Zyal, the lovely princess of Caltswahn, can see how weak Reisor is. She has the strength to be a hero—but no one will let her. Why can't he be more like that?

Then there's the Master Reabehd. A hyper-intelligent squid whose tentacles stretch out for miles. He guards a treasure that, though sought by all, may be worse than death. He sees Reisor's desperation and Zyal's frustration as an opportunity to complete his perfect plan.

For unlike the foolish schemes of mortals, the Reabehd's plans never fail.

INTERESTED IN MORE? THE STORY CONTINUES IN BOOK TWO,
BREKH'CHA: DRAGON'S FANG.

READ *BREKH'CHA,* CHAPTER ONE

TWO YEARS AGO

Thunder rolled across the night. Massive boulders soared through a lightning-streaked sky, crashing with stone-shattering booms into the city's wall.

Before the wall stood rows of soldiers. With each crash, debris pelted their armor like stone raindrops. Still they stood without speaking, beating their armor—taunting the city. Drumming their shields with their swords, stomping the muddy grass with spears and boots. Soaked with rain.

On the wall soldiers were shouting. Catapults cranked as men ran to and fro. Archers loosed a volley of deadly arrows. Still the army before them did not break rank or cry out.

"What do they want?"

A soldier turned to his commanding officer. "We don't know!" He pointed at the army. "We have no idea where they came from!"

Lightning silhouetted them as a boulder pierced the wall. More cries.

"Keep firing! They cannot lay siege so easily!"

"Yes sir!"

The clanging of a thousand breastplates rose in pitch with the rain—the defiance of an unknown army staking claim to an impenetrable city. As defenders pointed and yelled—catapults firing on both sides, boulders crashing, lightning fracturing the night— none noticed a shadow scaling the eastern parapet.

He rolled over the wall as a boulder landed meters away. Coming to a crouch, he raised an arm to shield himself from the debris. Not bad so far. But how long until they noticed?

He adjusted his black hood, scanned the landing—then crept

along the inside wall, ascending a staircase. Perfect. He leapt to the first landing, rolled to his feet and paused. Had someone spotted him?

He narrowed his eyes, pointed ears twitching. The defenders still seemed distracted...

No. The thunder was playing tricks on his ears. He was safe.

He leapt to the ground, ducked into an alley and took off. According to the map, the tower should be just beyond this intersection

Sidling up to the corner, he peeked around it. Two guards.

Lovely. He blew out his breath as thunder rolled, then picked up a stone. Tossing it over the guards, he waited for the clatter.

"What was that?"

He dashed past while their backs were turned. Way too easy.

Now for the tower. It loomed before him, lit windows adorning its face. He could start climbing at the right edge, but no, that was too visible...

Ah. A darkened window just meters away. He could climb into that...

Yes—perfect. He began scaling the wall, betting those soldiers were still investigating his lame diversion. A few more seconds—

Lightning! Very nearby. He blinked, black sparkles clouding his vision. Thunder clapped his ears as he punched out the window's glass. Punching was careless and loud—but he had to get inside! If someone had seen him...

He opened the window and rolled inside. The army diversion was working surprisingly well—but the longer he stuck around, the more likely his luck would run out.

That, or the rain. Not much difference either way.

His eyes adjusted to the pitch black, a fancy bedroom forming in the darkness around him. A large bed held a snoring couple.

He crept past, saluting them as he reached the door. He always liked married couples. So funny in their feuds, when they really loved each other. But this one was sleeping peacefully. Apparently some people could sleep through anything.

He opened the door a crack and peeked out. The hallway was quite clear. A few torches burned, but no major lighting.

Excellent. He ran past closed doors, shoes silent on the stone. Reaching the spiral staircase, he stopped to listen. No footsteps...

He sprinted up, counting stairs. Third floor…fourth floor…

Fifth floor. Now things would get more interesting.

The guards were doubled here, so he would have to find an empty room again. He knocked on one door. No sound from the other side—someone was asleep, or the place was empty. He picked the lock and slipped in.

These rooms looked so comfy. Obviously only the wealthy lived in this tower. He crept past another couple and made his way to the window.

Now that he was higher up, perhaps no one would notice a crawling shadow along the tower's edge. After all, people usually didn't look at the top of a tower when watching for intruders, right?

Or maybe that was just wishful thinking. Only one way to find out.

He leaned out the window—looked up, plotted his course—and began his climb up the wall. The stone was somewhat slippery, but his gecko gloves were working quite well. His climbing shoes still slipped a bit. That was unfortunate.

Reaching the top window—it was dark—he procured a protractor scalpel from his cloak. Cutting a circle in the window, he adjusted his footing—

His feet slipped. He skidded down the rock—*handhold, he needed a handhold!*—and barely found the windowsill with his free hand. Setting the protractor on the ledge, he tried for a better grip. These climbing shoes were still better than the last pair…

With a grunt, he hoisted himself back to his position. Now for the protractor—

He knocked it off the ledge instead of grabbing it—and watched it plummet to the courtyard below, raindrops rolling down his cheeks.

Really. Clinging to rocks near the top of some tower in a lightning storm, climbing shoes that didn't work as well on wet rocks—and now this. Most people would've failed right here.

He shook his head. Reaching into his cloak, he pulled out another protractor scalpel. That's why he had a spare.

Finishing the circle, he blew out his breath. Still shouldn't have happened.

Pop! The circle fell in as he tapped it. Reaching in, he felt for the latch and—*click*—pulled it. These openable windows. If they were just sealed shut, some break-ins would never occur! The risks people took just for occasional fresh air!

The window opened with a creak—he froze, pointed ears perked. Silent inside. He leapt in, lightning flashing behind. Closing the window, he checked for residents. This bedroom was empty.

The lounge was supposed to be nearby. The king would be there.

He tucked the protractor scalpel in his cloak, reaching the door. Opening it quietly, he peeked out. No one in the hallway.

So much for security. They must've figured the lower floor detachments would do their job and devoted more manpower to the siege. Not a terrible idea—unless they knew what was going on.

He crept along the hallway to a large room. A fancy yet cozy chamber with torches, carpeting and a fireplace. The crackling fire blended with distant peals of thunder. Nice lounge.

And reclining on the sofa, back facing him, was the target.

"Hello, Ilár."

Ilár sprung from the sofa and spun to face him. Scanning his cloak, he swallowed. "Who—who are you?"

"Interesting question." He grasped his hood with one hand. "One that deserves an answer." Pulling back the hood, he narrowed his eyes. "Recognize me?"

Ilár scrutinized his black hair, blue eyes, narrow chin—and his eyes widened. "No—no, that's impossible—"

"Not impossible!" He advanced on Ilár, fists shaking. "Just unlikely."

"That can't—" Ilár stumbled back, shaking his head, "—that's not possible!"

"And yet here I am." He pointed at the king. "So where are they?"

Ilár swallowed, rubbing his bathrobe with his thumbs. Glancing back, he murmured, "I—I'm not sure what you're talking about—"

"Yes you are!" He raised his right forearm, where a grappling hook served as his gauntlet. "You know where this comes from!"

Ilár stared at the grappling gauntlet. "Yes—but I don't—"

"Enough stammering! You know where they went."

"I really don't—" Ilár stumbled backward again, nearing the balcony. Lightning silhouetted him as his shaking palm found the archway. "I'm—I'm sorry. I honestly don't know."

"How? They didn't contact you?"

The king shook his head violently. "Never."

"I don't believe you."

"Why would I lie?" He stepped backward onto the balcony, raindrops pelting him. "I have nothing to gain."

"Except my trust." He advanced on the retreating king. "Now tell me where they are."

"I can't!" Ilár was shouting over the thunder. "All I know is they disappeared!"

"That's not good enough!"

"No one knows where they are! No one—" Ilár backed into the railing and gasped, tumbling over the rail.

"Ilár!" Siege lunged after the king—but too late. He looked over the edge, searching the void below. "Nooooo!" He hung his head, gripping the railing. "No…"

He inhaled sharply, thunder cascading. The mission was a failure.

His body went rigid—was that a gasp? He spun to see a maid fleeing the lounge. He'd been spotted! Donning his hood, he calculated. Could he climb? No, too risky. They were aware of his presence—he might as well paint a target on his back.

He bolted through the lounge, down the hallway—trying to keep his footfalls quiet—and into the bedroom. Lightning illuminated the window as he closed the door.

Yanking open the wardrobe, he blew out his breath. This was a stupid idea.

He shoved his soaked arms through one of Ilár's robes, jerking it into place over his cloak. Actually, this whole mission was stupid. A desperate chance gone sour.

Scoffing, he made his way to the bed. "Ilár," he whispered, crawling beneath the covers, "I never wanted you dead."

He was so sure the king knew…

"In here!"

He froze. He was facing away from them. And Ilár's bathrobe covered *most* of his wet hair, right?

"Be silent." There was a "shh" and some footsteps. "There, see? The king is sleeping. There is no emergency."

He heard a woman's voice. "But that's—I know I saw—"

"Don't disturb us again." He heard the door creak. "Close that as quietly as possible. And next time you have a bad dream, keep it to yourself!"

"It wasn't—it wasn't a dream—"

"Yes it was. The king is right there." The door closed. Now there were only muffled voices.

He sighed. Apparently no one supposed an infiltrator would be stupid enough to crawl into the king's bed. *Hey look! What a wonderful hiding spot! No one will see me here!* Smirking, he began pulling off the covers—

"Wait a minute." He heard the door creak.

He flipped the covers back on. What now?

"Something's not right."

He was about the same size as Ilár...right—how could he forget. He needed to *sound* like he was asleep.

He started snoring. Everyone had a different snore—but maybe his would be close.

"Nevermind." The door shut again.

Snoring. He almost chuckled.

Throwing off the covers, he leapt from bed. He had to climb out *now*—before they found the body. Wrestling the bathrobe off—wet clothes could really stick—he procured a climbing line from his belt.

Tying the line to a bedpost, he perked his ears. Rappelling was noticeable, but he needed to move fast. Not that it mattered in the end—he had already failed.

Licking his lips, he jerked the knot in place. Ilár, why?

☆ ☆ ☆

Birds chirping. Rays of morning light silhouetted rows of immobile soldiers. Before them stood the city's wall, cracked and pocked with craters. A few guards milled before it, but the real conflict was happening before the silent army. The city's general and his advisor were arguing beside a catapult.

The erstwhile intruder observed from a distance, crouching in shrubbery. He spotted the general and his advisor, then squinted, zooming in closer. Like binoculars. His eyes were so convenient.

He saw their mouths move but couldn't pick up the words. He

perked his ears—there. Now they were tuned to that spot on the field.

"How is this possible?"

"It's—well, it would appear—"

"Are these the soldiers that besieged us!" Spit was flying from the general's mouth. "Is this the army that would lay us waste!"

"So far as we know, sir—"

"These are wooden dummies in armor! Machinated puppets!" He kicked one of the "hostile soldiers." Its head bobbed, but it didn't topple—courtesy of the pole holding it up. Some water spilled from a bucket on its back. "There's no life in them!"

"I know, sir—"

"How did these things move?" The general advanced on him. "I want to know how they stomped and fired catapults!"

"Sir!" Someone wearing an engineer's vest stepped from behind a catapult. "I think I have an explanation."

"Really!" The general raised his chin. "Let's hear it."

"The buckets, sir," the engineer began, "each one has a bucket on its back, and it's connected to a lever." He made motions. "When rain filled the buckets to a certain level, the lever would turn—and action would occur."

"Action? You mean catapults firing?"

"Firing, soldiers beating their armor, you name it." He spread his hands. "It's brilliant."

The general murmured something, pulling a leather pouch from his breast pocket. "That's unbelievable," he said, opening the pouch. He stuffed a brown wad in his mouth, then began chewing. "The brazenness—was everyone sleeping when he set this up?"

The advisor exchanged a nervous glance with his engineer. "It seems—it seems the culprit rolled the dummies in on catapults while the rain made it hard to see—it looked like an army marching up detachment by detachment. He must've looked like another soldier—"

"Are you serious?" The general spat on the ground. "So we have no idea who did this?"

"Sir!" Someone wearing a messenger's tunic ran out from the city. "Sir, we have a description!"

"A drawing?"

"Of the culprit, sir!" Gasping, the messenger held up a paper.

"The maid spotted him."

The general snatched it from him, chewing furiously. "This is a regalite. He's the one who killed the king?"

"Yes—yes sir."

His engineer studied the paper. "Then he must also be the one who created the siege."

"No." The general narrowed his eyes, then spat on the ground. "He *was* the siege."

☼ ☼ ☼

They were calling him "The Siege." The regalite who laid siege to an entire city and assassinated its king! What a brilliant maneuver! What a fiendish rogue! Keep a lookout!

On another day he might've laughed. But rolling in those armored dummies was a pain. As it was, he couldn't believe the whole scheme actually worked.

Except for the part where Ilár died instead of answering his questions...which made the whole thing a failure after all.

He clenched his fists, staring at a poster bearing his face. The maid had definitely spotted him. And of course she would have a photographic memory.

Tightening his hood, he surveyed the market square. Vendors were shouting their wares, shoppers were haggling for deals—no one noticed him yet. But he couldn't keep a hood on for the rest of his life.

He rubbed his chin. The whole kingdom would be looking for him.

He made his way down an alley, cloak swishing. What a disaster. His search was over. He needed to find some secluded corner of the world—

Wait. He stopped. What if he could turn the situation to his advantage? Make his notoriety work in his favor?

"The Siege"—sounded catchy.

No, no. Too long. People would probably abbreviate it to "Siege" anyway. Which—he cocked his head—actually sounded pretty good.

Siege. It was decided.

He looked over his shoulder, ears perked. The market square was bustling as guards shoved their way through. People were being checked. Soon they would come his way.

"Fine," he whispered, adjusting his cloak, "find me." He ducked around a corner in the alley. "Just not yet."

He scurried down the alley, footfalls silent on the cobblestone. First he needed to build his résumé.

✫ ✫ ✫

THE PRESENT

Dust rose along the plains as an armadillo-like creature rolled at breakneck speed. He skidded and bounced to a stop, uncurling into a standing position. Now straightened, he might have been mistaken for a human—if only his silhouette were seen. He spread his clawed fingers, sniffing the air with his armadillo snout. Gleaming in the bright sun, rubber-like hide covered the top of his muscled arms, the front of his legs, his head and his back. His chest was strong, gleaming like burnished bronze. A utility belt with pouches wrapped around his waist. His bare feet were spaced apart, claws digging into the browning grass.

A herodon, he was called. He served as a scout for his mercenary captain.

He spotted something near the horizon. A large cart, rolling along by itself. Dust rose behind it like mist from a lake on a cold day, distorting the plains beyond it. Everything seemed to shimmer in the heat, and the creature shook his head.

A mirage. That had to be it.

But the speed it was moving…had to be sixty miles an hour. Almost as fast as the herodon himself could roll. No cart could move that fast—even if horses were pulling it.

He shook his head. Had to be a mirage.

The herodon curled into a ball and rolled parallel to the cart, keeping his distance as he headed for camp. Grass crunched beneath as he accelerated. Mirage or not, that cart would not beat him.

☼ ☼ ☼

Dane stuck his elbow out the window, eyes half closed as the sun burned overhead. They hit a bump, but the spinnivan kept rolling. He let his breath out.

Man, this was boring. Day three of their stupid trip from Ayphae to—what was it again? Caltswahn, right? He didn't know. He just wanted to be there.

He let his eyes wander to the front seat, where his older brother Reisor was driving. Blonde hair, blue headband to match his tunic. Reisor wore the same thing literally every day. His brother actually *liked* the silence.

Dane tilted his head back, letting out an exasperated sigh. Seriously, *why* was this taking so long? He stuck his face out the window, the wind tearing through his mahogany hair. Nothing but plains stretching as far as the eye could see—though the way the heat made everything shimmer and warp was kind of cool.

Okay, enough of that. He turned to his left, where his sister Feselea sat in the other seat. Fes was asleep, head lolling from shoulder to shoulder with each bump. Straight red hair falling down her shoulders, her lips slightly parted. She looked so peaceful asleep.

He could change that. Dane tugged at her hair, and she yelped. "Dane!"

"What? Couldn't resist."

"I was finally asleep!" She growled in frustration, turning away from him. "I couldn't sleep last night with your snoring the whole ride—"

"Yeah, well what am I supposed to do about that?"

"Cut it out!" Reisor turned back to them from the driver's seat, gripping the steering wheel. "We are *not* going to argue about snoring again!"

"Why not?"

"Because you're both acting like kids!"

Dane crossed his arms. "You wanna run that by me again?"

"Yes. You're behaving like a *child*."

Dane's jaw clenched. "You're only a few years older than me, bro. And I'm twenty."

"So you say. But you're getting tied with basidiothread in ten seconds if you don't settle down."

"Settle down?" Dane's eyebrows shot up. "Are you kidding me? And how do you even *have* basidiothread? Isn't that from Ayphae?"

"Yeah. The Marden packed it in with our other supplies. He gave us plenty of food and material, remember?"

Dane did remember. He rolled his eyes. "Whatever."

"I'm serious. I will tie you up right now. I will stop this car—"

A massive bump. Dane and Fes knocked their heads against the ceiling, but Reisor—of course he had his seatbelt on—only jerked in place. A huge bag leapt out of the passenger seat as their spinnivan jerked sideways, tumbling out the window.

"My tarballs!"

Reisor slammed on the brakes, knuckles white against the steering wheel. They skidded to a stop, dust rising around them as Dane looked out the back window. The bag was still tied shut.

"Get them quickly," Reisor whispered, gritting his teeth, "and strap them into the passenger seat this time."

"Don't tell me what to do." Dane opened the door and hopped out in one fluid motion. The fact that his tarballs were in that seat was ridiculous. Just because he and Fes couldn't decide on who would get the passenger seat didn't mean Reisor should give it to a stupid bag. Reisor needed to back off from playing the parent.

Hang on. Something was wrong here.

He stopped, ears twitching. Nothing. He heard no insects, no birds—nothing.

He spun, scanning the plains. A breeze swirled the grass, ruffling his hair. Shouldn't there be insects or something? Maybe cicadas?

No, wait. There *was* noise. A dull, faint pounding, like marching.

Dane turned, searching the land. There—just on the horizon, he spotted a line of moving dots. Was that an army?

He squinted, willing his eyes to zoom in on the dots. The dots grew bigger in his vision, like he was looking at them through a telescope. Whoa! He gave a start, and they were dots again. He'd heard "zooming in" was something all regalite eyes could do—but every time he tried, it startled him. He shook his head and tried again.

There. He could see the markings on their glistening black hides, the notches and pouches on their belts. He saw their fangs gleaming in the sunlight, though the creatures reminded him more of human-like armadillos. They were marching as one, snouts held high.

"Dane, come on!" Reisor leaned out the window and beckoned. "How long can it take?"

Right. Dane needed to grab the tarballs. He took one step toward the bag—

And watched as a hole opened up and swallowed it.

"Dane?"

"Uh…" He took a tentative step. Dirt was falling back *up* into the hole, as if time had reversed. Now it was just a patch of dry grass on the plains.

The ground had eaten his tarballs.

Dane heard the spinnivan door open behind him. He turned as Reisor stepped out. "Dane, why—" his brow furrowed. "Where did your tarballs go?"

"I…I'm not sure." He turned to the spot, swallowing. "A hole opened up and, uh, they're gone."

"Gone? Like that?" Reisor scanned the plains, as if the bag would pop up somewhere. He let out an exasperated sigh, running a hand through his hair. "This is completely ridiculous."

"What's that on the horizon?"

Now Feselea was out of the spinnivan. She pointed toward the moving dots. "I think I see an army of some kind. Are they—" she fell as a hole opened beneath her, yelping.

Dane and Reisor lunged toward her—but too late. Dane stopped before the hole, peering into darkness as grains of dirt fell back into place. "Fes!"

"Feselea—" Reisor fell to his knees beside him, clutching his head. "No, no, no…" He growled in frustration, arms shaking. "No! How is this happening!"

"Give her back!" Dane was shouting at the ground, fists balled. "She's my sister!"

Their spinnivan jolted, cargo jostling as a bigger hole opened below it. They stumbled back, nearly falling as it tumbled into the darkness.

"Dane—" Reisor gasped as the plains swallowed him.

"Reisor!" Dane lunged for him—but no. His brother was gone too.

His eyes darted around the plains, and he raised his fists. "So that's it, huh." He leapt aside as a hole opened beneath his feet. "Oh, that's not how it works! You have to come and get me!"

Fissures were opening everywhere. He leapt to and fro, grass falling from beneath his feet. He wasn't going down that easily.

"I can keep this up all day!" He stuck his tongue out, barely dodging the next hole. "You'll never—"

Wait. Maybe the holes actually *went* somewhere. If he hopped in one…

Yep, that was a good move. He could find his siblings! He dove headfirst into the nearest hole.

Darkness. Sharp points scraped his arms and legs, and he bounced off what felt like a giant stem. Something bumped his leg hard—tumbling, tumbling down—then empty space for a second. He hit the ground on his feet—and pain like fire shot up his legs before he collapsed.

Rolling to a stop on his back, he tried to focus. Oh, man—that hurt. He drew in his breath, teeth gritted. The only thing he could see was bright daylight in the opening far above—and that was disappearing fast. Grains of dirt were rising all around him—he felt a slight tug on his body, but not enough to lift him—filling in the hole. In seconds, the light was gone.

Then he felt nothing.

☼ ☼ ☼

Siege narrowed his eyes and zoomed in on the herodon army. Their greaves sported mercenary markings. But what would they be doing out here? These were dangerous plains. Soon the holes would begin.

And where was their leader? There. A particularly bulky herodon led the army. His stride was confident, so Siege assumed he was experienced enough to know where he was going.

What? Right beside the herodon general—was that a humanite? And dressed in that armor…Siege knew that armor.

He zoomed in further. That face! Could it be? It'd been so many years—but there was no mistaking...

The humanite raised a hand, and the general followed. Herodons snorted, jostled their comrades, stomped the grass—then halted.

Smart. Right before the Pereth region. They definitely knew where they were going.

The humanite and general turned to face their army as Siege tuned his ears to them. Maybe he would get some answers.

"We have now reached what is commonly labeled the Brekh'cha Caldera's Pereth region, where holes may swallow armies whole." The humanite sneered at his army. "Make camp here—quickly—and at dusk we roll. I will supply you the coordinates shortly."

Yes, it was Titanius. But what was he doing hiring mercenaries? Unless he expected to fight an army, it made no sense.

"What about you?"

The general was addressing Titanius. Titanius arched an eyebrow. "The holes do not bother me, Hrossar. They swallow only the incompetent."

"Very well, sir. Will you be entering Brekh'cha behind us?"

"Obviously," Titanius hissed through tight lips, "as otherwise, you would be hindered significantly for my sake."

None of this made sense. Why would Titanius be entering Brekh'cha? His quarry would be nowhere close.

"While we're camped, you will also be assessing battle schematics," Titanius continued, handing Hrossar a scroll. "Memorize them."

"As you wish, sir."

Siege studied the humanite. The hunter had changed so little. Cruel eyes, shining metal armor—clearly polished every day—an equally polished shaved head, more brazen without a helmet...and of course, the whip. He still stroked his electrified whip. Perhaps it was the only thing he had any care for, as it had probably served him better than many of his attendants.

Siege scoffed. If Titanius still *used* attendants.

But apparently he did, because here he was! This time it was a lovely mercenary army. Herodons, even. Walking, talking beasts that could curl up like an armadillo and roll across anything. Rubber hides. Short snouts that snorted and whined. Retractable claws on their feet and hands, small ears like a cow—and superior combat capabilities. Often hired as mercenaries.

He recalled one of those awkward nursery rhymes that didn't really rhyme: *Remember, son, that fast one may run, but none can outrun the herodon.* "Herodon" didn't rhyme with "un." It rhymed with dawn. Morons.

Siege wondered how long it would take before they got fed up with the draconian hunter. If they weren't already.

Hrossar rolled up the scroll. "Done."

"Excellent." Titanius stroked his whip. "Set up the tents."

The tents. Now Siege wouldn't be able to eavesdrop! If it was too far away, he needed to see it to hear it. He would just need to get closer.

What would bring Titanius to Brekh'cha? Siege himself was only here for the rumors that herodons were in the area. This realm was rarely traversed without reason.

"Titanius," he whispered, zooming out, "you're smarter than this. There's nothing here for you."

At least it didn't look like it. But what did Titanius know that Siege didn't?

Siege adjusted his cloak. He would simply take another approach. If the tents blocked his hearing, there was always the more direct method.

He smirked. Time to pay Titanius a visit.

☆ ☆ ☆

Voices. Somewhere above Dane—light shining in his eyes! He squinted. "What—"

Liquid filled his mouth. Delicious and sweet, like everything he'd ever wanted to eat combined, but not disgusting somehow. That was weird.

A tingling feeling filled his body. He heard cracks and felt fiery pain shoot through his joints. Then everything felt very pleasant.

"That ought to do it." The source of the light in his eyes was talking. "I think his bones are all mended now. The helenberries worked. How are the others?"

"Just fine. Still a little dazed, though."

"Aye, those concussions, they heal a wee bit slower. That's alright." The light stopped shining in his eyes. "How are you, lad?"

He blinked. Two boulders slightly larger than he was stood like pillars on either side. Ethereal yellow light filled the cave like it was lit by a central campfire. But no flickering...so no fire. And a scent like strawberries filled his nose. He tried sitting up.

Whoa—head spinning! "Oww!"

"Easy there, lad. Give it a few."

Did that rock just talk? Yep, both of the rocks beside him had mouths. And as he looked closer—whoa. They had eyes too! With irises like gemstones. The boulders were *perfectly* round with stubby legs, and muscular arms of stone poked out their sides. The light seemed to gleam on their smooth surface, like they were polished marble. One was holding a sharp shiny rock—definitely the source of that stupid light in his eyes before.

"Are you alright, lad?"

Now the other one was talking. Dane must've hit his head *ridiculously* hard.

"I don't think he speaks Laru."

"Bah! Of course he does, Tohen. Everyone speaks Laru."

Laru? There was a name for his language?

He scratched his head. Well of course there was. Stupid question. "Yep. I speak—uh, Laru."

The other one laughed. "Maybe he lost his memory!"

"I'm fine!" Dane jumped up. The cave was spinning in his vision, but he caught himself by leaning on a boulder—or person, or whatever it was. "My memory is just fine!"

"Easy there,"—the boulder-thing wrapped three stony fingers around his elbow—"no one likes a hand in their face."

"Oh." He took his hand off. "Right." He should sit down to stop the spinning. "Okay."

"Now what's your name?"

"Um..." He looked at Tohen. "I'm Dane."

"Dane! Now that's a fine regalian name! I'm Tohen!"

The other rock removed his fingers from Dane's elbow. "I'm Kelmor!" He held up two stony fingers. "But you can call me Kel."

Wow! Now that he was paying more attention, the Kel boulder-thing was made of some reflective rock that kind of changed between jade green and black when you looked at it from different angles. "Okay, Kel." Dane held up two fingers. Maybe that was supposed to be hello.

"You new to the world, Dane?"

"Stop giving him a hard time. His brains are addled."

The way they rolled their r's was kind of funny. Dane half-smiled. "What are you?"

Kel pointed at himself with a rocky thumb. "I'm a labradorite, and my friend here is an obsidianite. Great boulders, lad—you blind?"

"No!" He cleared his throat. "Of course I knew that."

"Right. You'll be yourself in a minute."

"So where are you from, Dane?"

He stared at the first boulder. "Um…" He didn't really want to talk about it. "Well, Tehone—"

"Tohen."

"Tohen. Yeah, I'm uh not from around here—"

"Oh, ya think?" They laughed again. "You look regalian."

"Dane!"

He spotted Reisor sprinting toward them. "Dane, are you okay?"

"Yep." Reisor was already better. Maybe he was given the juice first.

"Feselea's still recovering. She'll be here soon."

"Okay." Dane tried standing up again. Agh—still spinning!

"We were just entertaining your friend here." Kel patted Dane on the back, causing him to stumble. "Are you the head of this group?"

"Yes." Reisor put his hands on his hips, looking around, "And we have a spinnivan somewhere—"

"And a bag of tarballs!"

Kel raised his hands. "Whoa, whoa there! One thing at a time!" His face popped out from the rest of his body, connected by a stony neck. He peered around. "You mean that curious wheeled contraption? We haven't made pebbles nor rockslides of it."

Reisor and Dane followed his finger to the overturned spinnivan. The supplies were scattered around it like it was Fes's living space. And beside those—

"Wow! What is that?" Dane pointed at what looked like a river of glowing red-orange goop. Most of the light in the cavern was coming from it. "Can I touch it?"

"*You* can't," Kel said, patting him again—he lurched—"but we can." He motioned to Tohen. "Show him."

"Lad, this here is a substance called lava." Tohen dipped his feet in the glowing goop. Steam erupted as he gave him a thumbs-up. "It'll burn your legs off."

"How come it doesn't affect you?"

Dane turned to see Fes approaching. "Hey, Dane." She pointed at the lava, then focused on Tohen. "I've been eavesdropping. What makes you immune to the lava?"

"We're geolites, love. We're made of rock."

"Your friend told me, I know. But..." Fes tapped her chin. "Your friend here—" she pointed at another boulder-geo-thing, "—your friend also told me lava was melted rock. So how come you don't melt?"

"Oh, we melt alright," Tohen answered, chuckling, "but at much higher temperatures. It would take a real pressure cooker to juice *us*!"

"Which we have yet to see," Kel added, walking across the lava to their spinnivan. He flipped it over without any effort, and a spinning mushroom whizzed feebly like a spinning top. "Not sure what's wrong with your wagon, but these wheels have had it."

"They're spinners." Reisor strolled over, then stopped before the lava. "Is there a way—"

"Of course!" Kel walked back across the lava, motioning to another boulder. "Fetch me a helenberry shell!"

A head and arms popped out from the boulder, and he waddled over to what looked like a strawberry bigger than he was, but with thorny skin like a pineapple. And...oh wow.

"That's an insanely big briarpatch," Dane breathed, craning his neck. Stretching to the ceiling far above, a massive briarpatch with vines thicker than Dane curled tons of different ways, with a multitude of tiny thorns and big, thorny berries. The briars wound around the whole cavern. "What is that?"

"You've never seen helenbriars?" Kel accepted the helenberry. "What, do you live in a hole in the ground?" He laughed at his own joke. "Ah, I'm just teasing. Who are you people?"

"We're…" Reisor shifted, averting his eyes. "We're just travelers."

"I can see that!" Kel punched the helenberry. It split cleanly in half. "Where're you going?"

"Um…"

"Can I ask another question?"

Kel turned to Fes. "As many as you need, love."

She pointed at the lava. "When I fell in this cave, everything was dark. What happened?"

"That was low tide," Kel explained, scooping out the helenberry's insides. "The lava tide has come in now."

"Oh. So it operates on—wait a minute…what's a tide?"

"You don't know what a tide is?" Kel furrowed his brow. "You really do live in a hole, eh? I'm no fancy expert who could explain, though."

"Oh." Feselea's cheeks were a little red. She hated not knowing things. "Um, okay. Tohen, do you know?"

"I…I don't want to explain it right now." Tohen seemed almost impatient. Maybe he wasn't the type to answer a lot of questions. "Ask me later."

"Maybe someone else'll tell you." Kel turned his focus to Dane, a scoop of helenberry in his palm. "Want some? You still don't look very good."

He took the fruit and stuffed it in his mouth. How could something taste *so* good? "Do these just grow here?"

"All by themselves," Tohen said—he was scooping out the other half. "They've been over-harvested to extinction everywhere else. But we can't eat them." He tapped the shell. "We just sell the meat or use it to revive people, then use the shells to canoe on the lava."

"Canoe?"

Kel smiled at Reisor. "Which is what you're about to do."

"What—" Reisor stared at the shell. "We're going to float on the *lava*?"

"Unless you're heavy as an aragonite." He barked another laugh, then patted Reisor hard. "It's alright, lad. Not everyone gets my humor."

"You're an odd stone, that's for sure."

"Eh, more or less." Kel's head popped out from his round body again, like it was its own appendage. He settled his head close to his round body, giving himself just enough distance from it to allow things like nodding. Dane got the sense that this was Kel's preferred posture. "Now can we fetch a shell for this here lad—"

"I don't need one!" Dane was feeling much better after that last mouthful. "I can make it across."

"I don't know, lad. That's a good meter and a half—"

"Just watch me." Dane took a running start and leapt across the lava. Ow!—heat almost singed his legs. "Easy."

Kel beat the ground—was that supposed to be clapping? "Not bad! I'm impressed."

"We all are," Reisor mumbled, shaking his head. He put his shell on the lava, crawled in and pushed off. His shell started drifting across.

"Boring."

"Also much safer. Dane, how are you going to carry everything back without a shell?"

Everything—wait. "My tarballs!"

"I saw them over there." Fes looked at him with raised eyebrows and pointed. "Have fun."

Dane spotted his bag of tarballs nestled in some briars near the ceiling. He cocked his head, then shook it. "Yep. Maybe."

"We need more shells anyway." Kel crossed the lava. "This wagon-thing is dead. We'll have to transport your goods on shell."

"Transport where?" Reisor was pulling out supplies and arranging them in different piles—trying to sort them, Dane guessed. Pointless, but whatever. "To the surface?"

Now Kel laughed hard. "You really aren't from around here! It's far too dangerous up there because of the sink-holes." He pointed up. "Do you want to get knocked out again?"

Reisor stopped sorting. Glancing at Fes, he asked, "What are we supposed to do then?"

"Get your goods to Ticora, and they'll provide you with a proper underground transport."

"Ticora?"

"Aye, lad. It's the capital."

Reisor looked around. "The capital of what? This is a realm?"

"All of this." Kel spread his hands. "Welcome, lads and lass, to Brekh'cha."

ABOUT THE AUTHOR

 Everything Ian writes puts a new spin on fantasy as you know it. And when he's not writing he's imagining his next book. He gets so involved in the worlds he's creating for his books—and the characters he's developing—he can forget what's going on around him!

Ian loves science and incorporates it heavily into his fantasy worlds. He also loves philosophy—and since he hates going with the crowd, he resolves to take the reader on a journey of questioning and suspense, watching the characters struggle with interpreting and reacting to unfolding events.

Living in and around the Colorado mountains, Ian and his wife enjoy exploring the outdoors—soaking in the sights, sounds and smells of creation. But they are most passionate about their strategy games, usually spending hours or even days "nerding-out" on one game alone.

Find Ian online at:
https://www.ianvroon.blog
https://www.facebook.com/ianvroon.blog

Sign up for Ian's newsletter
to get information on all of his latest releases here:
https://ianvroon.blog/newsletter-sign-up/

Tell others what you think. Leave a review on Amazon
http://amazon.com/author/ianvroon/

If you enjoyed reading *Tales of Brekh'cha*, don't forget to recommend it to a friend. If everyone who reads this can get two other people to read it, I'm in the gold. That means more books more quickly. We can do this together.

Made in the USA
Middletown, DE
09 May 2022